CLEO BROWNE

Jules

Tombs Security + DRMC Crossover

Contents

Trigger Warning

This book deals with badassery in all its forms.
Please be aware that in order for these characters to be badass,
this book contains content that some readers may find disturbing,
such as alluding to SA, graphic descriptions of violence and
torture, and R18 sex scenes.

Hey Readers!

Thank you so much for picking up Jules' book and for joining me on this crazy ride.
This book marks the last of the Tombs to fall and also my one-year Authorversary.
Thank you so much, every one of you out there who not only gave my Tombs family and the DRMC a chance but also for reaching out and interacting on social media. I love that I get to chat with every one of you, and we can share laughs, thoughts, and moments that I would not have had had it not been for a funny little lady whose particular flavor of autism is "murdery."
Thank you all, and I hope you enjoy the last Tombs book.

Or is it?

Who the heck is that?

Devil's Rose MC

Marx - Pres

Rhodie - VP and Enforcer + Tuesday Tombs (Chewy) Icer

Rider - SAA

Wire - Secretary/Hacker + Remy Wright

Jovie (Wire and Remy's adopted child)

Tank - Member + Mira (Doll) Campbell

Switch - Medic

Judge - Member

Sniper - Member

Fox - Member

Nitro - Member

Savage - Member (ex Death Rider) + Nat

Dex - Member (Ex Death Rider)

Jimmy - Prospect

Takoda - Prospect

Tav - Prospect + Blanche (Pixie)

Niko, Sage, Cove, Elio (Tav and Blanche's children)

Tombs Security

August (Gus) Tombs + Ana Tombs

Jules Tombs + Violet Davies
Tav Tombs + Blanche Landry
Niko, Sage, Cove and Elio (Tav and Blanche's children)
Tuesday (Chewy) Tombs + Rhodie
Sidney (Pops) Tombs + Debs Taylor (Mother of Ana)

Bartashev Bratva

Roman Bartashev + Sasha Bartashev (BFF's of Ana)

Prologue

Jules

Shit, did I leave the TV on last night? Why the hell can I hear a baby crying? Rolling over gingerly, I check the time. Just after 2pm. Way too early for me to be up after last night's activities. With the DRMC in a quiet patch, it seemed the perfect time for Fox, Nitro, and myself to play. With their female contacts and my membership to Vibe, Rose Grove's sex club, we spent the evening drowning in pussy. It's a fucking hedonistic feeling having my cock balls deep in a girl's throat, my tongue in a pussy and my fingers buried deep in another. It's no secret that I very quickly bonded with the MC brothers over our shared interest of voyeurism, group sex and sharing women, although Fox and Nitro seem to share a little more than that. Not that it's any of my fucking business.

The incessant crying continues and I know I'll have to turn that fucking TV off. I have to piss anyway so I may as well kill two birds with one stone. My muscles groan as I stretch, rolling out of bed and stumbling into the ensuite, doing my business and then groggily making my way to the open plan living room.

Scrubbing my hands down my face, I do a double take when the crying gets louder and yet the TV screen is black. Swiveling, I tilt my head to pinpoint where the noise is coming from. Gus may live next door, but not once have I heard his kid cry this loud. Heading toward my front door the crying grows louder. I throw it open, confused when I'm met with Tav's Littles and Wire's kid on my front porch.

"What the fuck?"

"What the heck Unca Jules?" My gaze follows Jovie and Cove's wide-eyed stares to a baby carseat perched on the wooden bench on my porch. A baby carseat complete with an angry infant yelling at us. One that isn't my brother Gus's baby.

"Whose fucking baby is that?" I glare at them. That's all I can do at the moment.

"How should we know? They were here when we got here," Cove loudly answers. The kid has no inside voice whatsoever. Elio just stares at me.

"Why are you here? Did my brother put you up to this?" I squint at them. I'm sure this is probably some bullshit prank of Tav's. A fucking loud prank because this baby won't shut up.

"Aunt Ana is babysitting us." Jovie shrugs. "Anyways, whose baby is that? And why did you put them on the porch?" Her little face screws up in confusion.

"Are you referring to the baby as 'them'?"

"Well, yeah. Do you know what kind of baby that is? If you don't know what they are then they're a they/them." I stare at the 8 year old like she has two heads. What type of fuckery is this? From the conversation, all I can glean is that none of us knows where this baby came from.

"I can't think. How do we make it stop crying?"

Jovie's eyes drift back to the baby while Cove squints at me. "We're kids. You're the grown up. You should know. "

"Yeah, but don't you hang out with the babies at the club-house?" I prompt.

"The babies have mommies and daddies." Elio says in his robot voice, gazing over my shoulder.

"Yeah, where's the baby's mommy, Unca Jules?" Jovie asks.

We all look at the baby in the car seat. It miraculously stops crying and gives us all the stink eye.

"Oh! They look just like you Unca Jules! You must be the daddy!" Cove claps and stomps her feet, the baby moving its focus to stink eye her.

"What are we looking at?" We spin around at the feminine voice behind us.

"Ana! Thank fuck!" I let out a breath, my shoulders relaxing.

"The baby we found on Unca Jules' porch! They were crying lots and we don't know where the mommy is but Unca Jules could be the daddy cos they both do that face thing," Cove info dumps.

"What face thing?" I frown at the kids.

"They? Do you not know whether it's a boy or a girl? Do you know where they came from?" Ana asks, ignoring my question.

"No, we only just found them." Great now I've fucking caught it.

Ana pushes past me, scoops up the carseat and flicks her head at the kids to pick up the bag sitting next to it. She walks into my lounge, places the baby on the coffee table and starts unbuckling it.

"You check the baby bag for anything that helps tell us who the hell this baby is and where they came from. Oh, and someone pass me the baby wipes and a nappy."

We stare at her until she rolls her eyes. "A diaper. Pass me a diaper."

As soon as she lifts the kid from their seat a horrible stench permeates the air. Now, having to clean up my sisters' messes I have a strong stomach but this, this is enough to take down the toughest of men.

"Hey bay- oh my god Jr not a-fucking-gain son! I just changed you!" Gus moans, coming through the door with my nephew, stopping abruptly. "Who's fucking baby is that?" He looks around the room, bewildered. I know if he didn't have Jr, or Junior, in his arms he'd be popping those fucking antacids like Tic Tacs. My brother doesn't like surprises.

Ana waves something in the air, "Found the birth certificate and other paperwork. Her name is Juno, she's three months old and you're listed as the father Jules." Ana coos at the baby, clean clothing on and the foul diaper nowhere to be seen. "Juno is a cute name, goes with the rest of the Tombs' names."

"Who's the mother?" I manage to rasp out.

"Do you know a woman named Eloise Greenlake?" Gus asks, reading the birth certificate over Ana's shoulder.

I wrack my brain but nothing is coming to me. I mean, I don't date women, I don't sleep one-on-one with them. Whoever this Eloise Greenlake is must be mistaken.

"She does look a lot like you Jules," Ana says, turning the baby to look at us. She has whiskey colored eyes, much like my sister Tuesday's, and a hell of a lot of black hair.

"I dunno. Jules is way too ugly to make a kid that cute." I give Gus the dead eye, ignoring the fact that this kid looks almost identical to Jr at the same age.

I know I'm not the only one to notice, as Ana stares between the two of them. "Aw what a little sweetie," she coos. It makes her feel some type of way because she gets all soft eyed.

Shaking myself off I know I have to get this baby out of my house. It can't belong to me. I'm not built for kids or relationships or family outside of the ones I have. There is no room for anyone or anything else. I'm a selfish fucker and I can not and will not share my space. I list out in my head more reasons why I cannot be this kid's father. I'm too busy. I have a dangerous job. I don't have the time. I am somehow fucking not right on the inside. I don't have the emotional intelligence to raise something or someone. My chest grows tight and my stomach clenches, but I ignore it. That's panic rising but I can control that. My mind needs to rationalize what it needs to and once it does my body will follow suit. Moments pass as my body comes back into itself and I watch my family gently touch the baby's face, hair, hands.

"I gotta get this kid to the MC. See Fox and Nitro. There's a good chance it could be one of theirs." I stomp to my room, throwing on clean clothes, socks and boots, only to return to a wide eyed Ana.

"Holy crap are you telling me that the mother is probably someone from one of your orgies? Oh my god!" Ana looks like she's going to fucking keel over with glee and then she bursts into laughter so intense she has to hand the baby over to Gus as she collapses on the floor in a fit of giggles. Gus somehow manages to cradle both babies as he waits for his wife to calm down. The kids are obviously bored because they've fucked off to do whatever it was they were doing before they found this kid.

"Right, let's load up, I need answers." I stride to the door, press my key fob unlocking my SUV, and throw the door open, ready to get in when I hear a throat clearing.

"Ah, you gonna strap your kid in?" Gus asks, shit eating grin on his face.

"Nah, brother, why don't you take them in your vehicle? You know how all that shit's meant to work." Slamming the door behind me I start the car, jolting when the back passenger door flies open.

"Your kid rides with you." Gus somehow in 11 seconds flat has the seat locked in, the diaper bag beside it, and some fucking giant sunflower mirror thing pointing directly into my rear view meaning I get to see a baby stink eye everytime I check behind me. The kid and I stare at each other until the door flings open once again.

"I'm riding with you." Gus says, looking straight ahead.

"What the fuck? Don't you trust me? Gus, I've saved loads of mothers and children from shit situations. I'm sure I can drive a baby to the clubhouse." I grumble.

He side eyes me, watching with his beady fucking eyes that look just like the baby in my rear view. "In these rescues have you once carried a child? Held a baby? No? Didn't fucking think so. Just drive the car so we can get this 'whos' the daddy' ruse over."

"What? It - she - fuck, the baby, could belong to Fox or Nitro," I say, pulling out of our drive onto the road heading toward the clubhouse.

Gus snorts, not even answering me. Dickhead.

I need this SUV to go faster. I have to get to the clubhouse, sort this shit out and find the baby's real family. All while hoping against hope that the baby's real family isn't mine.

Skidding into the MC compound ignoring the almost naked blue man coming out of the clubhouse, I fling open my door and storm to the back passenger side. The baby glares up at me and I stare back, realizing I have no idea how the hell to get it out of here and into the clubhouse in the fucking hopes that Fox may be the daddy. Yeah, it must be his, he has that dark hair and shit.

"Fuck sake, move," Gus's fat elbow digs into my rib as he pushes past, presses something and releases the kid from my back seat before shoving it into my arms.

I fall into step behind him, walking through the clubhouse doors to the usual pandemonium.

"Why was that man blue?" Gus asks, before he's shoved out of the way by his wife, Jr strapped to her chest.

"You bitches started the 'Welcome Mira Strip Show' without me!"

"Serves you right for being late. What the hell were you doing anyw- whose baby is that?" Blanche stops mid-sentence, spotting the baby carseat looped over my arm.

All eyes in the clubhouse turn toward me, silence descending over the nosy fuckers.

Clearing my throat, I address Fox and Nitro, "Does this belong to you?"

Fox's brows fly up, almost disappearing into his black hair-line. "Why the fuck would that belong to me?"

"Because it was left on my porch and I'm guessing," my eyes dart toward the kids who are sitting on the couch in a row watching this go down, "Earmuffs kids," they all put their hands over their ears, but watch with eager eyes. "It belongs to one of us because I don't fuck with women solo. If you get my drift."

"Wait, wait, wait." Tav, steps up, hands in the air. "Are you saying that someone left their kid on your porch thinking you're the father but in actual fact that kid could belong to any one of you due to your extracurricular activities?" He turns, waving his finger between us. He stares for a beat and then collapses on the ground, pissing himself laughing. Much like Ana did.

While I wait for the laughter to subside, and Fox and Nitro to take this kid from me, Pops has made a beeline for the kid and has been staring at it, hands on knees, crouching, with a serious look on his face. He reaches out and gently turns the baby's head, looking at god knows what.

"What did the mom look like?" Nitro asks, snapping out of his shock.

"Dunno. Her name was on the birth certificate, an Eloise Greenlake?"

"Lou? Shit. She left town a year ago, never heard from her. That's probably why. She was growing your spawn," Nitro chuckles.

"What the fuck makes you think it's mine?" I growl.

"Besides the fact that it looks exactly like you?"

"Accept it. It's yours," Pops interrupts. "That's a Tombs kid right there. See the ear? We all gotta pixie ear on the left side. Sorry kid, but you're fucked." Pops' grin spreads wide across his face, Fox and Nitro breathing a sigh of relief and the clubhouse all making noises of congratulations.

I stare down at the face in the baby carseat. A face I know well because I stare at the same fucking face in the mirror every damn day.

Fuck my life.

Chapter 1

Jules

The snuffling sound from the spare room starts and I know I have about 3.2 seconds before Juno decides to scream her face off in starvation. It's been like this every day for the past two weeks and I'm running on fumes. Yeah I have family living around me, but the assholes decided the best way for me to adjust to this "new phase of my life" was to throw me in at the deep end. At least I can still count on Mama Debs. She helps out as much as she can, but between her hours at the clubhouse and having to run around after Pops who insists he needs her to sponge bath him, it means I've been spending more time with the baby than I would like.

I pull my big ass out of bed, make my way to the kitchen and heat up the premade bottle Mama Debs left behind after getting Juno to bed. Leaning against the bench I curse the fact that even though Tombs Security may be hot shit in the world of security and tech, it's not damn near enough to find someone who doesn't want to be found. After ditching her kid on my porch Eloise Greenlake fell off the face of the earth. Any close relatives she had are all dead. DNA testing came back saying the only family the baby has is the Tombs family. So, unfortunately for Juno, I'm the only parent she's got. Poor kid deserves the world, but I can't give it to her. Something inside me is broken. I'm not sure if it happened when my parents were murdered, or if I was born this way, but I've long come to peace with the fact that I don't feel the same types of things other people do. Other men would see a baby they made and feel a surge of love. I look at Juno and while I can now admit that we share DNA, I don't feel love. Protective? Yeah. I mean she's a helpless kid. Love? No.

Letting out a sigh I make my way to the spare room, shaking the warmed bottle, trying to murmur comforting sounds to the baby screaming in her bed.

"Yeah, I'm here." I place the bottle on the dresser and lean in to pick up Juno, awkwardly resting her against my shoulder as she screams blue murder. I've learned in our time together that she would rather eat immediately than wait for me to change her and then eat. I know it's probably not how things are meant to be done, but it's how we do shit and it works for us.

I sit in the poofy rocking chair the Ol Ladies gifted me, fumble around until Juno is in the crook of my arm, lean over to pick up the bottle and touch the nipple to the bottom lip of her open, wailing mouth. She shakes her head a little and then latches on like a rabid dog. I chuckle as she starts sucking like her life depended on it, wide, whiskey colored eyes glaring at me like I'll steal it away at any moment. We sit like this, staring at each other, just like we do every day at 5.30am which is when she decides she's ready to greet the world. If I'm lucky she'll go back to sleep after this.

We rock gently, the warmth of her little body seeping into me, relaxing me while she finishes her bottle. I burp and change her, feeling pretty fucking proud that I managed to do it all, with a quicker time than yesterday. Doing these things, making sure she's fed and clean, that's easy shit. I've had pets before as a kid and took my animal care really fucking seriously. Feeding, changing, keeping her alive and well I can do. It's the emotional shit I'm not cut out for. Which is why I've been secretly looking at alternative care for her. I'm sure my family would kick my ass if I told them I was looking into adoption. I'm well within my rights as her father to give her up, I'm just not sure yet.

Looking down at Juno in the crook of my arm, she shows no signs of going back to sleep. I decide she may as well sit in her UFO looking seat thing and glare at me while I workout. I mean what else is there to do? Sit down and have a heart to heart about why her old man is a dud? Fuck no.

"Come on, kid. Let's work out."

Three hours later I find myself hovering on Lovely's porch. Gus very generously gave me two months paternity leave, to "settle into fatherhood," but I'm fucking dying not being able to go into the office and talk to the men and women who work for us. I'm out of the loop and I don't fucking like it.

Lovely's door swings open as she steps out, eyes on her handbag as she searches for something. Little Bee kicks and waves her hands in excitement when she sees me, Lovely's head snapping up at the movement before she realizes I'm here.

"Hey Jules," she says in her sweet voice, smiling wide, "and hello to you too, little missy," She coos at Juno, who frowns back. Lovely waves it off, giggling. "I will never get over how frowny your daughter is."

My gut clenches when she calls Juno my daughter, but I have no time to investigate the feeling. I came here for a purpose. Clearing my throat I address her, "Lovely, I was wondering if you wouldn't mind keeping an eye on Juno for me for a few hours?" I use my best smile. The one that the club girls would drop their panties for.

Lovely's shoulders slump and I know I'm shit outta luck. "Oh Jules, I'm sorry, I'm working at Devil's Big Tow today." She gives me an apologetic smile before brightening, "I've officially finished my computer training with Remy so I'll be working reception and Bee will be coming with me. I'm not sure I can handle two little babies and the job. I'm sorry." Her brows furrow and I wave her off. She needs this more than I need to go to work. The work that has me on leave for another six weeks.

"It's okay, Lovely. You need to get to work and start making bank." I do my best to give her a smile as she laughs at my joke. We all know that she doesn't need the money. But she does need life experience and I won't cheat her of that.

"Hmm, maybe pop into the clubhouse. Mama Debs or one of the others may be able to keep an eye on her," She grins at Juno and shakes her little hand, waving it about until the baby rips her hand away. Lovely chuckles and shakes her head.

Stepping off the porch I watch them load up, and then decide to do the same. I already had Juno's crap packed up in her baby bag so I figure I may as well follow Lovely out.

"Come on, kid. Let's see if Nana will have you."

Violet

"Moss Davies! You never did tell me what happened with that orc man with the Maui hair. You know the one that ordered my innocent, gentle husband to deliver organs to that nice lady? I knew I should have punched him as soon as I saw him. I told you didn't I? That he had a very punchable face. Coming into Flora's Buds and causing havoc like that? *Dios mio*, what did we ever do to deserve that type of behaviour?" My mother throws her hands up in the air, not even letting my brother answer her.

Dad pats her hand and murmurs something to her as we all settle in, knowing that it will take Dad at least a couple of minutes to calm our mother down. Once she seems sufficiently settled Moss shovels some "mild" chilli into his twin's open mouths before answering.

"Well, we haven't had any more complaints about him, but I did pass your message on to the Devil's Rose MC so perhaps they had a word?" Moss's lips twitch and my sisters and I all look the other way so we don't burst into laughter.

"Oh, they're such nice boys!" Mom claps, "How is Johnny? He was always a lovely boy. It's such a pity that you stole his girlfriend from him and then married her. I told you that she wasn't the one for you didn't I? And then to run away from you, and her two adorable baby boys? Well, that Whorecules can stay away for all I care." Mom harrumphs. Dad pats her hand and my sisters and I cackle with laughter.

It's true though. The head of DRMC was the star quarterback at high school, and somehow, my brother Moss managed to steal his girlfriend. Next thing you know, close to two decades has passed, they're married, Moss has been made sergeant, his wife has given birth to twins and then poof! She disappears leaving my brother with two boys and all of us having to scramble to help him out. The fact that Mom can come up with so many names for the woman never ceases to make us cackle.

"That's the best one yet!" Jasmine, my older sister, and Moss's twin cackles.

"Yes, Mom, they've lovely boys. I'm sure they had some words with the orc man to make him think twice about his actions," Moss says, trying to put more food into his kids' faces, even though both Heath and Reed are wearing more than I think they've eaten. "Anyway, enough about him, what happened to Josh, Vi? I thought he was coming for dinner?" He gives me a shit-eating grin.

"Yes! Where is Josh? You've been dating for three months now and he's never come to dinner." Mom laments, "Is it my food? Does he not like my cooking?" She clutches at her nonexistent pearls, horrified that someone may not like her food.

"My love, how could someone not like your cooking? You are a master in the kitchen." I roll my eyes, my dad is such a suck up.

"He's never had your cooking, Mom, because he has tummy troubles. I told you that. Besides, we've only been dating a little while."

"See, this is why you need to date within your own culture." All eyes dart to our white father., "Sometimes outsiders' stomachs struggle with our food. Look what happened to Whorelando Bloom," Mom gestures toward Moss, "She couldn't handle the love and spice I put into the food and it drove her away,"

"She drove away with Matt from accounts Mom," Moss replies drily.

Mom waves a hand at him and continues lecturing me. "It's the same thing."

"May I point out that Dad is white?" I gesture to my father who smiles gently at me.

"Yes. But his love for me overcame his inability to handle spice. Now look at him! He's thriving," Mom beams at my dad and pecks him on the cheek.

"He also takes huge doses of Tums and Mylanta," Jazz whispers, making me snort..

"Enough about Josh, perhaps next time. I can make him his own boiled chicken if he wants to join," Mom beams and then turns to my sisters, interrogating them one by one, lamenting that none of the other children have significant others.

"Oh, I had Tav Tombs' little boy join my class today," Jazz says, interrupting the interrogation. "He's on the spectrum, and I'm not sure exactly how much he likes art, but he did draw some very detailed anatomy pictures using pastels. It was very impressive."

"Oh I love the Tombs! Such a nice family," Mom claps. "They were very helpful in investigating that Orc man. Jules helped me with all the cameras. You girls know that he is single, right?" Mom eyeballs Jazz and Lily, who nod and avoid eye contact. "All the siblings have coupled up except for him. Sidney must be so proud. I cannot wait to feel that feeling once three of my babies are coupled up. I'd take all four of you coupled up, but Moss has bad taste in women so maybe just make sure you girls find someone nice," her eyes flick to mine, "Who can handle spice."

We eat in silence for a beat, and I know at any moment that silence will be broken by my mother. She's not one to sit quietly, and whatever crosses her mind will come out of her mouth.

"Violet, I've been thinking about your role in the shop," Mom starts, eyes darting toward my dad who looks everywhere but at me.

"Huh? Is there a problem"

"Yes, I believe there is. It's time for a shake up. I'm firing you." Mom nods her head decisively.

Everyone around the table stares at me while I stare at mom. Did she just? "You're *firing* me? I'm your only employee!" I balk.

"Yes. That's exactly what I'm doing. Don't you want to do something more with your life than work in the family shop? You need to get out there and find your passion!"

"My passion was nursing but, well, we know how that turned out." I mumble.

"I know *mija*, you were asked to leave because you care too much –"

"Care too much? I had to escort her out of the clinic she worked at because she assaulted her patient's family member!" Moss glares.

"I never assaulted anyone! I threatened her! And that was her fault for not taking better care of her mother!" I point across the table at him.

"Ahp, ahp, ahp!" Mom raises her hands, making the same noise she uses on the cats when they don't listen to her, "Either way Vi, you need to find your passion again, because it's not the gerberas," She points her chubby finger at me before spinning to look at Dad, "Papi, did I tell you what she did? She almost killed a whole shipment!" Before dad can say anything she turns back to the table, "She has the black thumb! My own child cursed, unable to touch natural beauty without it shrivelling up and wishing for death, *Qué hice para merecer esto?* What did I do to deserve this!" She raises her hands up, shaking her fists in the air while my father fans her with his napkin.

"Is this the menopause? Is that what's happening?"

We all stare at Moss in horror, but none more so than Dad, whose eyes are the size of saucers. He even leans back in his seat and I'm sure I see his lips mouth "I'm sorry," to Moss because Mom is about to blow. Everyone knows that you don't question a woman's hormones. Especially if that woman is an overly dramatic florist with the ability to hit you with a thrown sandal from 15 feet away.

"Oh Moss, *mi amado hijo*, you're about to find out exactly what is happening."

* * *

"It'll be OK, Lettie," Lilly says, patting my shoulder and calling me the childhood nickname I loathed.

"Yeah, Mom and Dad wouldn't leave you destitute while you find your passion," Jasmine snorts, handing me the next dish to put away.

This is what we've done our whole lives after dinner. We line up, Lilly washes, Jasmine dries and I put away while Moss divides up all the leftovers into the 1 million tupperware containers Mom owns.

"What the hell am I going to do? I can't go back to nursing. People in town still call me 'Violent' instead of Violet, or 'the angry nurse'." I look at the ceiling and growl.

"Have you thought this could be a good thing? Remember when I got sick and had to drop my law studies? I was able to use my talent for art to build a new career that I love. Mom firing you could be the best thing that ever happened to you." Jazz shrugs. "Oh hey, speaking of the job I love, now that you're unemployed, do you want to come and be a life model for my kids? Moss pulled out - " Jazz narrows her eyes at our brother, "so I'm in search of someone who can sit still for a while so the kids can draw them. What do you say?" She waggles her dark brows at me.

I let out a sigh. It's not like I have anything else going on. This might be the thing I need to perk me up a little. "Count me in, why not? I don't have anywhere else to be thanks to mom firing me."

"You'll get over that *mija*, and you'll thank me!" Mom's voice drifts down the hall where she was very clearly eaves-dropping.

"Does your school need a nurse?" I ask Jazz, I mean, if I'm going to be there anyway, may as well try my luck.

"Ah, no offense but there's no way a school full of special needs kids would hire anyone that threatens people to take better care of their family members. The only role we got for you is modeling. Sorry Violent."

My eyes narrow as I look at my sister, "Why do you have so much trouble finding life models, anyway?"

"No reason." She smiles wide.

Moss snorts so hard he has a coughing fit, all us girls walking right by him ignoring him. Well all of us except Jazz who spins her dish towel into a whip and whips him with it.

"Serves you right, reneging on your promise to my kids.

Shame on you!"

"You talk about them like they're sweet angels, but they're not! They're feral. I arrest people for a living and those kids ruined my self esteem in one afternoon." Moss says indignantly. "Trust me, Vi, they'll scar you and you'll decide to remain childless forever."

"No way! I love kids. I've always wanted them," I answer, stealing Jazz's dish towel and whipping it at him.

"You won't after spending an afternoon with Jazz's." Moss shudders.

"Yeah, yeah. What's the worst that could happen?"

Chapter 2

Well, my fucking plan backfired spectacularly. After yesterday's triumph at dropping Juno off to the clubhouse for an hour I decided to replicate that good luck. Instead the good luck gods told me to fuck right off. What began as a mission to the clubhouse to find a babysitter ended with me babysitting a sick Cove while her mom takes photos of a cheater from her parked car.

"Why couldn't Mama Debs have you?" I ask Cove as I hold the door to the diner open for her. Kid needed lunch and my cooking skills are nearly nonexistent.

"Because she had to take Pops to the doctor."

My head snaps down to look at the top of her dark head. "Is he OK?" Pops may be an asshole but he's my asshole.

"Um, she said something bout him pulling his muscles when he was banging against the wall," She shrugs nonchalantly as all eyes in the diner turn to her after hearing her yell that tidbit out. I feel a little queasy because I'm sure I can guess why and who he was banging against the wall.

"Do you need a high chair for the baby?" The blonde, bored-looking waitress asks. Service really went downhill since Rosie retired and the new woman took over.

I look down at Juno asleep in her car seat and shake my head no.

"Suit yourself. Booth for two?" I nod at her, making my expression cold so she gets the picture that her service sucks. "Police and kids under six eat for free," she says, chewing gum vigorously, looking between me and my brother's kid.

I stare down at Cove who looks up at me with her mother's dark eyes. It's bad enough I have to babysit, the least she can do is wrangle a free meal. I mean, I'll still tip well, but I'm not in the market of buying a seven year old a whole lunch knowing full well she's going to eat half a dozen fries and quarter of a milkshake. She must get the picture because she nods up at me, then turns to look at the waitress.

"I'm a police."

Snickering from behind me has me turning. I figured it'd be my shithead brother, come to laugh at my misfortune but instead I come face to face with Sergeant Davies.

"Sergeant," I nod

"Tombs." He tilts his head, looking at Juno. "Heard you had a baby. Congratulations. You look like shit."

"Single fatherhood will do that to a man," I reply, raising a brow. I know full well what happened to Moss Davies. His bitch of a wife left him with newborn twins almost two years ago.

Instead of taking offence he grins, "Touché Tombs." He takes another look at me, then the baby and Cove staring up at him. "How's it going anyway?"

I don't know if it's because I'm sleep deprived or if I've become desperate for adult conversation, but I answer truthfully. "It's fucking hard and parental leave is killing me. I need to get back to work, not babysitting a kid."

He's thoughtful for a moment. "But you're not babysitting a kid. You're parenting *your* kid. There's a difference."

"So you say. All I know is that I need to find a solution so I can go back to work."

He squints at me, rubbing a hand through his short stubble. "I've got a sister -"

"You've got three sisters if memory serves me correctly."

"Don't I know it," he mumbles. "Anyway, Mom fired her from the florist and she's looking for a new job. Maybe you could hire her to keep an eye on your baby so you can get back to work."

I stare at him, trying to figure out if he's bullshitting me. Who the hell fires their kid? Strike that, Flora is somewhat unusual so I guess it makes sense. I continue to stare at him, thinking the offer over. Do I ask for references or something? I mean sure, I may not be the most fatherly person around, but I don't want any random looking after the kid. Then I remember Tav saying that Elio is in his sister's art class.

"Wait, the teacher sister?"

"Hell no! Jazz is my twin and my main sitter. Not that one, the other one, Violet."

I try to think which one Violet is. All of Moss's sister's are beautiful, a spectrum of Latina looks, if that makes sense. Jasmine, like Moss, has black wavy hair and dark eyes. The other two have the same dark eyes I think, but one has chocolatey brown hair, the other lighter. All of them have Flora's deep tan, are average height and shaped like coke bottles. If coke bottles were plus sized with tits and ass for days.

"The middle one with straight hair." Moss offers helpfully. "Look, she was released from her nursing job a couple of years back for threatening a patient's daughter. But other than that she's solid and you know you'll do a check on her. If you're interested, give me a call, and I'll pass on her number." He side steps me to get to the counter where the new owner, Maia, waves a cup of coffee at him. "See ya later, Police," he says to Cove on his way past.

Cove waves to his back and then looks up at me. "There Unca Jules. Get the nice lady to look after Juno. Then you can go back to work and stop being grumpy."

I usher her to a booth seat and place Juno at the end of the table in her carseat. "I'm always grumpy." I say.

"Yeah, but you're way more of an asshole now," Cove replies, staring directly at me.

"Do your mom and dad know you talk like that?"

"Who do you think I learned it from?"

We order lunch and then I sit back and watch Cove, who looks perfectly healthy and not sick at all, coloring. I drink my coffee and let my mind drift to Moss Davies' offer. Glancing at Juno sleeping in her car seat I dig deep inside myself to conjure up feelings for her. Any type of feelings. I don't want anything bad to happen to her, so I know that much. But as for any paternal feelings, I'm getting nothing. I'm still on the fence about adopting her out to someone who can love her like she deserves. I may not be equipped for that, but I know my family is, in their own weird way, so maybe she won't turn out defective if I keep her around.

I stare at her dark lashes resting on her fat cheeks, all her hair sticking up wildly and admit that she is a good looking baby. When she's asleep. Awake she spends all her time glaring or frowning, but with my DNA I guess you can't blame her. Running my finger down her soft cheek I come to the conclusion that perhaps we need more time to bond. When Dayz was born I wasn't overly fussed on her, but now I would kill for her. I'm guessing that's what love is. Sliding my phone out of my pants pocket I call the local PD and ask for Sergeant Davies.

"Moss? It's Jules Tombs. Set up a meeting with your sister."

Violet

"Do you even know where you're going?" Lily asks. Apparently Moss told her to come with me for moral support.

"I'm sure it's down here somewhere. Trust me, I've been here before." I mutter, cursing the fact that Jazz's special needs school is arranged much like a rabbit warren. Could I have listened to the directions the school secretary gave me? Well, yeah. But unfortunately I'm Flora Davies' daughter which means sometimes I think I know better.

I look into a few classrooms before heading further into the bowels of the school.

"Are you sure that it was a good idea, scheduling this before your interview?"

I wave off my sister, "It's fine. I mean, what's the worst that can happen? All I'll be doing is standing at the front of the class while the kids paint me." My eyes dart to hers as her lips curl up, "Not like one of those French whores!" I hiss at her, knowing that's what she's thinking. That's the trouble with living with your sister your whole life, you know each other too well.

"Are you nervous?" Lily asks, looking into the classrooms on her side of the hall.

"No," I lie.

I am nervous. My nursing career crashed and burned and the only other place I've worked since then is my mother's florist shop. I don't even like flowers, so it was probably a good call on Mom's part to cut me loose. It's the passion for any career outside of nursing that I'm having trouble with. I've never been a nanny, but the skills I have are transferable, and it's still in the caring profession and that's what I miss the most about my lost career. Being able to care for someone. Mom said I was born this way, always trying to take care of people, even if my methods were a little aggressive. Her words not mine.

"Are you sure? It's OK to be nervous," Lily pushes, as we walk further down the hall.

"Well, yeah, but I know how to look after babies so I'll be fine. I mean, I babysat all through high school, and we're basically Moss's backup sitters whenever he needs us. If I can handle those twins, I can handle any kid." I say, full of confidence that I'm not really feeling. A lot is riding on this interview. Like me getting mom off my case and being able to do grown up things. Like pay rent.

"Aha! There it is!" Lily points triumphantly to the colorful door with huge cutout letters spelling out Jazz's classroom name.

We peek through the window as our big sister in her colorful teacher clothes wanders around her class.

"I have no idea what Moss was on about, look at those little angels!" I scoff at Lily, yanking the door open and leading the way.

Jazz's head snaps up and she holds her hands up in the air, signing as she speaks, "Macaroni Cheese!"

"Everybody freeze!" The kids all exclaim, in one way or another.

"So, you're the victims for today, huh?' A little ginger boy with giant glasses says, staring up at us with narrowed eyes.

"Rodney! These are our guests, please show some manners," Jazz scolds, then waves us in using both hands. "I hope everybody has their buttons on so our guests can learn your beautiful names." She slowly eyeballs her class and the kids hurry to stick their name buttons to their shirts. Half of them are upside down, but that's to be expected.

She directs me to a small raised platform and has me stand facing the class. The tables are arranged in a u-shape so the kids can all see me, their art supplies laid out in front of them. Lily grins from Jazz's side and throws me two thumbs up.

"Right class, so today's special guest is my little sister Violet!" She rests her hands on my shoulders and waits for the kids to cheer. Or something.

"Pirate is a funny name for a lady," A cute little girl with wonky blonde pigtails and downturned eyes states, looking confused.

The ginger-headed boy, Rodney throws his head back and laughs hysterically, as does a little dark boy in a wheelchair.

"Pirate is a terrible name!" the wheelchair kid whose button says "Marcus" yells.

A little girl across from me frantically pats her teaching assistant, her hands flying, wanting in on the joke. The teaching assistant doesn't hold back and I know the moment the joke hits because the little girl throws her head back and lets out an unusual honking sound that I'm guessing is a laugh.

Lily and I share a side eye. Maybe Moss was right. Instead of saying anything I wave to the class and say hello. Hoping they'll get over the Violet/Pirate thing.

"That's enough class! *Violet* has come to pose for us today so we can practice drawing people. How cool is that?" The kids stare at my sister as if she's lost her mind. Apparently my posing isn't cool at all.

Rodney, the ginger, puts his hand up and wriggles in his seat, as if desperate to say something. Jazz nods his way, "How come that other person isn't standing up there?"

"That's a very good question," I answer, turning towards Lily with giant eyes, imploring her to join me in the hot seat. Lily just smiles softly and shakes her head.

The little hearing impaired girl gets the attention of her assistant and furiously signs something, her little hands flying.

"Morgan would like to know why they don't look like you," her assistant asks.

My sisters and I look at each other. We all look alot alike, the only difference is our hair color.

"I think we look a lot alike," Jazz informs the class.

Quick as a flash a cute little boy with braces on his arms put his hand up, "No because that one has huge eyebrows. I don't have enough brown pencil to draw them that big." He frets, pointing directly to me.

Said big eyebrows fly up to my hairline as Lily covers her snort with a delicate cough. Jazz decides to ignore his question, but that doesn't stop the little turds from all nodding in agreement.

"Maybe Moss was onto something," Lily whispers.

"And the eyebrow one has a snaggle tooth!" another kid

yells out, pointing like I'm a circus freak.

"Her eyes are too big for her face, too."

"Why does she look all sweaty? Has she been playing outside?"

"Ah, excuse me, class!" Jazz holds her hands up in front of her, signing. "Remember that we are all people, with feelings and quirks that make us unique. Violet has very large eyebrows –" My head whips in her direction and I glare at her. "And she has crooked teeth and giant eyes and she does get a little sweaty, but these are all things that make Violet uniquely Violet. And I think we should celebrate that there's only one Violet in the world."

"Probably a good thing," Rodney, the evil ginger says under his breath but loud enough for the dead to hear.

"Moving right along," Jazz continues, "remember when I helped you write down what type of poses you'd like our model to do? Well, I've put them all into a special cup. We'll choose a pose at random and Violet will hold the pose for you to draw. Make sense?"

The kids perk up at the thought of drawing so they nod eagerly. Well, all the kids except one boy who looks asleep, a kid currently putting his pencil sharpenings in the hair of the girl next to him, and a little dark-haired boy who has been sitting very quietly lining his pencils on his desk top. Jazz makes a big show of shaking around her coffee cup full of suggestions, and even asks the kids to do a drum roll, resulting in a lot of out of time banging on the tables.

"And the pose Violet will be doing for us today is………. the body of a person who fell from a tall building and landed on the top of a car." The kids lose their minds like they just won the lottery and Jazz rolls her lips in between her teeth to stop herself from laughing. She turns and gives me a shit eating grin, "Well, Vi, assume the position."

Chapter 3

Jules

Where the fuck is everybody? I'm meant to be interviewing Violet Davies, and my siblings offered to keep an eye on Juno for me. So far I've walked through the Tombs Security building and aside from our recon team, I haven't seen anyone related to me.

Getting out of the lift on the top floor, I make my way through the offices, Juno swinging from the carseat in my hand.

"If you're looking for everyone they're at the clubhouse." Dayz's voice drifts down the hall.

"Why the fuck are they all there? They're meant to be working. And keeping an eye on the kid while I interview Violet," I growl, stomping my way into her office.

Dayz doesn't even look up, eyes glued to her screen. "We're always there. Which is why I've taken the liberty of changing the interview location to the clubhouse. We all spend large amounts of time there, and Juno's nanny will likely visit on occasion. Meaning we need to know the cop's sister is a safe person to have around the Littles." I stare at her. "Oh, and

Marx wants it there."

"When did Marx become *our* Pres?" She looks at me as if I'm an idiot before rolling her eyes. "Besides, we've already run checks. We even did a deep dive into that harassment case that got her fired."

Turns out that while the sergeant's sister may be known as "the angry nurse", she actually had a pretty good reason to threaten her patient's daughter. Around 6 months after Violet was let go, said daughter was imprisoned for neglecting her disabled mother.

"I know, that's why interviewing at the clubhouse would be best. The whole extended family is there, and we all gotta feel her out."

I tuck my finger inside my shirt collar and loosen it a little. Heat spreads through my body and I can feel my pulse start to rise at my annoyance with the situation so I tell myself to lock it down. I'm not like August where I let the stress get to me. My family has decided to be a pain in the ass so I will deal with it. I am in control of the situation. I can pivot and do the interview at the clubhouse. I'm zen as fuck and have all the background information I need.

"It'll be worth it," Dayz continues, "Anyone can look good on paper. But is she a douche? Will she be mean to the kids or judgey to the brothers? Is she skanky? Will she want to mount Fox and Nitro, leaving your child in the corner with a bottle full of juice?" She sounds like she's been spending too much time with Mira. Dayz turns to look at me briefly, before her eyes dart elsewhere. "More importantly will she wear perfume that gives me a headache?"

"I thought this was about the safety of the kids?"

"On a scale of usefulness, I bring more to the table than your baby. So my needs should come before hers." Dayz replies, eyes back on her screen. "I've finished now. Drive me to the clubhouse so we can meet your prospective nanny. I will be sitting in, just so you know."

I stare down at her as she puts her fidget toys back in their proper places. "Why?" As Tombs Security, my brothers and I panel interview every new employee. Dayz deemed it a waste of her time. Her wanting in on the interview is a new development.

"It's part of my role in the DRMC. I need to manage the safety of our families and the club."

"I thought that was Rhodie's job as enforcer and VP?"

"We're a package deal." She stands and gathers her things. "I'm ready." I give her a nod and she continues loading shit into her giant bag. "I'll go easy on her. I won't even ask hard questions. I just have to vet her for the club and whether or not she'll be a safe person around Chomper."

Chomper is a fucking alligator. Sure he might have a fucked up jaw so he has to be handfed, and he's got toes that curl up so his mobility is an issue, but still. Who the hell would take on a gator? Not wanting to argue any longer I wave her out ahead of me and follow her through the office and out to the parking lot where my SUV is parked. Unlocking the car I lean in and make sure Juno is secure. I'm getting faster at putting her in and out which I'm fucking pleased about. I have to shave another 20 seconds off my time to beat Gus, but I think it's an achievable goal.

"You're getting better at that," Dayz says in her emotionless voice, staring through the front windscreen.

"Don't really have a choice," I mutter back, shutting Juno's door and getting into the driver's seat.

"Sure you do." Dayz replies, as I start the car and make my way out to the road. "Loads of parents realize they're not cut out for this job and they give the baby to someone who is cut out for it."

I side eye my sister, she's sitting bolt upright, looking out the window paying me no attention. Dayz may not know how to read social cues or emotions very well, but she can read me. "My question is, why do you think you're not cut out to be Juno's father?"

We drive in silence. Dayz doesn't care if I take the time to think my answer through. Hell, she doesn't even care if I never answer her. I roll my shoulders and then glance at her. "I'm not soft. A kid needs softness."

"No they don't. Pops isn't soft and we turned out fine."

I slowly turn to look at her, but she's still gazing the other way. Nobody would ever look at us and say we were fine. Although they probably wouldn't look at us and say we were fully fucked up either so maybe she has a point. Suddenly she turns in her seat to look at me.

"You're scared and you need to not be. You need to change. Remember when I was just me, back before Rhodie? I was awesome then, but then I fell in love and found friends and now we have a big family full of people that are better at some stuff than we are. I'm a better person now, on all levels. Probably too good. You need to level up, Jules. Let our people help you." She turns back to the front. "And maybe this nanny. But I reserve judgement. We don't need snitches in our lives." She looks thoughtful for a moment. "Actually, if she snitches as bad as her brother polices, then we should be fine.

"Dayz, you know that Sergeant Davies is actually pretty fucking good at his job, right?"

She snorts, "He lets perps ride in the front seat. I haven't researched it but I'm pretty sure that's illegal."

"He lets people he knows are innocent ride in the front. There's a difference."

Her brows pinch and she squishes her bottom lip, a tell tale stim that she's thinking through what I've said. We travel the rest of the way in silence, the only sound the snuffling of Juno in the backseat. Flicking my eyes to the rearview my gaze catches her intense dark glare, making the corners of my lips twitch. Her little face softens for a moment, and I'm surprised at the sweet look on her face, transforming it from what I see every time I look in the mirror, to what I see when I look at my sister. I get a weird tightness in my chest and I tell myself to breathe and settle down. There is no way in hell I'm going to start taking antacids like Gus.

"We're the same, you and me. We weren't born to know what to do with feelings, but we can learn. I learned how to love Rhodie and all the men in the clubhouse. With help you can learn how to love Juno," Dayz murmurs as we pull into the DRMC lot. She turns to me, her gaze holding mine. "You're one of the best men I know, Jules. If anyone can successfully raise a baby conceived at an orgy, it's you."

"Thanks, Dayz."

She gives me a nod, her eyes looking over my shoulder. "Come on, let's interrogate the new nanny."

Violet

Pulling into the clubhouse parking lot, where the man on the gate directed, I'm overwhelmed by the number of bikes and cars here. And the fact that thanks to Jazz's kids and my tight scheduling, I have arrived at a job interview with two bright green hand prints directly on my boobs. Moss was right, those kids are feral.

I take in my surroundings and admit to myself that I have no idea about MC life or even Tombs Security life. I have two options. Panic, or think of this like all those times we had Christmas with my mom's side of the family. People and kids everywhere, chaos, noise, cooking smells and laughter. I can do this. This is just a big family, waiting to get a look at the fresh meat hoping to be employed. Easy does it. I take some deep breaths, inhaling and exhaling. On the last inhale I choke on air as my eyes meet the dark glare of a true to life god. I've seen Jules Tombs in passing, I mean he's been into my mom's shop a few times when I've been out the back trying not to murder her plants, but holy shit, having his dark gaze on me has sent an electric pulse straight to my crotch and momentarily wiping my memory of sweet, cute, blonde accountant Josh.

Shit! Josh! I look down and quickly whisper to my vagina that she's taken, and to pull herself together, then tip my head up, smile at Jules Tombs and exit my car. Like a normal person. I am Violet Elena Ximena Davies, I can do anything and my mom and dad believe in me, I whisper as I try to pull myself together. I'm here to score a job looking after a sweet little girl, and maybe kick start my passion for a new career. Not ogle her dad. Besides, I'm suspicious of overly good looking people. They have terrible personalities a lot of the time. They never had to cultivate a personality or sense of humour because people have always fallen over themselves to do whatever hot people tell them to do. Well not me.

"Jules?" I ask, playing it cool, holding my hand out to shake.

He stares at me, his gaze moving from the top of my head, to the tips of my toes, only hovering for a moment on my hand-printed tatas. He nods once, then ignores my hand, tipping his head towards the door. I was right! Hot guys are rude. And I guess I'm following him. Which is fine because I get to see the backside of him which is as delightful as the front side. The man is the epitome of tall, dark and handsome. He stops abruptly inside and I bump into his hard body, eliciting a grunt from him.

Peering around his large body, the body that smells divine and has me reminding myself again that I have a boyfriend, I notice a large group of people staring at me. Well, a large group of women staring at me. The men are all pretending to not stare but I can still see their eyes darting to my boobs and away, in a not very stealth way.

Taking the bull by the horns I wave and give them all my best smile. "Hi! I'm Violet, nice to meet you. Ignore the shirt, I was helping out in my sister's art class."

"Oh, you were the latest victim," A short-haired pregnant woman snorts. I vaguely remember Jazz saying Tav Tombs' kid was in there.

"Your kid isn't ginger with glasses that make his eyes look huge is he?" I ask, indicating my boobs and praying that she's not because that Rodney kid is a menace and I can't be in the same vicinity as him and hope to keep my sanity.

She barks out a laugh, shaking her head. Phew.

"Have a seat, Violet," Jules says gruffly, abruptly cutting in and indicating a seat at a table in the middle of the room.

Everyone who isn't a Tombs seems to make themselves busy, milling around in this sort of common room area, while Jules sits down across from me. A chair scrapes the floor and Tuesday sits next to him. Then Sidney Tombs, who I recognize from around town, takes another seat, and before you know it the whole Tombs family is sitting across from me and this whole thing is feeling a little Shark Tank-y. If Shark Tank had Lori Greiner with an alligator strapped to her chest.

"Quick fire, what would you do if you locked the baby in a car on a hot day?" Grandpa Tombs asks with a squint, one bushy brow raised.

Relishing the fact that he's dived straight in and saved me from nervous chit chat, I dig around in my bag for my keys and hold up the tool attached to my keyring, "Smash the driver's side window to get access to the vehicle, the keys and the baby."

He purses his lips and nods slowly.

"Juno has a rash, isn't eating and is running a fever. What do you do?" One of the brothers asks. I'm not sure which one, but this one has a beautiful tanned woman beside him with a baby on her lap.

I work hard not to roll my eyes. I'm a trained nurse, this is easy shit. "Depending on her age I would assume she's teething. I'd give her Baby Tylenol, something cool to chew on and make an appointment for her with her pediatrician if I was concerned or needed further medical advice."

They all share a look and the one I'm guessing is Tav Tombs, because he has the short-haired lady in his lap, leans forward. "Sometimes we share care of the kids together. Are you open to having two extra children around even if one of them enjoys blowing things up?"

Wait, what? What sort of question is that? I don't think about it, I just answer. "As long as you are happy to have things exploding then I'll be sure to keep an eye on them and keep the baby away from exploding stuff. I guess." I shrug, I mean, surely that's hypothetical, right?

Throughout this weird quiz Jules Tombs has sat silently, watching me answer his family's questions one by one.

"Your brother is a Sergeant. Perhaps the worst sergeant in the world, but the law nonetheless. If you were to see questionable things would we be able to trust you not to snitch?"

I stare at Tuesday Tombs thinking through her question. Moss might say that the MC is full of good men, and women, but I know they can't always be above board. I've read MC romance books. I know that sometimes there are grey areas. I'm guessing sometimes DRMC, and in turn the Tombs family, may have to step into the grey every now and then.

"If it's questionable but for a good cause I doubt I'd need to say anything to my brother. I mean, I might snitch if I saw you hurt someone who didn't deserve it. But outside of that scenario, not a word."

They share a look, and I notice the MC men and women who are trying not to eavesdrop share a look as well. The Pres, sits in the background, arms crossed, intense look on his face. I would feel intimidated but given that I'm still sitting here, I'm guessing they don't see me as a threat. Yet. Taking their silence as approval, I lean forward, holding Jules' dark gaze.

"What else you got?"

Chapter 4

Jules

She stares at me waiting for me to ask her something. I stare back wanting to know everything about her and nothing at all. I may have to share my space with her while she looks after Juno, but that doesn't mean we have to be friends. Or anything other than employer and employee. Even if my dick is interested in seeing more of her. I ignore him. That's just a physical reaction to a beautiful woman, and fuck me if she isn't beautiful. I'm actually shocked that Moss Davies has a sister this hot. I mean, I knew they were attractive, but fuck me. It's like sitting across from Salma Hayek, but the Salma in From Dusk Til Dawn.

"The role is 7am til 6 pm. If I have to work late I will prearrange hours with you. Sometimes I go away for work and you will be expected to stay on the Tombs property for those days. Will that cause any problems with your significant other?" Out of the corner of my eye Tav's head slowly turns in my direction, but I choose to ignore him. Everything I have laid out is what I need. What I don't need is a husband or boyfriend kicking up a stink or staying at my house while I'm away.

Her dark brows furrow for a moment as she thinks through what I've said. She must come to a conclusion because her face relaxes and she nods my way. "Sounds reasonable. My boyfriend Josh is a sweetheart so he'll understand, there won't be a problem there."

"I will need Josh's surname so I can run a background check. I don't want any weirdos near my kid."

"Fair enough. It's Baker. He works at Milton and Co accounting firm. He's a great guy so I'm sure you'll find nothing alarming. Other than his love for Lego figurines." She smiles at her joke and I quickly raise my hand to my left, stopping Cove in her tracks. The kid is obsessed with Lego, and I have no time to open that can of worms.

I need to finish this interview and according to plan, ask her to hang around for a drink and to meet the rest of the family and the club. That way we can observe what she's like with everyone and if she smells satisfactory for Dayz's sake. Also, having the women interrogate her will be the make or break on whether this whole thing is a good idea or a huge fucking mistake.

She sits looking at me and my family, seemingly relaxed despite the circumstances.

"Does your mama know you're here interviewing to become a nanny?" Pops asks, his bushy brow raised.

"Yes, sir. She's the one who's pushing me to give this a try. She fired me from the shop so I could find my 'passion'," she says in finger quotes as she rolls her eyes.

"Do you think cleaning up puke and shit could be your passion?" Pops' face scrunches up.

"Ah, yeah. I used to do a lot of that when I was a nurse.

Unfortunately, being let go means it's a little hard getting another nursing role in this town." He squints at her, then nods, tagging in Gus to ask a follow up question.

"Why were you let go, exactly?" Gus asks, face impassive, knowing full well why she was let go. The question is, will she tell the truth?

"Look, I'm sure you've done your research. I threatened, not assaulted, threatened, Homer Gaskin's wife. But in my defence she was her mother's main carer and she was neglecting her something fierce. Bed sores, infections, you name it. I, um, may have offered to chain her to the bed and let her scrawny, rotten ass fester until she felt what her mother feels on a daily basis."

Chuckles can be heard around the common room, causing Violet's tense look to soften into a smirk.

"Good on you, girl. I would have done the same. Or worse." Pops smirks, Violet grinning back at him.

"What's something that makes you happy?" Tav butts in. He always asks these types of questions in interviews. Apparently what brings people joy says a lot about them.

"My family," Violet answers, without blinking.

"Your biggest weakness?"

Again, without hesitation, she answers, "My family."

Pops squints at her, rubbing a hand down his stubble. "Alright girl, biggest fear?"

I lean back, crossing my arms, I'm sure I can guess it'll be something like 'losing her family'.

Her face screws up a moment, before she pulls her shoulders back, and stares at me, then my family. "Getting into a street fight and whoever I'm fighting rips my top and I have to fight with my titties out."

I blink once, twice at her answer, the whole common room silent until Pops throws his head back and laughs like a hyena. The Ol Ladies start yelling out their agreement and my gaze meets Violet's, a small smile on her lips.

The laughter dies down and my sister stands abruptly, "Well, that's all we need to know. Stay for a drink." She wanders off to the bar, where Rhodie kisses her face off, poor Chomper squished between them.

Violet's wide eyes follow before looking back at me for permission. Well, that's a pleasant surprise. I nod, and she offers a small smile, getting up and making her way to the bar with Ana and Blanche flanking her.

"Well, brother. What do you think?" Tav asks, his eyes following his Ol Lady.

"I think in terms of care she will be good. She's a trained nurse, will be good under pressure and from a large family so good with feelings and shit." I answer, watching her chatting away.

"So, a thousand times better than you?" Tav smirks.

"Exactly."

Before I can get up and get a well earned drink, I'm surrounded by half of my sister's girl gang. Mira plops down in front of me, Nat on one side and Remy and Lovely on the other.

"You know what this is like?" Mira starts, and I know that there's no point in stopping whatever she's going to say, "this is the classic nanny trope. She'll be in your home, raising your child, you'll notice how good she is with Juno, she'll notice you're distant and need encouragement. Over time you'll come to find that the brightest parts of your day are when you arrive home and your little girl calls your name, Violet setting the dinner table with food she's made by her own hand." My brows raise higher and higher as she sighs, "You'll ruin what you're building of course, because you'll try and put space between the both of you, you're her boss! You can't fall in love with her! She'll leave your home and you'll smell her scent on your things, it'll cause you to go on a bender until your brothers, both biological and MC hit you with some home truths where you'll hunt her down and in a public display declare your love." She slumps after her monologue, as if exhausted by her creative imaginings.

"She has a boyfriend," I deadpan.

"Oh, in THAT case I bet he's a terrible boyfriend, and over time she will come to see that you will treat her so much better and -"

I abruptly stand and leg it from the table, the women cackling at me rushing away. I have no problem with the Ol Ladies, but there is no way I can fall for Violet. I'm her employer and there's a huge power imbalance and shit! Isn't that exactly what Mira just word vomited at me?

A hand lands on my shoulder, grounding me and chasing away the seeds that Mira planted.

"If you're interested we're having a little party later this evening. Just us and some girls, what do you say?" Nitro smirks at me, knowing that this is the shit I live for.

Or was. "Not tonight. I have Juno and I don't need another one."

Fox snickers, "What? Do you think you have super sperm or something?"

I shrug. "Who knows? All I know was one night of debauchery and I have a kid that I have to hire a nanny for. I don't need anymore coming out of the woodwork."

They share a nervous look, as if they never once figured that our activities could come back to bite them on the ass. I know I never did. I was more concerned with how many girls we could fuck in an evening.

"Jules, little miss wanted her dad," Mama Debs says, drawing my attention to her with Juno in her arms.

The little girl not only has a frown, but her little lip is pushed out, as if she got the raw deal by being in Mama Debs' arms. Any other kid would kill to be there, all safe and warm and loved. Instead Juno wants to come to me, the guy who is stiff and uncomfortable with contact of any kind. Well, other than fucking.

Mama Debs hands her over and Juno hides her face under my chin, letting out a sigh. My chest tightens and as I do every time, I ignore it.

Mama Debs rubs her back, smiling, before her gaze finds mine. "I'm proud of you, *tama*, you stepped up when I know how easy it would have been for you to walk away." She gives me a soft smile and runs her hand over my hair, like she's done a thousand times before.

The first time she did it freaked me out a little. But since then I've come to enjoy the warmth. I give her a tight smile and look toward Violet, at the bar laughing with some of the MC brothers.

"You'll be making a good call hiring her. She'll be a good influence on you both." Mama Debs' gaze moves from me to Juno. "It'd be nice to have a granddaughter that smiles, rather than frowns."

"I don't think she's a miracle worker," I reply drily, making Mama Debs laugh.

"You never know, Jules, she may be just what you need."

Violet

I'm surrounded by women and I like it. It reminds me of when my sisters and I get together, which lets face it, is all the time. You've heard of helicopter parents? Well, we're a whole damn helicopter family. Always up in each other's business.

They all speed talk over each other, and I would be worried about not knowing all their names, but they have those leather vest things on with their names on the front, although, I'm pretty sure some of them are nicknames, given that Tuesday's says "Chewy".

"How come your vest thing says Chewy?" I ask. I'm not sure if it's polite to ask, but you never learn anything if you don't ask so I go ahead anyway. The worst that can happen is they call me a nosey bitch.

Tuesday looks down at the leather patch over her breast before looking up at me. Or, moreso, over my shoulder. "It's called a cut. You get them when you become an Ol Lady. And the guys nicknamed me 'Chewy' like 'Chewsday'. Rider came up with it." She beams at the big, blonde biker that seems to be in the thick of annoying some of his MC brothers.

"Oh, Oh! As the newest recruit let me do the introductions!" A statuesque blonde says. She's dressed head to toe in color, her curly blonde hair in a ponytail.

The women share glances, and try to hold in their laughter. It's clear that these women are good friends, and they know that whatever is coming my way will be a lot.

"Have at it," Tuesday, or, um, Chewy gestures.

The blonde pumps her fist, hissing "yusssss" under her breath. "OK, I know it's a lot. It was a lot when I first got here. So I'll give you the cliff notes version. Chewy you met, and fingers crossed you'll be working for her brother, these two-" She points two fingers to two dark haired women, one I recognise as Tav Tombs' woman, "are sisters, Blanche and Lovely. Blanche belongs to Tav and she's preggo with a little Tombs. Lovely belongs to herself," her eyes dart to Marx before darting back, "and has a little girl named Bee." The one named Lovely smiles and waves. "This is Nat; her man is that hottie over there," Mira looks around the common room before pointing out the tall, dark-haired bearded man with bright blue eyes. "Remy here is Wire's woman, they're hackers and computer dweebs and he's that tall, dark, drink of water over there," indicates another good looking man. "And Ana you would have seen next to Gus. They have a giant son named after Sidney Tombs but they call him Jr. Oh, and my man is the big, blonde, biker hottie. We met in jail." She beams and turns toward said big, blonde biker, who even from across the room must feel her eyes on him because he turns and gives her a dazzling smile that transforms his whole face, taking him from menacing to golden retriever.

"I feel like I'm going to struggle here," I sigh.

"Because there's so many people?" Remy asks with a worried look on her face.

"Nah, too many people is fine. I'll struggle because everyone is so hot," I lament.

"Wait, is that a problem?" Remy's nose screws up.

"Yeah, because in my experience hot people are assholes."

The women throw their heads back and cackle, "Well, we never said they weren't assholes," Nat says between guffaws.

Chewy frowns at me for a moment, a puzzled look on her face. "You're really hot. Are you an asshole?"

I take a sip of the beer the prospect handed me. He looks really young and a lot like Blanche and Lovely. I'm not overly sure he's even old enough to be serving alcohol, but that's not my problem. "Um, thanks for the compliment, and in answer to your question, that would depend on who you ask."

Chewy narrows her eyes, as if trying to figure me out, but is interrupted by the rest of the women laughing at my sentiment.

A big man wanders over, nodding at everyone, "Ladies," he booms, before knocking twice on the bar top then turning his head to me. "I've worked with you before, haven't I?"

I take him in, my eyes widening in recognition. Usually he's in scrubs with crocs, today he's in boots, jeans, a black tee showing off his sleeve tattoos, and his cut. "Dr. Hansen?"

He nods, brow furrowed. "There's two Davies nurses. Are you the one that cries or the angry one?"

My hand flies to my chest, "How dare you accuse me of being the crying one! That's Fiona Davies. She's the blonde that shagged Dr. Carter in the supply room. Sheesh."

He nods again, this time with a smirk. "Ah, so the angry one then. You're the one that restrained that drunk in the ER waiting room that time, yeah?"

My eyes dart, hoping no one else heard that. Of course everyone, including Jules Tombs is looking this way, because Dr. Hansen has the voice of a fog horn. "Yeah, that was me," I mumble and then avoid eye contact.

A booming laugh shakes the loud ginger's body as he throws his head back, "I saw it go down, that shit was magnificent! The way you twisted his arm and frogmarched him through the ER was chef's kiss!" He chuckles, wiping his watering eye. "Tombs better give you the damn job, that way you can keep that lot in check and we can relax around here for once."

"What the hell are you on about? We're fucking delightful!" Sidney Tombs yells across the room, looking set to kick some ass.

"Ignore them. They get jealous of our sweet skills," Chewy says.

I smile politely because I have no idea what type of sweet skills she's packing, but I know from the spicy MC books I've read, the Icer is the person who takes care of things. In a permanent sense. Before I can do a Flora Davies and ask a bunch of personal or inappropriate questions, Jules Tombs walks over, with a little girl plastered to his chest. If I thought he was hot before, then he's a supernova of hotness now. But still a little assholey so I know I'm safe from the hotness. Oh, and I have Josh. Mustn't forget Josh. We've been dating for six months and it's been the best relationship I've ever been in. He's yet to meet my family but I just know that with the love they show, and how thoughtful and kind Josh is, that they'll get on like a house on fire.

"Violet, this is Juno. If you're employed she will be your charge." He leans back slightly, looking down at his daughter, gently maneuvering her in his arms so she's facing me.

With them both looking at me with their blank faces it's remarkable how strong this family's genes are.

"Holy crap! I'm going to have to call my brother, a crime has been committed!" I blurt out, without thinking.

Silence descends and the tension in the clubhouse ratchets right up. The only sound is the stomping of Johnny, I mean, Marx's boots coming directly for me.

"Mind informing us what crime has been committed?" Marx growls down at me,

"Yeah." I point to Juno, "That baby is a thief."

Marx's brows pinch trying to figure me out.

"She stole his face." I gesture back to Juno and everyone in the clubhouse starts to relax.

Well, everyone except Marx. The Pres. Johnny Paxton. He glares down at me, then frowns a little, shaking his head. "I was hoping you weren't going to take after Flora too much, but I'm shit outta luck, aren't I?"

I smile up at him, "Yeah, sorry buddy. Flora's genes are strong. But I can assure you, I'd never snitch without a damn good reason. I don't work like that. You respect me, I'll respect you and you can maim as many people for the greater good as you like."

He rolls his eyes and gives me a nod, heading toward the bar.

"Phew! That was intense!" I say to no one in particular, before turning back to Jules. "But seriously, man, that kid is you all over. You copy and pasted your exact resting bitch face. It's uncanny."

Jules looks down at his daughter in his arms, and she looks up at him as if having a very grumpy, silent conversation. They must come to an agreement because Jules' gaze moves to his family, all leaning against the bar. They give small nods, before he looks toward Marx and Rhodie, who repeat the gesture.

"When can you start?"

Chapter 5

Jules

Footsteps thump down the hall and I just know that I'm going to be invaded. Flicking my eyes to the clock in the bottom of my laptop screen I note its 9.15am, so they left me longer than I expected.

"Morning, brother, how are you on this fine day?" Tav asks, flopping down in the chair across from my desk, not even waiting for an invitation.

I scowl at him, waiting to address him when Gus and Dayz are here, which won't take long as I can hear them coming now.

"Jules," Gus offers roughly.

"Hey Jules," Dayz follows, albeit slightly perkier.

She sits at the small conference table in the corner, eyes on her laptop, while Gus leans his big bastard body against the wall, arms and feet crossed.

He and Tav stare at me, while I stare back. I don't know why they're here and I'm not one for guessing, so I'll wait them out.

We sit in silence, the only noise the sound of Dayz tapping

away on her keyboard.

"Ugh, fine!" Tav throws his arms up. "How was your morning? Did you fret leaving Juno with Violet? Did you shed a tear, looking at your daughter, saying things like 'they grow up so fast!'?"

I glare at him and his lips twitch. He's fucking loving this.

"No, you asshole. I didn't feel anything. Violet knows what she's doing. I handed Juno over, and left."

They all stare, even Dayz has stopped typing abruptly.

"You didn't!?" Tav gasps, scandalized.

"I did. It's her *job*. Besides, Juno won't even notice. She's a baby and she's only known me for a few weeks." My reasoning is sound. A few weeks isn't enough to form a bond strong enough to result in separation anxiety.

Gus's brows lower, "I think you'll find that a baby will imprint pretty fucking quickly, there, brother."

I stare at him for a moment and then shrug it off. Even if she was starting to get attached, I still have work to do and Violet is well qualified to take care of her. She's a nurse for fuck's sake. Juno's probably safer with her than with any other woman. At least Violet knows what to do in an emergency. And I know that this morning they've just been hanging out around the house getting to know each other.

I can feel both of my brothers staring at me, so I lock gazes with Gus, knowing that Tav will get pissy at me ignoring him.

Gus's brow raises as he stares me down. "So you just walked straight out the door, not a care in the world?" I nod in reply, "And you haven't contacted them to check in to see how they're getting on?"

I frown. "Why would I? Violet knows what she's doing."

I finally move my gaze to Tav, giving him my famous blank

stare. I even add in a little frown, the one I know he hates. He frowns back, then his lips twitch and a knowing look comes over his face.

"You've been watching them, haven't you?" his smile spreads.

Fuck! I hold his gaze, giving nothing away. If I react too fast he'll think I'm being defensive.

"Oh, resting bitch face me all you want, big brother, but my money is on you checking in on them. And look at that." He looks down at his watch. "It's only been two hours since you left the house."

Gus has a shiteating grin on his face and I know he's happy to sit back and let Tav run this bullshit interrogation of sorts. It's not really an interrogation, not when the person asking questions has started answering them himself.

"So, two hours out of the house, I think you've checked the feed, hmmmm," he taps his stupid bottom lip, "four times? Once every half hour?"

How the fuck does he know? Has he been watching me?

"Actually, he's checked them six times." I direct my glare over Tav's shoulder to my little hacker sister who hasn't looked up once.

"Ohhh, I see. So the dump and run was really a dump and crawl away at a snail's pace only to then check in on them like a creeper. Got it," Tav nods and then throws his head back and laughs.

I fucking hate his laugh. He sounds like those hyenas from the Lion King. Not only is it a grating sound, but it always lasts for fucking ever, coming down from full hysterics to giggles. I tip my head back and stare at the ceiling tiles, counting them from left to right.

"Well, good to see you have a heart brother," Gus says, pushing off from the wall. "But don't forget, you can always work from home if you need." He walks out of my office, tapping twice on the door jamb before leaving.

Dayz picks up her laptop and leaves, not saying a word after snitching about my viewing habits to Tav. The big bastard is still in the chair across from me.

"You know, there's nothing wrong with worrying about your kid. It's natural."

When I don't reply he gives me a pitiful look and a huge sigh. "Fine, I give up. But one day, it's going to sneak up and kick you in the balls, just how much you love your daughter. It happened to me with with my kids, it'll happen to you with Juno." He stands and starts moving toward my door, turning to back out as he singsongs, "Mark my words, Jules."

I wait until I can hear him further down the hall before I do a cursory glance around my office and then log in to the camera feed in my cabin. My checks are running a few minutes behind thanks to my annoying family.

I flick through the rooms. They've been mainly in the lounge for the past two hours, but seeing my empty lounge on the screens means they must be somewhere else in the house. I cycle through the rooms and pull apart the images, noticing where some things have been tidied or other things have been filed. Huh. No sign of them. Maybe they're on the deck? I tap into the outdoor camera and take a look around. Still no one to be found. I cycle through the interior cameras again in case I missed something, but still nothing. A quick check on our perimeter cameras show's her car parked exactly where she left it, on a ridiculous angle between mine and Pops' houses, pretty much blocking the path.

My fingers tap on my desk and I wait for my body to relax. No point in getting worked up about nothing. There is no real trouble the two of them can get into. Unless you count the scum that Tombs Security investigates on a regular basis. Not all people trafficking is women from poor countries. People would be astounded if they found out that the lovely couple in their cul de sac aren't the biological parents of their kids. Enough money means you can pretty much buy a nuclear family. Kids are taken everyday to sell on the black market to infertile couples. I close my eyes, and breathe, consciously focusing on lowering my heart rate. I'm sure they're fine. I mean, they may have just popped over to visit Pops. My shoulders loosen and I tap a few keys, bringing up the tracker I put in Juno's little carseat. And the one in her baby carrier thing. And the one in her diaper bag. It may be a little much, but this kid is in my care and it will never be said that I wasn't doing my absolute best to keep her safe and well.

The location of all three trackers light up in a cluster on my screen, meaning all three of them are together. That's good. Leaning closer and squinting I check the map, then the satellite images of the maps. How in the fuck did they get to town if Violet's car is at home? And why the fuck did they go to town? Violet never said anything about taking Juno anywhere. 20 minutes ago they were at home, where I saw them safe and sound. Don't they know what type of people are out there?

Standing abruptly I snatch my keys from where I've left them on my desk and stride out of my office, crashing into Gus on the other side of my door.

"What the fuck! Move!" I growl, Gus's brows flying up.

He opens his mouth to speak, then closes it, tilting his head to assess me.

"I don't have time for your bullshit, get out of the way, Gus."

I barge past and make my way to the elevator, mashing the button incessantly until it opens. Stomping inside I hit the ground floor button, watching the doors close in, cutting off the view of Gus texting. Then his fat hand shoots out and jams into the doors before they close and he climbs in with me.

"So, brother, where are we going and who are we dealing with?"

Violet

I dance around to the tinny music in the supermarket with Juno frowning at me from her position in the shopping cart. I have never in my life met a baby with resting bitch face. It's almost crazy. But then I guess you see her dad and it's a face she comes by honestly at least.

"What else do we need, girl?" Sidney, or Pops, as he told me to call him, asks.

"Well, do you want them healthy or unhealthy?" I'm not sure if he's a healthy eating type of guy normally. I mean, for his age he's in good condition. Still very spry, but I guess love will do that to a man, and whoa, does he love his woman!

He's told me a million times how amazing a cook Debs is, so I'm not sure how I've ended up here, at the supermarket buying ingredients for tamales, but hey, it gets me and Juno out of the house. As lovely as Jules' house is, it's very manly and expensive looking and not overly comfortable. He seems to really like architectural type furniture so his couch looks amazing but it's as hard as a brick. It'll be interesting to see if he ever changes that out, now that he has a baby. My brother's house is full of soft squishy furniture with no real edges because his kids keep walking into things. In their defence, they're only two and head height to a lot of stuff. I'm sure they'll grow out of that. Eventually.

"What'll happen if I opt for the unhealthy ones?" Pops asks, his eyes narrowed.

"Nothing, they'll just taste infinitely better." I shrug.

"Unhealthy."

"Good, grab the lard for me?"

Pops hustles off in that direction and I push the cart further into the store. Before I can get through the frozen section I'm stopped in my tracks by a 6'2 wall of man with a scowl deep enough to make a normal woman crap her pants. But alas, I'm not a normal woman and a big grumpy man isn't going to scare me. Although he does make my down belows tingle. I ignore that and hold his eye contact to see if he'll move.

"What the hell are you doing?" Jules growls at me.

"Shopping. What the hell are you doing?"

He looks taken aback at my question, but recovers a lot quicker than I expected. "I'm the one asking questions here. Why the hell are you here and not at home?"

Oh, so that's how he's playing it? "I am employed to nanny your child. The contract is completely clear on my tasks, which all involve child care and some housekeeping. What the contract does not state is that I have to do all of that from your home. Also, as a ground rule, I refuse to answer questions if they're barked at me." I mean mug him for a moment, which probably isn't that intimidating given that he's a foot taller than I am and made of muscle, whereas I'm made of cheesecake.

"Hmph," he grunts at me, "As the father of the child you are caring for, it's my right to know where she is at all times and if you are to leave that you inform me of this. I wasn't informed that you would be leaving."

My eyes narrow at his wording. How *did* he know we left the house? And how did he know where we were? Glancing around the supermarket I look for clues as to how he knew where to find us. Pops doesn't seem like a snitch, and he also doesn't look the type to put up with any shit. Turning to look behind me I notice the other two Tombs men, both hiding unsuccessfully. If they were here earlier Pops and I would have seen them. Turning back to Jules I narrow my eyes, mirror his stance and then it hits me. The family owns a high end security company.

"Are you *tracking* me?"

He scoffs, crossing his arms over his chest. "Not you. Her." He nods to Juno who is smiling up at her daddy, the first real smile I've seen her give.

Huh. For a man that shows little affection, it's kinda heart–warming that he cares enough to have a tracker on Juno. Heartwarming and a little crazy but hey, there are worse things to be.

"Fine, so you tracked us here and the plan was to interrogate and or scare me enough that Juno and I stay home forever?" His eyes dart to his siblings for help. I spin toward them and they jump, then take off further into the store.

"Yes. I guess," he mumbles, rubbing the back of his neck.

I stare him down, trying to get a read on the man. He acts disinterested about most things, and then has a freak out about us leaving the house. I know that he has to work overnight sometimes, and my brother has alluded to the fact that Tombs

Security works alongside the alphabet agencies and the MC, so maybe he knows something I don't know? I decide to cut him some slack. For the moment.

"Well, how about I send you a message if we leave the house and we leave it at that?"

Before he can answer Pops comes around the corner, slowly at first then speeding up when he sees Jules. "What the hell are you doing here? Violet is with me today, so stop sniffing around and get back to work. Fuck's sake," he grumbles.

"I should have known you'd have something to do with this," Gus says, coming to join us in the middle of the aisle.

"What the fuck is that meant to mean?" Pops growls.

The Tombs start to bicker about something amongst themselves. Well, Gus, Tav and Pops do. Jules is glaring at me saying something but I'm mesmerized by the scene taking place over his shoulder.

"Violet, I asked you a question," Jules voice breaks through momentarily and I'm not sure whether I should pay him attention or find this kid's parents. "Violet! Are you listening to me?"

I really want to tell him that actually, no, I'm not listening to him, but I can't. Because right there behind Jules' back, that ginger bespectacled kid from my sister's class is making the blowfish face that you do on windows. From the inside of the frozen meat case. I have no idea how he crammed his chubby body in there.

"Violet!" Jules growls before he whirls around and stops. Frozen in place. "What the fuck?"

"What?" a chorus of Tombs voices all call out.

We all stare at Rodney for a moment before Gus snaps to attention, "Shit, how the hell did he get in there?" He walks over and pulls the door. It doesn't budge. He investigates the door for a moment, tugging here and there. "It's like, fixed shut. I think the kid might be stuck."

"I'll go get the store manager, you lot figure out how to get him out of there." Tav races off as Jules, Pops and I all look at each other.

"He's a tubby fucker. I'm sure that'll keep him warm until we can get to him," Pops says very seriously. So seriously in fact that I burst into laughter.

Jules stares at me like I'm insane. "There's a kid stuck in there, Violet. Who knows how the fuck they'll get him out."

"He looks really wedged in there," Gus agrees.

I roll my eyes, damn men. "Here, watch Juno for me," I tell all three of them, Tav still off in the store somewhere.

"What are you going to do?" Gus eyes me, "No, seriously Violet, this is an actual emergency. Probably will need the fire department or something."

I ignore his comments, storm up to the door and knock directly where Rodney's mouth is wide open, pressed against the glass. He leans back so he can see me better, then a wide grin covers his face as he yells "Pirate!" clear enough for everyone in the vicinity to hear.

I let out a sigh, then concentrate on the matter at hand. "Rodney, get out of the meat case."

He smiles wide, but refuses to budge. He got in there himself, he can get himself back out. "Rodney, get out of there, right now." He shakes his head and blowfishes the glass door again. He thinks he's winning, but I have his number. I slap my hand against the door before threatening, "Rodney, if you don't come out of there right this minute I will tell Miss Davies that you were being naughty, and naughty boys don't get to use hot glue guns do they?"

His eyes go huge and he starts to wriggle sideways like his life depends on it. I step back and take my position at the cart handle. Juno is wide-eyed watching the goings on.

"How the hell did you get him to move?" Pops asks.

"His name is Rodney and he's the kid who painted my boobs the day of the interview. He's in my sister's class and covets the hot glue gun. He's been working on his behaviour to earn enough stars to use it. He's almost there, so I threatened to take that away from him." I shrug.

All three men slowly turn to look at me. We stare at each other, the only noise the sound of Rodney's big, pale belly dragging across the glass of the door to the frozen pizzas.

"I bet you were a mean nurse," Pops says, eyeing me.

"Hey, this is the manag-oh look! He's getting himself out," Tav says, just as Rodney pushes open the door next to where he was wedged and steps out into the aisle.

"Not cool, Pirate, not cool." He points and narrows his eyes at me before waddling away.

"Pirate?" Pops says, turning to look at me.

"Don't ask." I turn my attention to Jules. "So, you were saying?"

He stares at me a moment, "Fuck it. Just tell me if you're leaving the house." I narrow my eyes at him. "Please."

I nod once. "Better. It's amazing how far you can get with good manners, you know."

Gus and Tav snort and Pops smirks and waves the middle finger at Jules as we head off to finish our shopping, Juno frowning at the world from her carrier.

"That went well, girl," Pops says after a minute.

"What's that?" I ask, grabbing the things we need off the

shelves and throwing them in the cart.

"Your first showdown. Jules is an asshole of the highest order. Love him, but he's a moody pain in the ass. The fact that he knows you're not a pushover is a good thing."

"Hard to be a pushover in my family. You'll be destroyed at the mere whiff of weakness."

He nods once. "I'm going to love having you around girl, I think you're exactly what he and that baby need."

Chapter 6

Jules

"Jules, how's fatherhood treating ya?" Flack asks as soon as I walk into the clubhouse. Remy's father is like the jolly uncle every kid has growing up. Well, from what I've seen in movies and shit. Both of my parents were only children.

"It's... something," I answer truthfully.

Life is a hell of a lot easier now that I have Violet. I get to go to work and do what I enjoy, with people I enjoy working with. Like our recon team, not so much my pain in the ass family. The evenings are still a struggle as Juno likes to fight going to sleep, but we have our morning routine set so at least my life is exactly as I like it until around 6pm.

Flack's eyes narrow and he screws up his face a little before letting out a breath. "I know how you feel, kid. Both my girls were the result of fucking around with club whores. Sunny's mother fucked off and left her with me. Like you it was a fucking shock to the system. I was in a 1% MC, had no idea what the hell to do with a kid. But there were people who knew more than me and taught me everything I know."

No offense to Flack, but I feel like my life is a fuckton more organised than his, so I guess if he can get his shit together and raise a baby, then so can I. I think through his words. "Wait, what about Remy's mom?"

"That was another matter. I had to share Rem with her crack whore hooker mother. Took me a while but I managed to get the bitch to give her up when she was four. Four years too long if you ask me."

I nod. I get what he's saying. He stops me as I turn to walk away.

"Family is more than the people that share your blood. They're the people who have your back. You've had mine and I got yours if shit gets a little too real for ya. Can't offer to babysit, but I know what it's like to think that you'll never love that little lump like she should be loved."

My brows pinch as I look into his rugged face. "What if I can't?"

He shakes his head at me, before stepping close and slapping a big hand on my shoulder. "The fact that you're worried about it shows you can. Trust your gut. It's never led you wrong before, right?"

I jerk my chin at him. He gives my shoulder a shake and swaggers back to where he came from, waiting at the bar for Niko to get him a fresh beer. I give a quick wave to Tav's eldest and take a seat in the recliner near the couch.

I'm not sure how DRMC became the place the Tombs family likes to hang out, but it is what it is and I don't question it. It's like a home away from home. Even Juno likes visiting, although that's probably because there's lots of kids around. She stares at them as they run around and make noise and do the shit kids do. She frowns the whole time, but every once in a while I've noticed her hands waving and her feet kicking.

I glance at my watch and take a few deep breaths to calm my irritation. My siblings are all meant to be here as we have something we need to run by the MC in Church tonight. As soon as they arrive we can get this shit started. I need to be home by 6pm, to relieve Violet. She doesn't mind if I'm a few minutes late here or there, but definitely not on a Wednesday, which is her family dinner night. The first and only time I was late on a Wednesday she tore me a new one. She also made me call her mother to tell her why she was going to be late. The woman is a menace. Both Violet and her mother. And yet, even though she is a huge pain in my ass, I respect the work she does for me. Every night there is a cooked meal waiting in the oven. Juno is bathed and in her little pyjama things. I don't know what she uses, but Juno's skin is looking a lot better and her hair always smells nice when I get home. Sometimes she even stays and holds Juno while I eat dinner. She talks and I listen. Sometimes I ask her questions. She's my employee so I try to keep a little separation between the roles, but it feels like over the few months she's worked for me that we've become friends. It's fucking baffling and weird as I've never had female friends before. Hell, I've never found anyone whose company I enjoy enough to want to keep them around. And that's the hard part, if I want to keep Vi around for Juno I have to keep my moods in check and my cock in my pants, which is proving a lot harder than I thought. Turns out the fucker doesn't care if we employ her. He wants what he wants, and he wants Vi.

"What? No, that's not what happened. Pops was meant to get rid of it and he just shoved it in there until it fermented and exploded! I had nothing to do with that shit!" Tav yells as he and the rest of my family walk into the clubhouse.

I sometimes wonder what we look like to outsiders. My brothers are tall, big guys. Dayz is beautiful but with way too much hair, and Pops looks like every other retiree around in his polo shirts and chinos. Then there's me with a RBF so strong Juno inherited it. Add to that the fact that we are noisy fuckers who argue a lot, and well, shit, I'm amazed anyone takes us seriously.

"Jules! You tell him!" Tav whines.

My brow raises. "Tell him what?"

"That it was Pops' fault that a cow exploded behind his house."

I'm well known for my impassive, unexpressive face, but at that sentence my brows fly to my hairline without hesitation. I don't even answer him. Instead I look from my grandfather to my sister and I know it was probably both of them.

"I have no idea what you're talking about," I answer. Because I don't. And I don't really want to know, I have places to be.

"Oh my god! Everyone did you know Elio blew up a cow with Pops and Aunt Chewy?" Cove yells as she comes racing through the door, Sage, Elio and Blanche following her.

"See!? I told you Gus!" Tav crows.

The MC brothers that are now all in the common room waiting for Church roll their eyes. Except Rider who is kneeling in front of Cove wanting all the gory details.

Boots stomp and Marx's annoying as fuck whistle calls us all to attention. "Church!" he bellows and everyone falls into line.

We file in, the brothers not even questioning that Gus and I file in alongside them. Everyone takes their seats, Gus and I on some extra office chairs that have been placed at the table for us.

"We still have two guests yet to arrive, so I'm going to start with general business. Tombs, I expect you to keep your mouths shut outside of those doors." Marx glares at us and I glare right back.

Marx doesn't need to worry about us telling anyone what their little MC is up to. We have more important shit to be doing. Regardless I give him a nod and Gus agrees to whatever the fuck Marx was asking.

Tank's huge fists bangs on the table to everyone's attention. "Just wanted to let you know that Lovely is doing a fucking amazing job at DBT. The reception is tidy and welcoming, customers love her and she's a fucking demon when it comes to paperwork. She's implemented a new system and we've had no overdue payments since she came on."

I watch Marx as he takes in the news. He puffs up with pride and I can't fault him. I feel a little proud of her, too. I've watched her grow since she's been living next door and it's been quite a sight to see.

"Good, that's good." He goes to say something else but is interrupted by banging on the door.

Rhodie stands and strides toward it, pulling it open wide enough to talk to whoever is on the other side. There's some grunting before Rhodie turns and makes his way back to his seat, Moss Davies and Roman following close behind. I guess if we're going to do this, we're going to need all hands on deck.

Moss sits in an office chair next to Gus while Roman stands over Rider, staring, until Rider gets sick of being eye fucked and moves to the other shitty office chair next to me.

"Bossy fucker," he grumbles as he flops down, legs outstretched, arms crossed over his chest.

"Thank you for agreeing to meet," Marx says in a voice that's not really too friendly. Roman tends to bring that out of people.

"Hmmph," Moss grunts. "I'd love to know why I'm sitting in Church with the head of the Bartashev Bratva."

"Your guess is as good as mine, Sergeant," Roman replies.

Marx stares at Gus who gives him a nod. "Gentlemen, there is trouble brewing in our little patch of the world."

Violet

I flick Jules a text before loading up little miss grumpy face and slamming the door. It's Wednesday night dinner and there's no way I can be late. Which is why I decide I'll take Juno to the clubhouse to wait for Jules.

Sliding into the front seat I buckle up and check my rear view to make sure I have a good view of my little buddy. I smile when she gives me her RBF. In the time I've been her nanny I've grown really attached to her. I feel like she's a lot more like her father than even he realizes. Sure she looks a spitting image of the rest of the Tombs family, probably favoring Tuesday purely because she's a girl, but aside from the scowl she inherited from her father, she also has a similar personality. At six months old you'd expect her to be babbling away to herself, rolling over and generally doing a bunch of baby stuff. Not Juno Tombs. No, she's happy to sit in her little seat and judge you. Which I find hilarious.

We pull into the clubhouse carpark and I park next to Pops' old beat up truck. I figure I may as well leave my keys and other crap in here, I mean who would be stupid enough to steal from an MC? I gather all Juno's things, unclip her seat from the base Jules added to my car and lug her and her belongings inside.

"Oh, hi Violet!" Mira comes bustling over like she hasn't seen me in ages and gives me a friendly hug, her arms wrapping over all the things I'm carrying. She's one of the nicest women I've ever met, and one of the most random.

Mira is, I guess, kinda like what would happen if Tuesday was a lot more social. And maybe better at reading social cues. Jules shared with me one evening that Tuesday is neurodivergent. It was over one of the dinners I had made and I had stayed behind a little later than usual to hold a fussy Juno while he ate. I have to admit I quite like those dinners. I wouldn't call us best friends, but I wouldn't call us strangers or the guy who always rubs me up the wrong way when he demands stuff and doesn't use manners, either. Anyway, his sharing Chewy's diagnosis made me wonder if he is also on the spectrum but doesn't recognize it in himself. I've seen it a few times before when I was working at a small medical center where I trained. A whole family came in focused on the one child they knew to be neurodivergent but didn't pick up the signs that both parents and the sibling were all on various points of the spectrum as well. I suspect Jules' coldness is actually an inability to be able to voice or even recognize what he feels.

The other women greet me one by one and I head toward the table they're sitting at.

"Vi, did you know Elio and Pops and Aunt Chewy blew up a cow?" Cove all but yells in my face. If I didn't know better I'd think she was Dr. Hansen's, I mean, Switch's daughter.

"Not only did I know, but I think I saw some chunks as they rained down over Jules' house." I was shocked and grossed out about the whole ordeal, but when I peeked out the window and saw the three of them out there unbothered, I figured it was probably safe. Fucked up, but safe.

I place Juno's car seat on the table and take a seat just as Mama Debs greets me with a warm hug, "Are you hungry *kotiro*? I have fettuccine keeping warm as we speak," she smiles, eyes glowing.

I'm shaking my head before the words even come out. "I'd love to, but no, thanks. I have family dinner tonight and Flora would *kill* me if I ate elsewhere. Besides, tonight's the night that Josh is coming to family dinner, and I need enough space to finish his food when Mom's not looking."

"Why would you finish his food?" Remy asks, brows pinched.

"Flora Davies likes to make her food with love. And by love, she means chilli. Josh is a nice guy, but I doubt he has the intestines to handle too much of Mom's love."

The women all snicker. Well, apart from Chewy whose brows are pinched. "Why do you date Josh?"

I glance around the table, trying to figure out where left field, and that question came from. "Um, because I like him?"

This makes Chewy frown even more, a spitting image of Juno who is doing the same thing, but at Jr who is strapped to Ana's chest. "I saw him when we were running through the security background. You're conventionally beautiful. Josh is conventionally not. So, I just want to know why you, a conventionally beautiful woman, would date him. Is he very funny?"

I think about it for a moment and the answer would be a resounding "no".

"Oh, she's thinking too hard. She's going to say no!" Nat cackles, Ana joining her.

"No! I was going to say –"

"Too late! Sorry Vi. You hesitated. You can't come back from that one," Remy adds.

I let out a sigh. "Fine. He's not funny. But he's super thoughtful and kind and he laughs at my jokes so I feel that makes up for it."

Chewy turns her body toward me, her gaze over my shoulder somewhere. "So, he's really good at sex then?"

I choke on my saliva, sending me into a coughing fit. Hands start pounding my back and a glass of soda materializes in front of me thanks to Niko who's running the bar tonight. I guzzle it down, the bubbles tickling my throat and soothing the coughing fit.

"Um, yeah, he's okay," I finally answer, to get Chewy to stop interrogating me.

"Oh no," Mira whispers, "That means he's bad." She looks sad on my behalf. In fact, everyone except Lovely looks sad on my behalf. "When you're with someone you really want to be with, making love is magical." Mira says, with hearts in her eyes. I've seen her with Tank, they're such a sweet couple. "Oh, the dirty fucking is really good too."

"Rhodie let me peg him for Christmas." Chewy informs us. "It was very romantic and my thrust game is very good. He said I wouldn't be able to keep up without getting tired, but I proved him wrong. I'd make a really good man. I'm good at fucking."

I stare at these women and make a note to get my sisters to the clubhouse. They would *love* this. Especially Lily. She may be quiet, but she's a little freaky.

Pops comes out of the kitchen from where he's been "helping" Mama Debs with dinner and scoops Juno out of her car seat before plopping down in the chair next to me. "What are we talking about ladies?"

"About how good Chewy would be at fucking if she was a man," Blanche says drily.

Pops nods as if that's a totally normal thing to say, "Well, yeah, of course she would be. It's hereditary." He nods as if that's a fact and blows a raspberry on Juno's belly, making the child's hands wave as her face stays neutral.

Before any of us can question whether that's a weird statement or not, the doors to Church fling open and men, good looking men, so many good looking men come spilling out. Like a clown car of hotness. Jules is with them, talking to Nitro and I have to admit that man is stupid hot. His gaze raises and lands on me, widening a moment before darting to look at the clock on the back wall.

He stomps over, taking a moment to gaze down at Juno in Pops' arms. She gives him a gummy grin and I watch as a smile slowly takes over his face, mirroring hers. I'm frozen in place, watching a moment I have to admit, I thought would never happen. I know deep inside that he cares for his daughter, but I wasn't sure he had it in him to show it. Watching them smile at each other warms my heart.

For 0.23 seconds before he glares at me and barks, "What are you doing here?"

I sigh, before giving him "the look". The look that Flora Davies taught me. "I sent you a message that I'd bring her here in case your meeting ran late. Mama Debs was happy to have Juno if I had to leave early. Is that OK, your highness?"

He looks like he sucked a lemon for a moment before covering it up with his usual bland mask. "I knew I had to be done before 6pm."

I stare at him for a moment, wondering if I feel like a battle or if I should save that for Flora's interrogation of Josh in about half an hour. I opt to take the easy way out. This time. "I know, and I appreciate that. But I figured this would be easier for you. Besides, Mama Debs has made fettuccine and a peach cobbler for dessert."

His eyes light up and he must forget to be a moody jerk for a moment because he pulls a face at his daughter. Then remembers who he is and scowls at me. "Well, thank you for bringing her here."

I grin, knowing that I've irritated him slightly. "You're welcome, big guy. I've gotta get going." I turn to the table of women who have weirdly been sitting there quietly, watching the whole exchange. "Thanks for the enlightening sex talk there Chewy." I turn back to Jules frowning at his sister. "I'll see you tomorrow."

He gives me a nod and I lean over Pops' shoulder, saying goodbye to Juno, "See ya tomorrow little chickadee." Juno stares at me, but flaps her hands so I take that as a wave.

I wave to all the brothers, and then stop abruptly when I see one of them is my own. "What are you doing here?" Surely he wasn't in Church?

"Well hello to you too, little sis! Like you, I was here for work." He smirks at me and I know he's keeping a secret. That's his secret keeping face. "Need a ride to dinner?"

"Nah, got my car. Last one to get there has to tell mom her chilli is too spicy!"

Chapter 7

I watch Violet sprint toward the door, stopping long enough to fist bump Rider as her brother yells after her that he's going to use his sirens.

"I'm not losing, Violent! Mom will fucking freak out if I tell her its too spicy!" The door slams behind them and half the clubhouse has moved to the windows to watch Violet peel out, then Moss.

"Sibling relationships are weird," Chewy says, ignoring Blanche staring at her.

I try to hide my smile. My siblings and I are like any other group of siblings. Except our hobbies tend to run a little less vanilla, I guess. Thinking about my siblings is a great way to get my cock to go down after watching Violet jiggle her way out the door. She throws me into a tailspin. My body is attracted to her body, because fuck me, she's built like a wet dream. Any man alive would look at her and feel themselves stiffen. Then my mind takes over and reminds me that she has a boyfriend, and a mouth and attitude that I'd rather not take on. Besides, I'm not a one woman man. That just invites trouble into your life. The thought of trusting one person, not only to have your back but with your heart? What if they die? What if they betray you? No thanks. I'll stick to groups of women with no expectations other than a good fuck.

Shaking off my thoughts I glance over to where Pops is trying to make Juno laugh by blowing raspberries onto her fat belly. I think she likes it, her hands are waving and her legs are kicking, but her face is its usual mask of RBF. I'm sure other people would be concerned that their kid doesn't smile much. Not me. Or at least it wasn't me until last week when I fed her breakfast. After she had finished sucking the bottle dry she pushed the teet out with her tongue and then smiled. She smiled. At me. Her face lit up and her gummy, drooly mouth smiled wide and it made me feel like I'd been kicked in the chest. I've felt that feeling a few times since she came into my care. I'm still not too sure what the fuck it means, but I think it may mean that maybe I'm not completely screwing this up. She's warm, fed, clean and has a home. She also has a loud, bossy woman in her corner helping her to grow up right, and my family and the club. With that kind of support she has a chance to grow into a normal, well adjusted adult. I think.

Moving closer I lean over Pops' shoulder, catching Juno's attention. She smiles widely, kicking and waving like crazy, making loud baby noises that a couple of months ago would have pissed me off.

"Why the fuck does she smile at your ugly mug -" Pops whines before putting on a high pitched voice, "-and not my handsome face, huh, sweetheart?"

"Pops, we look the same. Calling him ugly is like calling yourself ugly," Tav says, herding his kids toward the serving hatch.

"Shut your cakehole, I'm far more handsome than you!"

"Come on Juno, let's get something to eat." I ignore my family trading barbs and pluck her out of Pops' arms. She nuzzles into the side of my neck, her hands gripping my shirt.

Before I can carry her to the kitchen hatch Mama Debs stops by with two plates of fettuccine, placing one in front of Pops and one for me next to him. Glancing around I notice everyone else has already gotten their food. Taking Violet's empty seat next to Pops, I realize it's been a while since I last sat and ate with everyone, and I have to admit it feels nice. The Tombs family changed the night Dayz snuck into the compound. We're a close family, but a little insular. Since that night the number of people that I count as family and that I know will have my back has grown exponentially. Perhaps Dayz had a point when she pressed me about learning how to be open. I'm surrounded by good men and women. Surely they can teach me a thing or two.

"Seems weird, eating with you staring at me," I mumble. Juno stares up at me from her place in the crook of my arm as if I've lost my mind. "But I guess until you can eat real food you'll just have to sit there."

"Who are you talking to?" Glancing over I notice Elio staring at me.

He's an unusual kid. Gets on with my sister like a house on fire, so I tolerate his questions much like I tolerate hers. Dayz has managed to grow into the person she is today because people were patient with her. Elio will need the same.

"Violet told me that I needed to talk to Juno. It's good for her development."

He nods his dark head. "Makes sense."

That's it. No segue into a conversation. He got the information he needed and has moved on. Looking into Juno's dark eyes I wonder what she'll be like in five years time. I've since given up the idea of giving her to another family. No one would be good enough.

"Jules," Mama Debs lays her hand on my shoulder, "How about Sid and I take Juno for the night? You can have some time to yourself."

My initial reaction is to say no, because I hate people doing shit for me. But haven't I already moved on from that attitude? I have a nanny now and I'm always looking for people to babysit if she's unavailable and I have shit to do. My eyes dart to Juno who frowns at me and I decide to take up the offer. Might be time to blow off a little steam.

"Thanks Mama Debs." She kisses me on my crown and I turn back to my meal, smiling at Juno for a moment. "You're a lucky kid, you get to stay with Nana and Pops tonight."

She frowns deeper and pushes out her lip and it makes my stomach hurt a little, but that could be because I'm shovelling food in my face, wondering what shit I should drop off to Pops' place for the night.

* * *

Two hours later I walk through the doors of the playroom that Fox and Nitro have reserved at Vibe. I'm strung fucking tight, it's been a while and not even my fear that I could knock up another loose woman will hold me back tonight. I give a chin lift to Fox and Nitro who are both splayed out on a velvet couch, women between their legs.

I pour myself a whiskey from the in-room bar and take a seat in the corner. "The cuck seat" the guys like to call it but I dont give a shit what it's called. It's where I like to start the evening. Relaxing my shoulders I take a sip, savouring the woody flavor as it burns down my throat, my senses filled with the sounds of moaning from the two girls sixty-nining on the bed behind the guys. Nitro taps the top of the head of the blonde sucking him off, pulling her to stand where he plunges two fingers into her pussy, pumping them roughly, causing her legs to shake and the obscene sounds of her pussy to fill the air. His movements get more and more frantic, her moans almost drowning out the two on the bed, then she explodes, squirting over Nitro's legs. He grins up at her, grips her hips and straddles her over his sheathed cock, allowing her to hover for a second before impaling her. I watch her ass ripple as she bounces on his dick, head thrown back in pleasure. The brunette that had been sucking Fox off turns toward me, straddling him reverse cowboy before sinking down onto his cock. I stare as he pumps his way inside her, his hand snaking around to rub her clit, his balls bouncing off her lower pussy, she pinches her nipples while keeping eye contact with me.

I take another sip, feeling the burn once more. I watch with hungry eyes, letting the sounds of pleasure invade my senses and yet.... My cock remains soft in my pants. I remain soft as one of the women on the bed climbs off and starts licking Fox's cock and the pussy his cock is buried in. My dick even stays soft when both Fox and Nitro arrange themselves to fuck the same pussy, both cocks pressed against each other in the same tight sheath.

I'm surrounded with sexy sounds and smells, mouths,

pussies and asses to give me pleasure but my thoughts keep drifting back to the woman I need to keep my hands off of. The one I enjoy talking to and accidentally pissing off, earning me a sexy as fuck glare, maybe even an irritated huff. My cock twitches at the thought and I know I'm well, and truly, fucked.

Violet

I'm late. Late for dinner. I'll never hear the end of it. I'm late because Josh decided that we should talk about family dinner and perhaps the commitment is a little more than what should be expected of him this early on in the relationship. I'm not quite sure what he's getting at. I mean, sure, we've only been dating for six months, but we've talked about our goals and moving in together at some stage. He's met my friends. And by friends I mean Jazz and Lil because let's face it, I don't really have a lot of those. But anyway, I don't feel like we're rushing into meeting my family. They're important to me and so is Josh so we conceded that he would come to dinner but bring his own vehicle in case the food is a bit strong for his tummy. I get it. I wouldn't want to shit myself the first time I meet my boyfriend's parents either. But still, tonight I saw a different side to my lovely boyfriend. The Josh I know is sweet and caring. This Josh was being pushed out of his comfort zone and became a little condescending and defensive.

I park on the street out front of my parents', waiting for Josh to pull in behind me. I wait on the sidewalk for Josh to join me, reaching out to hold his hand. I smile up at him and give him a gentle kiss.

"Violet! We're in public!" he hisses and I roll my eyes. He's always been a bit prudish in public. He keeps telling me that we need to project a successful, respectful image. I always thought that was crap, but then again I'm not looking to climb the corporate ladder. Or any ladder really.

I shake it off and tug Josh's hand, heading towards the front door. I grip the handle and swing the door open.

"Whoa, don't you knock?" Josh asks, looking horrified.

I stop in my tracks, "Wait, do you?" I look up at him in confusion. Never in my life have I ever thought about knocking when I enter my childhood home.

"Yes. Every time. It's my parents' home, not mine."

I stare at him for a moment like he's grown two heads.

"This is Vi's home, she's welcome to come and go as she pleases, right *mija?*" Mom says, arms open wide to draw me into a hug, giving me a kiss on the cheek before pulling back and almost shoving me to the side. "Josh! I'm so glad you could make it! Welcome, welcome! Vi told me about your tummy troubles so I made all the things much blander than usual so you can enjoy." She beams up at him and he looks like he wants the ground to swallow him up.

His eyes dart to mine, looking betrayed but I can't do anything other than pat his chest in reassurance. "I didn't tell her you had tummy trouble, I said you can't handle spicy foods."

He frowns down at me then follows my mother to the back of the house, where the huge open plan kitchen dining is situated. I freeze in the doorway, immediately sensing something is up. My brother and sisters are acting normal. Reserved. So I know something has gone down and they're putting up a front. My eyes dart toward Mom who looks like her usual self. I glance at Dad, because if anything was going on I know he would be the one that would give it away. Steven Davies is perhaps the nicest man to walk this earth. Other people would say he was whipped, but I know that dad has a spine of steel. Much like Moss he covers it up with his congenial manner, and he loves Mom and us kids to distraction, which means that if anything is going on and one of us asks, he'll cave. Immediately. Unless Mom threatens him, of course. I mean, he doesn't want to lose out on that "spicy sweet loving" as he calls it. Gross.

Staring at Dad who is trying very hard to avoid all eye contact, I realize that yes, something is up. But with no outward signs I'm going to have to play this one by ear until I can get to the bottom of this.

I narrow my eyes at my family and take a seat, Josh sitting next to me.

"Thank you for the dinner invite Mr. and Mrs. Davies," he says politely.

"You're welcome! I'm just so glad you could join us. It feels like I've been asking Vi to bring you to dinner for months and you've been too busy," Mom says, bustling around.

"Yes, well, as Violet knows I take my career very seriously. If it comes down to dinner with her family or advancing my career, I will choose my career every time."

I shoot him a look, as does every one else in my family. What the hell? I've seen Josh like this when he's with his Finance Bros, talking a big game, but never when we're together. Maybe it's nerves at wanting to make a good impression? Like trying to convince my dad that he's a guy that can support me or something? I glance at Jazz who gives me huge eyes as if to say "wtf?" I give her a little head shake and try to brush the awkward moment off.

I clear my throat. "Josh is very busy at work. Sometimes I don't see him for days." I smile at him and pat his thigh which is tense beneath my hand.

Mom gives him an incredibly fake smile and places the tamales in the center of the table a little roughly. As per usual, everyone talks animatedly while dishing up, giving me time to point out the dishes, what they contain, the heat factor based on historical evidence on how Mom usually makes them, and which ones are my favorite. He opts to dish up the smallest amount of everything, ignoring the stares from my family, including the grip my mother has on her cutlery. He gingerly takes a forkful of birria and moves it around his mouth before looking up at my mother and giving her a tight smile.

The knuckles on her knife-holding hand turn white as her grip tightens even more. I catch her eye and try to beg her, using only my eyes, to please, let it go. This is all new for Josh and he will get used to it. I mean, Dad did. Her shoulders relax and she gives me a curt nod.

"Vi, how is Juno? I know you said last week that she's teething again," Jazz asks, obviously trying to make small talk.

My thoughts move to the little girl I spend my days with. I've always liked babies, kids in general. I loved working with them when I was nursing, such cute little munchkins. I have a feeling everyone in my family is wired that way, to be carers of some description. Moss cares for the public by keeping them safe, Jazz with her special ed, Lil is a physiotherapist, Mom's a feeder and now I'm a nanny. I didn't for one second think I'd enjoy it, but I actually do. Watching that little girl grow and change is one of the highlights of being her caregiver. Even if her dad can be a bossy grump, I just know it's because it's the way he's wired. He's not cold, he's just unsure how to show he cares other than protecting.

I swallow my mouthful to answer her. "She's doing so much better. That tooth was a real dick coming in, but it's through now and she's back to being her stoic little self." I grin and then Josh catches my eye.

"Are you OK, babe?"

"You said 'dick' at the dinner table."

I give him a puzzled look. "Yeah. It's how I talk."

"Well, it's not very classy. Maybe just tone it down a little over dinner, OK?" He takes another tiny bite of birria and I side eye my family.

What. The. Fuck?

"Jazz! How are the kids in your class?" Dad practically yells across the table in a desperate attempt to deflect whatever the hell Josh has going on.

Jazz hits the ground running and tells us a story about that menace Rodney and how he escaped during PE to climb the jungle gym in skidmarked tighty whities to sing WAP.

My family is in hysterics and as much as I want to laugh I'm more distracted by the odd vibe I'm getting from Josh, which is weird because me and him have always been on the same wavelength. Or so I thought. Before my siblings or parents can launch into another story to make everyone feel a little more comfortable, Josh pushes his plate aside and smiles tightly at my mother.

"That was very nice thank you, Mrs Davies, but I'm going to have to pass on the rest."

Mom's eyes grow wide and she looks confused as all get out that someone has rejected her meal. One that she tried hard to tame. I know this because it's bland and awful. We're eating cardboard versions of her usual feast.

"It's just that it's a little too-" Everyone around the table's eyes grow wide with horror as we can all guess what he's about to say to mom. Trigger words. "-spicy."

The last word comes out in slow motion. My brother cringes and my sisters shrink back a little. Dad mumbles, "Settle," under his breath and my mother does the unthinkable. She pulls her shoulders back and smiles warmly at Josh.

"Oh, I'm so sorry! I guess you won't want to take any leftovers home then?" She smiles at him from across the table, hiding her true feelings as I can see her white knuckling the corner of the table.

"Oh, no, none for me thank you. I really need to head off. Thank you once again." He pushes his seat out and doesn't wait for anyone to say anything else. He doesn't even look at me as he strides toward the door.

"Maybe he needs to poop?" Lily asks, her brows pinched with concern.

I jump up to follow him out, catching up to him at the front door. "Babe, are you OK?"

"I'm fine Vi, I just, I should never have come here. Your family and the dynamics are just so different to mine. We don't chat at dinner or use foul language. It's just, I guess you're a different class to what I'm used to but hey, that's not your fault, I mean, your mom is an immigrant and all."

Gasps and the words "motherfucker" and "scoundrel" can be heard down the hall and I'm so shocked that sweet, kind Josh actually said that shit to me that my usual wit and sharp tongue are trapped in my gaping mouth.

"I mean, I knew you were latino or something, but I just didn't realize *how* latino you really are. And look babe, there's nothing wrong with that. I have a lot to think about. I'll call you." He leans forward and kisses me on the cheek, then pretty much slams the door in my face.

Turning slowly I gaze down the long hall at all my family members crowded in the doorway. "Did he just - was he j-"

"Yes, he pretty much said we're kinda shitty cos our mom is an immigrant."

I roll my eyes at Moss, "I know *that*, but did that greasy dweeb just break up with me?" I can feel my cheeks heat and the tears pooling in my lower lash line. What the hell? I *liked* Josh. Hell I thought I was well on my way to *more than liking* Josh and he pulls this shit?

"Oh Lettie, come on, you're going to get yourself worked up and blow." My dad's strong arms wrap around me and I bury my face in his chest. "It's OK sweetie, he was a scoundrel talking to you like that. You deserve more than a beige finance bro." I nod, wiping tears on Dad's sweater. "Are you hungry? Your mom made actual real food and hid it knowing Josh probably wouldn't last."

I lean back, taking in the look on Dad's face, and then Mom's. "Wait, what do you mean Mom knew he wouldn't last?" I ask, confused.

"*Mija*, I don't know whether you know this, but that man was terrible. He was bland like unsweetened oatmeal. No honey, no berries, nothing. Just plain, lumpy oatmeal. And then he ran his mouth and *dios mio* there was salt in the oatmeal! Blech! I even made the worst birria I've ever made to make him feel comfortable. I could feel the tears of my ancestors as they watched me leave out half the flavoring all so your beige boyfriend wouldn't crap his pants. Well, no more! If he can't see how perfect you are and how much love and chilli goes into our meals then good riddance!" Mom says with a flourish, pulling dishes out of hidey holes all over her kitchen. Dishes that taste like my childhood and family and home.

"I'm so embarrassed that the asshole had the balls to say that to me and I was shocked into silence," I lament over the chilli hot enough to give me a sweat moustache.

"Don't worry Vi, I'm sure someone else will piss you off soon enough and you can let loose and feel like you have your power back," Lil says, patting my hand in sympathy.

My mind drifts to the only person I know that pushes all my buttons without even trying. Jules Tombs. The man that tends to flit into my mind at the most inopportune times. I may dislike hot guys because of their usual lack of personality and manners, but I will concede that there's a lot more to Jules Tombs than meets the eye. Yes he may be moody and grumpy and lack basic manners and sometimes language skills, but I've seen him with his family, the MC family, the kids and Juno, and there's a big heart in that man. I'm just not so sure that he knows it himself.

* * *

I'm tucked up in bed, trying to read a new MC book, but instead I'm lamenting the end of my relationship with Josh. I may have already eaten a tub of ice cream that had tears in it. I mean, we'd only been seeing each other for six months but I really, really liked him and could see myself building a future with him. Now that the blinders have been taken off I can kind of see where Josh was a bit of a snob. He kept pushing me to take on nursing jobs, saying I was wasting my potential working at my

Mom's or nannying. Now I can see that the nice guy schtick was an act. He was always going on about having to project a good image for his career so I'm guessing he was with me because he thought I was hot. Well, now he has a hot ex-girlfriend that will kick his ass if I ever see him again. You don't say shit about my family and get away with it.

Rolling to get comfortable I'm startled by my phone blasting Fleetwood Mac's "Silver Springs". I changed it 20 minutes ago feeling the same anger as Stevie did. I'll haunt that man for life, I have decided. My phone continues to ring and I frown down at the number, sliding my thumb across the screen to answer it.

"Jules, is everything OK with Juno?"

"Violet," his deep tone washes over me and my ice cream addled brain, "I know it's late but we're being called out, I hate to do this but can I bring Juno to you?"

I pull my phone back from my face to study the time before making a split decision. "Stay there, I'll come to you."

"Are you sur-"

I don't even wait for an answer. Jules is incredibly professional. He wouldn't call if it wasn't important. Besides, Juno will be a welcome distraction to figuring out if I want to cry or punch Josh in the junk.

Chapter 8

Jules

Violet arrives like a bat out of hell and I'm impressed by how quickly she got here. Her home is on the other side of town and she sounded a little drowsy like maybe I had woken her. She quickly gathers her things and gets out of her car, rushing up to the porch where I'm standing. My eyes bulge as I've never seen Violet like this. Usually when she's working she wears jeans and t-shirts. Simple things. Because of the late hour she's in what I'm guessing is her sleep wear. An oversized tee that probably belongs to her boyfriend, a tiny pair of shorts and Ugg boots.

My cock, which wasn't working at the live porn show earlier, now roars back to life. Until I get a look at her face.

"What the fuck happened?" I bark at her with concern. She flinches and I try to soften my voice. "Sorry, it just looks like you've been crying."

She tilts her head at me, opening her mouth to say something, once, twice. "What would you do if someone told you that they think you behave lower class, but that's OK because you have an immigrant mom so it's not like you could help it?"

"I'd tell them to get fucked and to keep their distance because the next time I see them I'll kneecap them," I say without hesitation.

She gives me a wobbly smile and pats my shoulder. "Thought so." She turns to walk into the house, not asking any questions about why I needed her here at this time.

"Vi?" She turns back, looking worn out by whatever happened, "take my bed. If I'm back early I'll crash on the couch." She raises her brow as if to argue that she'll take the couch but I cut her off, "Do it, Vi."

Her brows dip as she scowls, "You're a bossy asshole sometimes, you know,"

"I know."

"Good. I didn't want you out there thinking you were a gentleman or anything." She deepens the scowl before rolling her eyes and huffing, "Thank you, Jules. Be safe."

I watch her walk into my bedroom and I linger, for once not wanting to head out. But the Computa's have finally managed to link some shit together so an emergency meeting has been called.

"Jules! Roll out!" my bastard brother Gus yells out as he climbs into his SUV. Dragging myself from thoughts off the woman in my bed, and Juno in hers, I close the door gently, locking it behind me and head out to meet the rest of our crew.

* * *

"What have we got?" Marx asks, once we're all assembled at

the clubhouse. Because of the hour none of the kids or women are here except Dayz and Remy.

Wire, Remy and Dayz all share a look then Remy taps on her keyboard, sharing their screens onto the big screen.

A photograph of a bleached blonde woman with a tight bun, sharp cheekbones and pumped up lips fills the screen.

"This is Candice Rogers, owner of Happy Values Adoption agency. She is currently in negotiation with 147 prospective families." Dayz states.

Photographs of cute kids ranging in age from baby to older school age start popping up on the screen.

"These four have all been taken in the last six days from towns within a 3 hour radius from here," Chewy says, staring at her laptop screen.

We were waiting for this. We knew that children in the South were going missing at an alarming rate over the past six months. Up until now we couldn't find concrete evidence that it was all linked. No matter how good Tombs Security is, sometimes it helps having contacts with people in the underground. Enter DRMC and Roman Bartashev.

"Happy Values is a private adoption agency that has grown exponentially over the last two years, placing them as the top adoption agency in the South. The only problem being the rumours and accusations that the children aren't given up, they're taken. From playgrounds, front yards, malls, even purchased on the dark web. So far we, working with the FBI, have rescued and returned 14 children, but the rate that Happy Values is growing means that they're going to have to start sourcing more children to sell to desperate couples," Gus adds.

"I have word of a container coming through the port on Friday. From Mexico." Roman says, looking bored. I know he's playing a character, the disinterested Russian. I also know his business runs both legally and illegally through the port, Roman paying them good sums to keep things clean. The last thing he needs is a truckload of kids going through the same routes he uses. Not only is it bad for business, but he draws the line at human trafficking.

"I'm sure there are a shitload of containers coming in from Mexico on Friday," Savage challenges.

"Da, but a container carrying bell peppers would need to be refrigerated, and this particular one is not."

Everyone in the clubhouse shares a look.

"What does your contact say?" Marx asks Gus. I'm always happy that Gus takes the lead. I wouldn't deal well with being interrogated every fucking time we have shit going down.

"They've been quiet. Either they know something–"

"Or they're waiting for us to do their job," I reply drily.

Tombs Security have been working closely with the FBI for a while now. Usually we're called in to help transport people saved from trafficking, helping return them to their families. Other times we've been called in to track the traffickers and shut down their operations. We have a fuck ton less paperwork to work through, meaning, as long as the FBI are okay with it, we can complete our contracts in any way we please. Our current contract is what has us, DRMC, Bartashev Bratva and Sergeant Moss Davies working together.

"Our personal intel tells us they'll transport all the kids through Rose Grove, whether they were taken locally or they shipped them in on the container Roman mentioned. Happy Values takes ownership of the kids and rehomes them. Once they're out of state they'll be almost impossible to trace, so we need to grab them once they hit town," Gus says.

"Rehoming? Is that what we're calling it?" Judge mumbles.

"It sounded less rage inducing than 'selling'," Gus answers. "We need to remember that for some of these people, they think they're adopting through a reputable business."

"Instead of a greedy bitch who doesn't give a shit about where these kids come from," Sniper says, his voice dripping with disdain.

Gus nods in agreement. "Computas, you got anything?"

"Happy Value's bank accounts are filling up steadily. From what we could hack each couple pays between $30,000 and $60,000," Wire says, trying hard to keep the growl out of his voice.

"Why such a big range?" Rider asks, looking around the room.

"60 for a baby, 30 for an older kid," Wire answers, his jaw clenched tight.

A crash sounds out and I snap my head to the left to find Sniper, hands on hips, taking deep breaths.

"You good, brother?" Marx asks.

"No. But I will be," Sniper answers, pulling himself together before turning back to the screen.

Looking around the room I can see the tension rising. No one wants a shipment of kids coming through our town. Not if we have the means to stop it.

"So, what's the plan? How does this usually work?" Moss asks. The few interactions I've had with him have been intriguing. He's different to his sister in that he doesn't come across as such a blunt instrument. Where Violet will tell you exactly what she thinks and feels, Moss covers his thoughts and feelings with his congenial nature. Which makes him more dangerous.

All eyes move to Dayz, who is sitting staring at her screen. She looks up suddenly, seeing everyone's attention on her.

"Roman, when containers come through port and get loaded onto trucks do they drive straight through after processing or do they usually need to fuel up somewhere?" Dayz asks, head tilted to the side.

The port Roman has a hand in is around an hour outside of Rose Grove. Due to the highway configuration anybody travelling north will go through here. Taking into account that Happy Values headquarters is four hours north of us, that truck and its cargo is set to drive straight through the middle of DRMC territory.

"Trucks driving north stop at The Diner. It's fast, cheap and preferable to the truck stop outside of town," Roman's husband Sasha says, speaking on his behalf.

Dayz nods once, then taps on her computer. "We need trackers on that truck. We will also need people inside The Diner, I want eyes on that driver. We need to know if he's travelling alone or in a convoy."

"So, we're running a sting operation?" Moss asks, looking impressed.

"No. We're running a 'take down greedy bitches and save the children operation," Dayz answers. Rhodie is looking at her like she hung the moon and can't help himself, he leans over and eats her face off for a few moments before letting her get back to work.

"I hate how her scheming makes you horny," Tav bitches to our future brother-in-law.

"Don't care," Rhodie grins.

"So, we're just running surveillance?" Savage asks.

"For the meantime. We take this guy down, Happy Values

has a new driver within the hour. Our best bet is to track them to where they keep the kids, go in and get all of them out of there. We also need hard evidence to bring Candice Rogers and her whole operation down," Dayz finishes.

"If this woman is clever enough she'll be the face of the company and she'll have employees to do her dirty work. So, why don't we send someone in? We have a shit ton of couples. Why can't one of them go undercover or whatever and try and get in from the inside? A two pronged attack," Savage suggests.

It's not a bad idea. Everyone exchanges glances. Most of the couples have children already. All except one.

"It can't be me." Dayz says bluntly. "No one will ever believe that I'm desperate for a child. Besides, Rhodie has neck and hand tattoos. Candice Rogers isn't going to give us the time of day."

"I'll do it," a soft voice says, all of us spin to face the mouth of the hall.

"Lovely? I thought you were at home?" Remy asks.

"No, Bee and I are here tonight, I'm doing the early breakfast shift for Mama Debs. Her and Pops are on a date night," she answers.

"Shit, I wondered why we weren't being interrupted every three seconds by that grumpy asshole," Rider says.

Marx blows out a breath, looking to let Lovely down gently. "Lovely, there's no way we could ask you to do this, it'll be da-"

"You're not asking. I'm offering. That could have been Bee's life if I never got her out of The Keep. I kept her safe and if there's anything I can do to keep all those other babies safe, I'll do it," she interrupts Marx. She's really come into her own since she's been out of that god forsaken place.

Marx's eyes narrow as he clenches his jaw. "Fine. But I'm

coming with you." He turns to Dayz. "Set up a cover story and a meeting."

Everyone in the common room shares a look. Fox and Nitro exchange cash and I watch as Sasha also slips them a bill and his predictions.

"Right. We have two days before that truck rolls into town. Roman, you and your men will be working the port. Tombs will have our teams on surveillance. Marx, we'll need the DRMC to be running point the whole time, I'll leave you to organize the men for that. Davies I'll need you on standby and keeping the heat off us. You'll also be our liaison with emergency services should we need them," Dayz commands.

Davies stares wide eyed at Dayz before grinning, "Bring on Friday."

Violet

The crunching of gravel jerks me awake and I lie in a daze staring at the unfamiliar ceiling. It takes me a couple of beats to remember that I'm in Jules Tombs' manly room. The walls are a bland grey color, the bed is a dark grey, the bedding more a gunmetal grey and there is very little furniture to be seen. There is nothing on the walls and no personal photographs are displayed anywhere. The room itself looks more like a hotel suite. It should be impersonal and uncomfortable, but instead I felt at ease, the scent of Jules wraps around me, easing the argument my head keeps having with my heart.

My head saying "fuck Josh!" My heart saying "but I liked

him and I'm not getting any younger." Now I have to start from square one in the dating pool, which is really more of a swamp.

Checking the time on my phone I note that it's not as late as I thought and I know that I'm not going to go back to sleep anytime soon. I throw the covers off, slip on my Uggs and pad into the kitchen, getting together the stuff I need to make some of mom's famous hot chocolate. I bought the ingredients that day at the supermarket when Jules freaked out about us leaving the house without notifying him. It's kinda amazing how far he's come from that day. I mean, he's still moody and can be difficult, but we're friends. I think that's based on mutual respect and trust. Even if he does forget that I don't particularly like being barked at.

"Shit, I didn't wake you, did I?" Jules says, quieting his deep voice.

"Nah. I'd not long been in bed but am having trouble sleeping," I answer over my shoulder, before looking back at the milk I'm pouring into a saucepan. "Want some?"

He moves to stand a little behind me, peering over my shoulder. I try to hide the shiver it sends down my spine and to my lady parts who not ten minutes ago were lamenting the loss of a judgemental asshole.

"It's hot chocolate, but Flora's secret recipe," I add, breathing in his scent.

"It can't be secret if you know about it," he says, moving to lean against the counter beside the cooktop, arms crossed over his chest, and one booted foot over the other.

"She doesn't know I know. My siblings set a bet that the first one to figure out the recipe gets one favor out of each of the other siblings to be used at any time, with no option to back out."

"And you figured it out?" His brow raises. I'm not sure if he's sceptical, or just being Jules.

"Sure did. I hid in a kitchen cupboard with it cracked open just a teensy bit to see what she put in it. Then I recreated it to make sure it was right. So far I have only used one favor."

His eyes narrow. "You have three siblings and you've only used one?"

"Yup. Lily's. Moss and Jazz still owe me. One day I'll cash in." We share a grin and go back to whisking my ingredients in the pan. That's the key.

"My siblings aren't as diabolical as yours, but we come close," Jules says, his lips tugging at the corners.

I give him a bored look and roll my eyes. "Chewy has an honest to goodness alligator as a pet. Her cut also states she's the Icer for the DRMC. I'm sure you lot are plenty diabolical." I turn off the heat, give the liquid chocolate concoction one last stir and then pour it into two mugs that Jules has placed on the counter in preparation. I put the pan in the sink and sprinkle a small amount of chilli flakes on the top. "*¡Ahí está!*" I hand him his mug and then turn to make my way to the hardest couch in the world, taking a seat.

Jules follows to sit in the hardest armchair in the world. "How was Juno? Any problems?"

I let the spicy hot chocolate sit in my mouth for a moment, soaking in its warmth before swallowing it down, the heat making me feel relaxed and gooey. "She woke up when your SUV pulled out and then got upset that I was here and not her daddy." I giggle remembering the face she pulled. "She was *pissed*. You should have seen her face!"

Jules chuckles and I freeze. I have never heard him make any noises other than growls and barks, so to hear a rusty laugh escape him is something to behold.

"Yeah, I'm sorry to say that she got a little too many of my genes," he huffs, a small smile tipping his lips up.

"Where is her mom? Shit, sorry, I was doing a Flora. You don't have to tell me." I make myself super interested in my mug, trying to avoid eye contact.

Jules is quiet for a moment, but then I hear him whisper, "Fucking open up," before blowing out a breath. "I don't know where she is. I found Juno on my porch one afternoon. Her birth certificate had me listed as the father but at that stage I figured Juno belonged to Fox or Nitro."

My brows pinch as I stare into my cup, trying to understand his words. "Why would you think she was one of theirs? Was the woman one of those sweet butts or something?"

Jules lets out a snort before a mask slips over his face, taking his face back to the blank visage I'm familiar with. "We, ah," he clears his throat, "I, um, I don't sleep with women one on one."

My eyes shoot up to face Jules looking off to the side. "What do you mean? You like tag team them or something?"

"Kind of." He shifts in his seat and I can't tell if he's embarrassed. Does Jules Tombs get embarrassed? "I like group sex. There's less, um, pressure, to form an actual relationship."

I nod, processing his words. So he likes orgies. Lots of people like orgies. The Greeks for one. They loved them and seemed to get on just fine. I frown as I repeat what he has just told me. He likes orgies because he doesn't like the pressure of forming relationships. From what I've seen of him he has loads of relationships and gets on just fine. He has Juno and his siblings,

Pops and Debs, and all the kids. He's fiercely protective of them. He's the same way with the MC. I tilt my head to study him, he's staring into the kitchen, still looking uncomfortable.

"Is it empty, not having personal relationships with the women you fuck?"

He looks a little startled, before his eyes drift to gaze over my shoulder. "Never really thought about it, its just fucking," he shrugs. "Do you feel fulfilled when you fuck Josh?"

"Well, I was feeling *filled,* heh." He rolls his eyes at my joke but I catch his lips turning up. "But that was before he decided to be an utter cocksucker and insult my family. I should have seen it coming, he was always a little weird about meeting my family. He would sometimes make comments that I wasn't living up to my potential. I kinda thought it was part of this course thing he was doing to 'find himself' and 'maximise his potential'. I think part of maximising his potential was having a pretty girlfriend."

"Beautiful."

"Huh?"

Jules clears his throat. "Beautiful girlfriend."

"Oh." I look down at my cup, still half full of hot chocolate. "Thanks. But yeah, anyway, that's over now. I can't go out with a man who talks shit about my mom. He doesn't know what she's been through to get to where she is today."

A realization comes over Jules' face and he sits straighter, stiffer. "He made you cry," he states, not asks.

I nod, letting out a sigh. "Yeah. And I was so mad at myself because I was so shocked that shy, kind Josh could say something like that, and I couldn't even react with anything other than shock." My shoulders slump and I try to flop back against the couch but it's too freaking hard. It's like leaning against a wall.

Jules scowls, his whiskey colored eyes boring into mine. "Want me to make him hurt?"

I bark out a laugh, and then quieten down, not wanting to wake little Miss Grumpy Pants. "No, Jules, but thank you. I'm already planning my revenge. But if it goes wrong, I might tag you in."

He sits staring at me for a moment before giving a stiff nod. "You need anything, let me know. Anything Violet. I've got you."

The air around me feels charged, heavy but not suffocating as we stare at each other. Then I remember I'm the reason he can work all day without interruption. I'm his friend, a trusted person to look after this daughter. That's all.

I clear my throat, and nod towards his mug, his hot chocolate untouched. "Try your hot chocolate, let me know what you think?" I smirk behind my mug and watch with anticipation running through my veins.

He blinks quickly, as if snapping himself out of a trance, brings the mug to his lips and takes a sip. Then another. Then he takes a large gulp before pulling it back and licking his full lips. "Holy shit! Thank Flora for me. It's fucking delicious." I gape at him and he throws me a wink. "We grew up with spicy food. You'll have to try harder than that," he smirks.

I narrow my eyes, "Fine. I know you're not very people-y if you can help it, but one Wednesday you are coming to family dinner. Flora is going to damn well love you."

He gifts me with a smile I've only ever seen him give his daughter and I feel blessed that he chose to send it my way. Blessed and panicky. I'm Joshless for six hours and I'm starting to crush on my asshole-y boss. Although, he's not really an asshole. He's just a little lost. And grumpy.

I make a show of stretching and yawning, the hot chocolate having worked its warm, chocolatey goodness on me.

"I should really get home, you don't need me taking up your bed," I move to get up when a growl stops me.

"Vi, get back in that bedroom. It's too late for you to be driving home, and you're not only tired, but you've had an emotional evening. You'll be shattered." I open my mouth to protest but he raises his hand, effectively shutting me up. "Please, Violet. I don't want anything bad to happen to you." The blank look on his face drops and his concern shines through.

My instincts tell me to run, that I'm tired and confused and he smells so good and I already love his daughter, but another part of me can see the man that he hides for reasons unknown to me. Hell, they're probably unknown to him too, so I will give in. This time.

"Alright. Only because you said please," I say, my eyes narrowed. "And because you're right, I am really tired." I rise up and move toward the kitchen, rinsing my mug and placing it in the dishwasher. Once I'm done I walk through the living room, making my way to Jules Tombs' room. Before I shut the door I look over to the man sitting in the dark, alone.

"Jules?" His head snaps up, his gaze locking onto mine. "Thank you. You're not as big an asshole as I thought." I tease, trying to dispel the tension in the room. He raises a brow at me, saying nothing. "Nah, you're more of a butthead."

I close the door gently behind me as the sound of his rusty chuckle fills the silence.

Chapter 9

Jules

"Do we need any more men on the ground?" Gus asks. "Marx and Lovely will be at the Happy Values main office. Their interview with Candice Rogers is at 11am. Sniper, Savage and Switch will be shadowing them, leaving Rhodie, Judge, Tank and Rider to sit tight in the diner. We have Wire and Remy working offsite surveillance. Dayz will be onsite in the van. We have access to all CCTV coming in and out of town, and the security cameras on the buildings surrounding the diner," Tav answers, staring down at his tablet. "Moss has commandeered four parking spaces for "road works" to keep them clear until our surveillance vehicles park there tomorrow."

"Fox and Nitro will be working the port as Roman's employees," I add, looking at my own tablet, checking off my to do list. It may sound lame as hell but I like routine, schedules and deadlines.

We run things as tight as we can. Any lapse or holes in our surveillance could be the difference between getting those kids out of there and never finding them, which is not a fucking option.

"Good. Ana had Dayz and Wire go through earlier. Roman wasn't happy about having some of his trucks wired up, but he'd rather that than have the port shut down due to trafficking. It's already on thin ice with the amount of drugs that have been found passing through. Innocent kids would shut down the whole operation," Gus says, staring at his computer. "Who have we got placing trackers on the truck once it comes in?"

Tav and I look at each other. So far I haven't pulled in my team yet. These guys are all ex-military, but prefer to stay on the right side of the law. This particular job is happening off the books, and my siblings and I would like to keep it that way.

"Dex and Flack will be on hand to place the trackers. Tum-Tum and Chef will be 'working' in the kitchen, so will be on hand if we need them," Dayz answers, her eyes not leaving her laptop screen.

"How the fuck did the MC pull that off?" Gus asks.

Dayz shrugs, "Easy. Paid her to let TumTum and Chef hang out in her kitchen, and the rest of the MC sit at her tables all day."

"She's a nice lady. Has a couple of kids, bought the diner with an inheritance from her grandmother or something," Tav says.

"Works well for us. Have we got any other intel?" Gus settles back into his office chair, the leather creaking under his weight.

"Wire's following a money trail. He can't be too sure but he thinks Happy Values is working with someone within organised crime. He just doesn't know who," Dayz answers.

I chew this over. It can't be the cartel, Roman took care of them. Savage's old club aren't up to fuck all these days so that rules them out. Maybe we have a new player or one of the many Louisiana crime families are dipping their toes in our waters? Regardless of who it is, it looks like we're going to have to get the information the old fashioned way - information gathering, undercover work and maybe checking in with some of my contacts on the street. Most people look at street folk and see them as pests, I look at them and see them as the eyes and ears of the city. They know shit no one else knows.

"Good. Looks like we've got this covered. I'm meeting with Dansen tonight. I'll give him a progress report." Gus always does the FBI meetings. He's better at staying cool under pressure. I've dealt with Dansen once before and I wanted to punch his face in. "Now fuck off and go do some work," Gus grins, effectively kicking us out.

I don't really give two shits. I've been distracted since Violet and Juno came to visit me at lunch. It wasn't a surprise as Vi had let me know they would be leaving the house and where they were going, but still. It was nice to sit and talk over sandwiches while Juno stared and frowned and then slept in her carseat. Having watched my siblings do the same thing with their families I never really saw the appeal. But once I had a taste of it I wanted more. Now we have lunch every time Vi and Juno run errands.

Heading back to my office I settle into my chair and let my devices sync. My siblings think my lists and spreadsheets are over the top but I don't give a shit. Opening my desk drawer I take out my burner phone and send a mass text to my street contacts letting them know we're running an operation tomorrow at the diner. Giving them a heads up not only lets them know to stay away, so as not to get caught in any shit if things were to take a turn, but it also puts them on alert to keep their eyes and ears open. I know that if anything looks fucked up they'll let me know in real time.

I know the MC often wonders how I made these contacts in the first place. I'm an unapproachable bastard at the best of times but this was a case of right time, right place. Turns out all it takes to gain trust is to listen and treat them as people. Probably helps that I've set up tabs at the diner, the medical center, a motel in town and the grocery store so they can have access to everything they need. I once tried to offer them permanent accommodation but they all refused, preferring to be free to come and go as they please. I'll never know what it's like to live with that level of freedom. I need rules, routines. Predictability.

Unfortunately since Juno and Vi entered my life I've had less and less of what I crave. And yet, I don't feel out of control or like I'm spiraling. I feel ... I don't know how I feel. Shit. Maybe I'm just tired and overthinking. I've been up almost 24hours, the couch was hard as a fucking rock so even after Violet went to bed last night, I couldn't get much shut eye. Letting out a long breath I shut down my laptop, grab my shit and make my way into the elevator, not looking back.

It's crazy but with our operation tomorrow I'm actually looking forward to going home. Even if Violet still seemed a little bummed this morning when we got Juno up and ready for the day. She looked like she'd been crying too, and I don't know what it is, but I swear to god if I see that Josh guy I'm going to make him pay. Violet is more than her background. She's beautiful and fierce and strong. She's no fucking angel, stubborn as hell, unafraid and unapologetic, but she's still someone that deserves respect and not a fucking dickhead like Josh.

Shaking off the thought I head out the door. I got two people I wanna see.

Violet

"And then little missy, do you know what he said? He said that I, *I*, was not classy. Like what the actual?" Juno frowns up at me and it makes my lips twitch, "I know! That's what I thought too!" I scoop her up out of her little bouncy seat and jiggle her in my arms, dancing around a little, just being silly gooses.

After waking up this morning wrapped up in Jules' very grey bedding, and his panty melting scent, I remembered that Josh was a dick and I was a wimp and then I had another cry. I know that Jules could tell I was upset over lunch, and I'm glad he decided to try and ignore my red puffy eyes. He frowned a lot everytime he looked at me, but I spend all day with his frowny daughter so it didn't faze me too much.

"It's just that I guess I built this whole life up in my head, you know what I mean?" Juno, in fact, does not know what I mean. "Looking back I can see now that what I thought was him being career focused, was actually him not wanting to hang out with me. Unless he had a dinner party or drinks where he wanted to parade me around. I don't even know why I'm so cut up! We were together for six months and most weeks we only saw each other once, maybe twice if I was lucky. What the hell possessed me to date a ham sandwich of a man and not recognise a relationship that had the expiration date of old milk?" Juno looks up at me with her dark brows pinched before letting out a little sigh and I'm damn sure she rolled her eyes at me too. "Rude," I whisper to her before dropping a kiss to the top of her head.

I move Juno to my hip, pick up the remote and then fiddle with it to bring up some latin music on Spotify. Nothing makes a girl feel better than bitching to her friends, in this case Juno, and then dancing out the sad with some good beats. Or so Mom says. It's something she would do when we were kids if we had a rough day. She always knew when something was up with us, so as a family we'd all surround the dining table, hash out what was going on, and then dance the rest away.

I crank the music up as loud as I think little ears can safely listen to, take one of her chubby hands in mine and dance us around the living room salsa style. There's hip swiveling and booty shaking, a little shoulder shimmy that makes Juno smile wide. I do it again and she throws her head back and lets out a squeal and a breathless honking noise.

"Holy shit! Did she just laugh?" A deep voice booms out over the music, making me spin toward the door and almost crap my pants in unison. Before I can yell at Jules for scaring the shit out of me he drops his stuff on the floor, strides up to us and eyes wide in wonder, whispers, "Do it again."

I hold Juno to my chest, one little hand in mine as I shoulder shimmy and dip her slightly. Her head tips back, dark hair flying as she grins wide and lets out another squeal and a breathless honk. I bring her back to upright and her baby chuckles have Jules and I sharing wide grins, both of us marvelling at little Miss Grumpy Pants' laughter.

He clears his throat and before he can back out I hand her over to him, his large hands brushing against mine as we exchange the little girl from my arms to his. As soon as Juno is wrapped up in his strong embrace she buries her face in the space between his collarbone and jaw, twisting her head this way and that, as if she's trying to burrow into him. He looks at me as if to ask how to get her to laugh, so I roll my eyes, take one of his hands in mine and start dancing, wiggling my hips, shuffling my feet in the salsa dance frame. Before long I have Jules shuffling this way and that with me, his body a little looser.

"Now shimmy, Jules!" I yell, shaking my shoulders, leaning forward and back.

He glances down at the little girl in his arms, staring at him as if he hung the moon and he shimmies. Well, kinda rocks and wiggles before making the same motion and tipping Juno slightly. As expected she throws her head back and squeals before breaking out into peels of laughter.

I laugh along with her then throw my hands up in the air, letting the music and joy flow through me. Flora was right, this beats moping around over an unsweetened oatmeal man.

"Shit, I didn't know we were having a dance party!" Pops' voice booms as he pulls Mama Debs through the door with him by the hand, and starts wiggling in front of her as if he was trying to get out of a sleeping bag without using his arms.

Jules and I share a wide-eyed look as Pops starts shaking very close and very low to Mama Debs before wiggling his way back to standing. He grips her ample ass with both hands and then pulls her into him, Lambada style. A snort escapes me, then a little giggle and I try to cover it with a cough but it's too late. Jules has already seen and rolls his lips between his teeth. His shoulders are shaking and he buries his face in Juno's shoulder, trying to hide his giggles.

The song comes to an end and Pops dips Debs low, before kissing her. Well, more like devouring her, both of them finally breaking the kiss, a little breathless.

"Thank you for the dance, my love."

"Sid Tombs, you are a silly man," Mama Debs says, hitting him on the shoulder as he pulls her to standing, looking a little flushed. "Anyway," she says looking around the room. "We came over to take Juno back to ours for a sleepover. We have Jr, Cove, Elio and Sage tonight, so figured grandkiddo sleepover it is. Is that OK with you, Jules? You can get some rest for your big job tomorrow."

My eyes flick to Jules at the thought of him going on a job. I don't know why or when it happened, but over the past few months the thought of him going out to make things safer for others, and being hurt causes me to worry. My stomach clenches thinking about Juno and what would happen to her if Jules was hurt or worse. She already has a mom who isn't around. I can't imagine her not having a dad as well.

"Um yeah, sounds good. I'll get her things ready," he says, tightening his arms around her a little.

"No need, I'll do it," I offer.

"Just the stuff she'll need for tonight, Violet, we have a crib and spare diapers and things. We'll just need her PJs and whatever else she likes to have in the evening," Mama Debs adds.

I make my way to Juno's room and smile at the changes that have happened over the time I've worked for Jules Tombs. When I first arrived Juno's room was as expected when a kid turns up randomly out of the blue. The furniture is plain white, the crib and changing table matching the dresser and a big, blue, soft rocking chair in the corner. But that's not what makes it a room for a loved little girl. There have been plushies turning up out of the blue every now and then. I know it's Jules buying them because there's no theme or rhyme or reason. They're just things I think he sees and thinks Juno will like. He loves his little girl but I'm unsure if he knows this.

He never refers to her as his daughter, or anything really other than her name or "the baby". He has started talking to her a little more, but it's more a commentary of what he's doing as he's doing it. No baby talk or high pitched voice, just the man communicating with a baby that has stolen his heart.

I live for the day when it finally dawns on him. It's one of the reasons I like to hang around for a while when he gets home. When I first met him I thought he was a cold asshole, but much like Chewy, they feel deep. They're just not sure how to get it out.

Gus and Ana's voices add to the voices in the living room so I double check that Juno has everything and take it out to a waiting Pops and Mama Debs. I mean, it won't be the end of the world if I've forgotten anything, it's not like Pops can't come next door for it.

"Hey Vi!" Ana in her accent says cheerily, looking more than excited for a night without Jr. From our conversations he isn't the best sleeper even though he's around seven months now. They've taken to co-sleeping and I just know that Ana is more than ready to spend a full night in bed with her man and no Jr in there with them.

"Big plans for tonight then?" I ask with a smirk.

She throws her head back and lets out a belly laugh before dropping a kiss on first Pops' cheek, then her mom's, and then 20 kisses for Jr before taking Gus by the hand and dragging him out the door without a word.

I laugh at the sight and then start to pack my things while Jules begrudgingly hands over Juno.

"Vi, when you arrive tomorrow just come straight to the big house, we can have breakfast before you and Juno start your day, *ne, kotiro?*"

I smile at Mama Debs and give her a quick hug as she and Pops head out the door. I pick up the overnight bag I brought with me last night and head toward the door until Jules' deep voice stops me in my tracks.

"Please stay."

Chapter 10

Jules

I'm not sure what the fuck I'm doing, but watching my brother leave with his woman, and Pops not only with Mama Debs but with Juno as well, all I knew is that I didn't really want to sit in my house alone. Which is fucking nuts when you think not long ago it's all I would have wanted. It's insidious how I went from preferring my own space, only venturing out to the clubhouse to hang out or fuck around, to a man who actually enjoys eating dinner with a baby and the woman who takes care of her.

Violet's dark gaze bores into mine for a moment, before a smile tips the corners of her lush lips and she places her bag down on the floor.

"Not wanting peace and quiet just yet?" She raises her perfect, dark brow. It's amazing how this woman can read me so easily but instead of sympathy for a 37 year old man who doesn't want to be alone, she instead teases, which goes a long way to making me not freak out about my sudden neediness.

"Something like that." I reply.

The latin beats playing over my ridiculously expensive sound system move from frantic to slow, the sound washing over me, causing the tension to leave my body. I hold a hand out to Vi, an invitation. She stares at it as if I might bite her, but instead of cracking a joke or making a snarky comment, I wait her out.

Her eyes meet mine and she gives me a quick jerk of her chin, having made her decision. Slipping her soft hand into mine, her palm swallowed up by my giant mitt, I pull her close and then start to sway. She relaxes into me, letting out a sweet sigh before jerking back and looking up at me.

"I can't guarantee that I won't squeal and laugh like Juno if you shimmy me backwards," she grins, almost stealing my breath with how gorgeous she is.

It's not the first time either. When I walked in the door earlier and saw her plump ass shaking to the beat I almost swallowed my tongue. I stood like a creeper, taking it all in, and much like Shakira, Vi's hips don't lie either. I had visions of her working those thick hips as she rode me and then, she shimmied forward and the most amazing sound came out of Juno. Instantly I forgot my cock and the images in my brain and all I could see was the most beautiful woman in the world laughing with the little girl that causes my chest to ache. It was so fucking magical that I had to demand she do it again, and again until she handed over Juno and it was my turn. Fuck, it was a moment that is seared into my brain.

Gazing down at Vi, her upturned face smiling softly at me, I can't help myself. I lean forward, closing the space between us and I take her mouth as she lets out a soft gasp. I start gently at first, tasting, teasing, but the little minx has other plans. Ripping her hand from mine she brings both hands up, gripping the back of my head, angling me where she wants me before she devours my lips. I probe her mouth with my tongue, and she meets me, taste for taste. She's not like anyone I've ever met. She's hard but soft, a smartass but sensitive. There's just something about her and even though she can drive me to distraction one moment, the next she can smooth things over with a few words.

My hands cup her face as the heat between us grows more and more intense. A shiver runs down my spine when she tugs my shirt out of my trousers and runs her soft palms up my stomach, over my chest where she rests them. I pull back and stare at her, half lidded with desire, her pupils blown wide.

"Two can play that game," I growl, staring her in the face as I tug her shirt up over her head and run my large palms up her soft stomach, a whimper leaving her bruised lips.

"Jules," she gasps and whatever blood isn't in my cock makes its way down south and in a hurry.

"Tell me that you want this," I mumble, sucking the soft skin at the base of her throat. "Tell me that you want me,"

She inhales sharply when I nip at the top of her breast, just above the lace of her bra. "Yes, Jules, I want you, so bad. Make me feel good, make me come," she whispers, her hands cupping my face as she tugs me until we're eye to eye and she's capturing my lips. That's what I needed to hear, her consent, her willingness to have me touch her, on top of her, inside her.

Running my hands down her body I grip her lush ass and drag her up my body until she's high enough to wrap those thick thighs around my waist.

"Oh god, Josh could never do this!" she cackles, and I give her ass a swat.

"You don't talk about that fucker when you're in my arms. In fact, you don't talk about that fucker at all," I growl. Fuck him.

She raises a brow at me and I scoff, "I'm not saying please."

She throws her head back and laughs, the tinkling sound soothing my anger. I kick the door to my bedroom closed and then toss her on the bed, my eyes devouring her as she lies back against the pillow, her messy bun askew and her cheeks flushed. Damn if she doesn't look like she belongs there.

"Take your clothes off, Vi." She stares at me for a moment. "Please."

She smirks, raising to her knees on the bed. "Yes, sir."

Fuck, I almost come in my pants as soon as the words leave her mouth, but I wont let her know that. Instead I raise my brow, "I thought you didn't like being told what to do?"

She shrugs one shoulder, her large tits bouncing gently now that her bra is dangling from her finger before she flicks it at me. "I didn't think so either. But now that I'm half naked and horny? I kinda like it." She bites her lip and gives me a little coy smile.

I let out a groan, running my hand down my face to try and get myself under control. How the fuck I have this woman here, in my bed, and she doesnt want to stab me or kick my ass for being a dickhead is beyond me. My eyes devour her as she rises to standing on the bed, her hips winding and rolling as she unbuttons her jeans, pulling the zipper down achingly slow. I swear I hear the sound of each individual tooth on that zipper being undone. Just when I think I can't take anymore she smirks, turns her back to me and ever so slowly peels the denim down her plump ass, over her thighs and down her legs, revealing a tiny black string hidden between her two, perfectly plump globes.

"Fuck me," I rasp, gripping my cock hard. Not sure if for relief or for punishment.

She looks over her shoulder at me, her pink lips ticking up., "What next, sir?"

Violet

I have no goddamn clue what has come over me. Never in my life have I been submissive in any way, shape or form, and yet, here, in this room, Jules telling me what to do has heat pooling between my thighs. I know he's an intense kind of guy, but seeing him like this, almost unhinged in his want for me, it's making me feel a whole bunch of things that I shouldn't be feeling. I mean hell, it's only been a day since I was unceremoniously and racistly dumped by a guy I really liked. Even if now the rose tinted glasses are off, I can see how flawed we actually were.

"Out of your head, Vi." My eyes shoot to Jules' whiskey pools, his pupils blown wide, gripping his cock through his pants. "Eyes on me, beautiful. There's no room for anyone or anything other than you and me. Got it?"

I nod my head, pulling myself out of my head.

"Need your words, Vi," he demands, unbuttoning his shirt slowly, one tiny button at a time, revealing a chest dusted with the right amount of hair. His hands stop when I don't answer, frozen in time. My mouth has stopped working, my brain foggy as the lust swirls through me.

"Y-yes, sir," I stammer because hot damn this man, gah! I need a taste, I can't just stand here with my tits out and my jaw hanging.

I move to the end of the bed, dropping down to bounce on my butt before standing toe to boot with Jules. I grip his belt, making short work of it while he peels his shirt off, revealing a hard chest, toned abs and a delicious happy trail leading down to the part of him I want to taste the most.

His belt comes free, and I quickly pop the button on his pants before shoving them down his thighs, leaving him in his tight black boxers that do nothing to hide his cock. The purple head peeking out the top, precum glistening in the low lighting. I swipe my thumb over it, massaging it in just a little before bringing it to my lips, and sucking in his essence. My eyes close of their own accord and a shiver runs through me when Jules growls, hooking me under the arms and tossing me on the bed. That's the second time he's done it and I'm loving the sheer savagery of his need.

Before I blink he's hooked my knees in his hands and folded me damn near in half, legs together, knees to my chest. I can't see his face from behind my thick thighs, but I know exactly what he's doing as he runs his nose up and down my pussy lips once, twice, only to replace it with his tongue.

A meep sound escapes before a long groan is pulled from me. Holy shit he has a talented tongue. At moments wide and flat, other times little laps, batting my center before sucking gently on my clit. My hips buck and my legs kick out, but he's not deterred. He slowly spreads my legs, wider, wider still until I'm almost in a split, pussy spread wide and bared for him.

"Jesus fucking christ, look at you." His gaze devours me, as if unable to decide where he wants to look first. "Arms over your head, grip the headboard and don't let go."

I open my mouth for I don't know what reason and a harsh

slap lands on my pussy before he licks the sting away. I frown down at him and he raises that stupid dark brow.

"Did I say you could talk?" He stares me down for a moment, before a smirk grows on his face, causing me to frown down at him. "Not another word, babe. All I want to hear out of you are your screams of ecstasy.

That cocky asshole! I should argue, fight back but oh my god that talented tongue of his has all thoughts flying out of my brain and my hips humping his stupid bossy face. The stubble from his face abrades my thighs, causing a delicious counterpoint to his soft, wet mouth. His rough hands hold me around my waist, propped just above my hips, as if they belong there. He devours my pussy, pulling me down onto his tongue and then pushing me up slightly, fucking me with his mouth.

My groans and pants fill the room and I can feel my core tightening, building up into something huge, something fucking awesome. I grip the headboard as hard as I can, white knuckling it as my legs begin to shake and my toes curl, my eyes slam shut and a guttural groan leaves my body as stars burst behind my eyes and the tension explodes out of me.

"Fuck yes, thats it's babe, cum on my tongue, give it all to me," Jules groans, lapping at me, as if trying to get out every drop.

I lay twitching and groaning on the bed, my core clenching over and over with my waning orgasm, wanting more, to be filled. Jules reads my mind because he kneels up on the bed, kneeing one of my wayward thighs out of the way, lining his sheathed cock up at my entrance. I don't even know when or how he put that on, but I'm beyond caring. If he doesn't fill me now, we're going to have problems.

"Please, Jules, Sir, whatever, I need you to fill me up, please!"

I beg, my words tailing off on a whine.

I'm not sure if we're still doing the bossy sir thing or not, and I don't much care at the moment either. I open my heavy lids, stare up into Jules' handsome face, silently pleading.

He growls and thrusts forward, sheathing himself in one quick movement and stealing my breath. He's huge, wide, filling me up until I feel like I'm going to burst.

"It's too much," I pant, wiggling my hips to accommodate him.

"No, it's just fucking right." He lays his weight on my chest and he feels so right. His chest hair grazes my nipples, making them impossibly tighter as he pulls his hips back slightly, and then rams himself back in, his heavy balls bouncing off my ass.

"Ugh, Jules! Don't stop, please, don't stop." I'm speaking in tongues now. First it was too much, and now it's not enough.

He leans back on his haunches, his hands going back to my waist, pulling me on and off his cock in time with his thrusts. His gaze is on my breasts, bouncing with the rhythm, and all I can do is drop my hands down to his powerful thighs, gripping onto them as the muscles ripple underneath my hands.

My head is thrown back with bliss and then I feel a pinch on my clit, Jules gripping my pussy in his hand. "Hands. On. The. Headboard," he grits out, jaw set as sweat rolls down his forehead, a bead dripping off his chin and down his fantastic chest.

I do as he says, and instead of loosening his grip on my pussy he leans forward and lets a string of saliva drip down onto my core, spreading it with his thumb. Sparks flare behind my eyes and I throw my head back, my body feels like one exposed nerve that is being toyed with by Jules Tombs. He powers in and out of me and the dam bursts suddenly, surprising me with its speed and intensity as my orgasm takes over my body, "Jules!"

"Fuck yes! Squirt all over my fucking cock, just. Like. That." On his last thrust his hips stutter and he lets out a long, low groan, his chest rising and falling rapidly, head tipped back looking like a fucking bronze god. "Fuck your pussy is squeezing me so tight holy shit, shit, shit," he groans again and his hips stutter once more as if he has more to give.

His head tips down to gaze at me and he stares for a moment, his heavy lidded eyes taking me in, from the top of my head down to where he is still connected to me. Inside me. His gaze comes back to mine and I see the look of the man that I met months ago. His walls have come back up and I feel exposed, stupid. He looks down at his cock, gripping the base with this hand as he withdraws himself, holding the condom in place because god forbid any of his cum leak out and into me.

He strides to the attached bathroom, and I admire the ass on the ass before I roll to my side, my post-coital bliss slowly leaving my body to be replaced with mortification. What the hell did I just do? With the man that has harder walls to break through than Fort Knox. I got caught up. Holy crap I had a boyfriend yesterday! I get up, scuttling around looking for my clothing, pulling it on hastily. Jules still hasn't said a word, instead he's staring past my shoulder as if he can't stand to be in the same room as me.

"Jules?" I ask, just in case I'm not reading him correctly. I know that he doesn't ever sleep with women one on one, which I'm guessing is some type of weird trauma response, but I thought he was on board with everything we did. He seemed pretty damn fine with it.

"Yeah, um, look, I just, I don't sleep with women like that, ever. And if you're waiting around for me to ask you to stay then you got the wrong man. I'm an asshole, Violet." Violet, not Vi. "You'll do well to remember that."

I set my jaw, ready to argue and then I think what's the point? Really? I have no business imagining anything other than what this was with Jules. A lonely man and an emotionally confused woman. That's all. No matter how much my heart thinks it wants it to be more. No matter how much the scene with him and me and his little girl in the living room burrowed into my heart and made me want things I have no business wanting. Not with this man, and not now.

I turn, walking out of his room, down the hall, through the open plan dining and living room, stopping only to pick up my overnight bag, and then I walk out of his house.

Chapter 11

Jules

For the fourth time in as many hours I wake up breathless. My chest feels tight and if I had a tingling arm I'd believe I was having a heart attack. Except I'm young. Ish. I workout every day, eat well, minimize stress and am healthy as an ox. I share genes with Pops, and he's fit as a fiddle. I take stock of my body, and take a deep breath, pulling it deep into my lungs before blowing it out. I'm in charge of my body. I do this three more times and the tight feeling starts to dissipate. My arms feel looser and my jaw unclenches. My mind tries to drift back to Violet and I refuse to let it happen. What happened between us was a mistake. She just got out of a relationship. I was horny. It was a rebound fuck. Nothing more. Except for the throat tightening feeling that it felt like a hell of a lot more. I have to shut that shit down. That's not me, and I need to remember that. We'll just go back to having a professional relationship and I'll join Fox and Nitro when they play next. Easy.

Rolling over I check my watch, it's only two hours before I

need to leave so I may as well get up and get my day started. I'm running on less sleep than usual but fuck, it is what it is. If I'm lucky all will go to plan. Roman, DRMC and Moss will play their part, along with Tombs Security and we'll have all the information we need to bring down Happy Values and that bitch Candice Rogers.

By the time I've finished with an extra long workout, showered, had breakfast and gotten myself ready, any tension I was carrying is gone. In its place, the focus I need to run my end of today smoothly. I think about crossing the yard to say a quick hello to Juno, but then have second thoughts. I'll get caught at Pops and Debs' and I don't want to be there when Vi turns up for work. She may have a reputation for having a temper, but so far I haven't seen it. I thought it would come out last night, but instead I got indifference? Disappointment? Either way, I need a clear mind, not be bogged down with shit that I'm not built for.

Grabbing my keys I head out, not bothering to lock anything as Vi and Juno will most likely be over after breakfast. Starting the engine I drive down the long drive, only slowing when Vi's piece of crap Honda drives past me. I side eye her, not wanting to stare her down, especially after last night, but it doesn't really matter. She clocks my game and returns my gaze with her middle finger held high and proud as her eyes never leave the road.

I huff out a laugh. Good morning to me.

* * *

"Everyone clear?" I call through the intercom in Dayz's big blue van. Well, it was blue, but is now black and fitted out with a surveillance system the CIA and FBI would be jealous of.

Our plan today is pure surveillance on our part, but that doesn't mean that a truckload of kids are going to be collateral damage. Roman is looking for the route this guy came in on and his pick up point contact. Moss is on hand for traffic control and keeping our sightlines clear once the truck driver is in the diner. The MC will have eyes inside. Dayz will take care of him once the kids have made it to the drop off point where Gus's contact Dansen will be waiting with orders to take down Happy Values and Candice Rogers. From there the plan is to work with the Landrys and their network to get these kids home safe. There's a lot of moving parts but we should be able to pull it off as long as we stick to the plan and keep open lines of communication.

"I saw Violet leaving your house," Dayz's voice in the silent van startles me.

"Hmmph?"

"I saw Vi leave your house. Late at night. After I heard moaning. I like her. Do you like her?" She turns to glance at me, at the same time Tav and Gus all lean closer to hear.

"Yeah, she's cool. Juno really likes her," I answer vaguely.

Tav snorts and I turn on him, "What the fuck are you snorting at? And why the hell is your big ass crammed in here with us?"

His lips twitch and he gives me an asshole-y look. "Because, big brother, I work here. Maybe you left your brain somewhere else. Like in Vi's pants?"

I shoot up out of my seat and almost decapitate myself as my head flies backwards thanks to my headset cord.

"Sit the fuck down and don't break anything!" Gus growls,

looking between me and Tav. "Fuck's sake, we're working," he grumbles.

Dayz carries on, unperturbed. "That's not what I asked. I want to know if you like her in the same way I like Rhodie."

"I wouldn't know. I don't like people in that way," I answer. I don't want to talk about this.

"Why not?"

"I'm not built that way." I don't have to turn around to feel the eyerolls Gus and Tav shoot my way.

Dayz scoffs, "Yes you are. You aren't me." She pauses then continues, "OK, you're a little like me. But not really. I try. You don't. I'm funny, you're not. You're afraid of relationships. I'm not. "

"She's not wrong, brother," Gus says under his breath.

I open my mouth to answer her, and nothing comes out.

"One day, you'll be old. Everyone would have moved on and found their people, including Fox and Nitro. No one will want you at their orgies because you're old and sad. Juno will grow up and move out and you'll be alone in your cabin." I turn toward her and find her wide eyes staring directly at me. "You act like you're a loner but you're not. From the day you were born you've had people. Mom, Dad, Gus, then me and Tav and Pops. You attached yourself to Mama Debs quicker than the rest of us. You have the MC." She shrugs and looks back at her screen.

Tav's hand lands on my shoulder and squeezes. Hard. "She's right, Jules. You're surrounded and don't see it. You're not an island, brother." I shrug his hand off and focus my gaze on the screens in front of me.

"You think you're broken and don't need people, but you need them more than anyone else I know. So stop trying to push them all away. That's a dick move," Dayz finishes.

I stare at her, swallowing the lump in my throat at my sister giving me some hard truths with very little tact. "When did you become so smart, Dayz?"

Her face scrunches a moment, "It was watching everyone fall in love. Everyone was all messed up in their own way. But they found people that understand them. That could be Violet for you. Or someone else. Or even two someones."

"We don't have enough space at Pops' dinner table for two someones with the amount of kids coming out of the woodwork, so maybe just stick to one someone," Gus says dryly.

Could I handle one someone? Vi's beautiful face and goofy, tinkling laugh drift through my mind and my chest starts to tighten. Shaking my head I push away thoughts of her as I take a deep breath and unclench my thigh muscles, muscles I didn't even know I was tensing.

"DRMC are on site," Tav says.

I flick my eyes to the tiny screen in front of me, seeing nothing out of the ordinary. Except the four big bikers walking into the diner. I zoom in a little closer, the cameras good enough to see straight through the large window and into the front seating area. DRMC takes up a large booth, the brothers all sliding in. Except Judge, who looks frozen in place, staring at something further back.

To the left of me Dayz squints and leans in closer, seeing the same thing. "What is he doing? Is he talking to the owner lady?"

Before I can zoom any closer Judge turns and storms out of the diner, his brothers all looking confused, but none going after him. I can hear Rhodie over comms assuring Dayz that they can still go ahead without Judge. If backup is needed they have us and various MC brothers dotted around. Hell if worst came to worst I'm sure Moss would jump in for a good cause.

Our shared comms alert lights up and I flick it on, making it so everyone with an ear piece can hear what's being said. I've run enough of these ops to know that it's better for everyone to be on the same page, than have one single person coordinating. This way everyone can adjust expectations and plans in real time. "Target is pulling out of port now. A driver and his buddy. If you're thinking of tagging the truck it could be difficult if one is on watch," Fox's voice says.

"I'll get Flack to run interference," I answer.

"Roger that," Flack's voice sounds out, on board with the plan.

"Heat detection gun showed at least seven small human sized heat signatures in the back."

My fists clench at Nitro's information. Dayz and I share a look and I know for a fucking fact that this guy and his buddy will be going straight to the Rev Room once we get hands on them.

Checking the time, we have about 20 minutes before our target arrives. The Diner may be on Rose Grove's main street, however there's a huge lot behind it perfect for trucks to pull in for a quick bite. There is no rear diner entrance, only an exit, however the DRMC has men in the kitchen, with easy access to the back exit if needed.

I watch my screens and religiously check comms for the moment the truck we are waiting on pulls in. Flicking my gaze between all my screens I concentrate on the traffic before flicking my eyes to the diner entrance.

"What the fuck?" Moss's voice rings out at the same time I yell "What the fuck is she doing there?"

There, on screen, is the woman I fucked and then sent away. Walking right into my fucking operation.

"I'm going to redden that ass," I growl to myself.

"You fucking what?" Moss yells into the intercom, deafening me and everyone else with an ear piece.

I throw down my headset and squeeze my big ass through the two front seats, throwing open the passenger side door and climbing out.

"Wanna fucking tell me what that comment was for?" Moss grumbles, stopping, toe to toe with me on the sidewalk.

"No time. We gotta get your sister outta there before that asshole arrives." I ignore his huffing and puffing. I got shit to do.

"This isn't over Tombs. That's my sister."

I want to argue with Moss but there's no time . My feet carry me toward the diner and the woman that's messing with my mind.

Violet

"Shit," I exclaim to my sisters, fumbling through the 1 million bags I'm carrying to find my phone. I forgot to send Jules a message letting him know where Juno and I are, and the last thing I need is for him to act like even more of a dick.

I mean I get it, he has stuff going on, and all that, but still. The least you can do after banging me like a screen door in high wind is shake my hand and say you had a lovely time. Not avoid eye contact and remind me you're an asshole.

I didn't say a word about what happened last night when I saw Pops and Mama Debs this morning, there was no way I wanted to get into that. They must have known something was up anyway, Pops' eyebrow waggling was off the charts, and so was Mama Debs' backhands to his gut.

"You know, I'm sure you can probably get those four bags down to two. I saw a nanny at the park, she had the car seat thing, and two bags. The baby one and one small one she kept her phone and lip gloss in," Lily says, pulling open the door to the diner.

I roll my eyes because I'm sure there are lots of great nannies at the park. Ones that don't over pack the bags or sleep with their bosses.

"Oh, no, we're not going to the back," Jazz whispers, corralling me and Lil to a table in the front window.

"Why not? The booth is so comfy. Besides if there was a shootout we'd be the first to die, sitting here. What if an out of control car comes speeding down the street and through this window?" I whine.

"What if Rodney was sitting at the booth right next to the only free one in here?" Jazz hisses.

My eyes shoot to the back of the diner and right there, flipping me the bird is that ginger Rodney kid. My shoulders slump and I sit my ass down into the hard wooden chair by the window.

"Fine. You win."

Lily grins and smiles up at the server who places three coffee cups down and starts pouring.

"Hiya, we already know what we're having, can we please get three all day waffles with bacon and banana and a side of fries? Oh, and a banana milkshake for me." I ask.

"Chocolate for me," Jazz says at the same time Lil asks for strawberry.

The server giggles, writes down our order and winks. "Gimme 10."

I watch her walk back toward the kitchen to drop off our order and by the time I draw my eyes back to the table I have my sisters staring at me. "Spill."

"Spill what?" I ask, busying myself with straightening Juno's blanket over her legs. She gives me a judgey look then frowns at my sisters.

"You're acting weird. First off, you never call us sounding all needy wanting to randomly have lunch. You're a planner to your core," Jazz says, giving me a harsh big sister look.

"And you've been radio silent about Josh. Two nights ago he insulted mom then ran away. That type of behaviour would cause you to be angry calling us all to bitch about him. Mom thinks you're having some type of quarter life breakdown or something."

I stare a Lil for a moment. "Why? Because I haven't been blowing up people's phones?"

"And Moss hasn't had to arrest you. Remember when Tony Di Santos cheated on you in high school with that Maddy girl and you keyed his car and then let a popsicle melt on the hood essentially ruining the paint?" Jazz makes it sound like I was crazed. Pissed, yes. Crazed no. I planned that shit.

"That's different. He broke my delicate teenage heart!"

"OK, what about that Gavin guy?" Jazz persists.

Lily's eyes get huge. "Ohhh Gross Gavin,"

I glare at her, "He wasn't *that* gross!"

"He had back hair so long it stuck out the top of his shirt neck hole. You went out with that loser and then when he dumped you publicly you stuck Nair in his shampoo bottle before you moved out."

A gasp and the scraping of chair legs on the checkered floor has me turning to see Mira, Nat, and Ana at the table next to us.

"Hi! We're from the DRMC. We're friends with Vi." Mira says cheerily to my sisters. "We're gonna come sit with you and get all the amazing sounding gossip. Good material and all that," Mira waves a hand in the air and then drags their table closer to ours, almost squishing Lil in the moving process. "You don't mind, do you?" she asks us, as she takes a seat in the newly formed six seater table.

"No way! The more the merrier. We're just here trying to figure out why we've been invited to lunch and why Vi hasn't retaliated against her douchey ex-boyfriend. I'm Jazz, this is Lil." Jazz says then smiles at the server who places our milkshakes in front of us.

Nat and Ana stare at me, while Mira claps excitedly. "Oh, pick me! I bet I know!"

"She probably does," Ana says. "It'll be some well known book trope that you're going through. Trust me. If she wasnt so, *Mira*, I'd think she was psychic." She shrugs, smiling up at the same server woman who drops fries off to the end of their table. She promptly takes a fry and dips it in ketchup before popping it in her mouth and letting out a long, low moan.

"Great, now we know what you sound like when Gus taps that," Nat teases. "Mira, hit Vi and her sisters with your prediction."

"Well, I heard about your little boring problem. Josh, was it?" I nod. "I think the reason you haven't retaliated is because you're not hurt by it."

My brows pinch and I use my gentle voice because I don't want to hurt Mira's feelings when I tell her that I think she's wrong.

"No, you're hurt by his insult, but not the fact that you aren't together anymore," she argues.

"Let me ask you this, what did you like about Josh?" Nat prompts, stealing one of Ana's fries.

"Well, before he insulted my family, he was nice. I knew he would never cheat on me. He had a good job. He had a good future planned out. We'd be able to afford kids and live in a nice neighborhood," I answer truthfully.

"Riiiight. And how did you feel around him? Did you want to tear his clothes off or get frisky in an alley or even make a mold of his penis and use it on him?"

"Wait, what?" I ask, bewildered.

"Oh, I mean hypothetically, of course," Mira continues, then waves her hand in the air to get me talking.

"Well, not so much all the extra spicy stuff. He was nice, and we had a very fulfilling bedroom life," I answer.

Jazz stares at me, then shares a look with Lil, then back to me. "What are you? Elderly? Did you also sleep in separate single beds and wear flannel pyjamas?"

"He just wasn't a tear my clothes off kind of guy!" I hiss at her, in my defence.

"Ohhh. He sounds like a 'make lover'," Nat whispers.

"A what?" Lil asks, looking intrigued.

Nat takes a long sip from her Pepsi and gets comfortable. "There are two types of men in this world and a rare unicorn. The first type are the 'make lovers'. They make love, all soft, gentle, fairly vanilla but they mean well. Then there are the 'fuckers'. The ones that tear your clothes off, bend you over the nearest surface and thrust away until you're a mumbling mess."

"They are also more likely to spit on you," Ana nods.

My mind flashes back to Jules, a string of saliva going from his lush lips to my clit as he thrust in and out of me. My body temperature rises and my core clenches in remembrance.

"Wait, what's the third? The rare unicorn?" I ask, trying to shake images of Jules from my mind.

"The unicorn is a man that can do both. Make love, and fuck."

Mira stares at me and her lips turn up, "And to wrap up that little lesson, ladies and ladies, the reason that Vi isn't cut up about Josh the Make Love man, is because she's recently been in the vicinity of a Fucker." She leans back in her chair, looking very pleased with herself. "You got over one man by getting under another. The question is, who could it be?"

"What the hell are you doing here?" Jules' voice growls through the diner.

Mira's grin grows even wider. In fact, everyone at the table is grinning at Jules, including his daughter.

"What does it look like I'm doing, Jules?" I answer, holding his blazing eye contact. I would look away, but fuck him. I'm not submitting to this guy again.

"You shouldn't be here."

"Why not?" I tip my head to the side, and notice my brother hovering close behind him.

Jules steps closer to the table, his body wedged between my two sisters opposite me. He places his fists on the table and leans over, almost nose to nose with me. "Because there is shit going down in here," he growls quietly.

I glance around the busy diner. Nothing looked amiss when we walked in, but now that I'm looking closer, most of the people in here seem to be connected to the MC in some way. A booth in the middle of the diner has Rhodie, Tank and Sniper sitting around it. Looking through the kitchen hatch I can see the two newly patched guys, Chef and TumTum dressed like greasy spoon cooks. There's some women I recognise from some of the businesses I know the MC own.

I look at the three DRMC women with my brow raised in question. "We're people watching," Nat says with a shrug. Turning back to Jules I hit him with the pants shittingly feral look Flora Davies uses when we've gone too far. "If it's safe enough for the Ol Ladies to be here, it's safe enough for us to be here." I gesture to myself and my sisters.

"Not with Juno it's not. You need to leave." Jules' jaw ticks and I'm pretty sure he has a pulsating vein in his head. Any other day I'd back down. But not today. Today I feel raw in more ways than one. I open my mouth to challenge him when the bell above the diner door rings.

The air in here feels like it's been sucked out, as two dirty looking trucker types walk in. Mira's eyes are huge as she watches them walk past, but then true to form she spins back to the table.

"I've never written a romance about a trucker. I mean, obviously my one would be hot, not like those guys. But do we think it could work?"

My sisters stare at her before turning their gazes on me. I let out a sigh, "Jazz and Lil, meet Mira slash Melody Baldwin."

"No. WAY!? I love your stuff! Holy crap, could I get your autograph?" Lil gushes.

Jules clearly has had enough of me ignoring him because

instead of walking away, he makes his way to my side of the table, sits in the empty chair next to me, grips my chair leg and drags me until our thighs are pressed together.

"If you're not gonna move, then neither am I."

Chapter 12

Jules

I have no clue what the fuck I'm doing. I should have kept my ass in the van and did my job. However watching Vi sashay her way in the diner and then sit at the motherfucking window made me lose my mind. Add to it Juno is here and I left my senses in the van with my sister and brothers.

The heat of her thick thigh seeps into me, and I try to act like I'm just a normal guy joining a bunch of women for lunch. Moss managed to make his way to the DRMC table, blending in nicely with the brothers. I on the other hand am getting a full creative breakdown on how Mira is going to write some trucker romance.

"Obviously he's been a bit of a player on the road, but maybe he's back in town after two years away from the woman that he spent one hot, memorable night with who now tends bar at the watering hole he decides to stop at. Seeing her again brings up all these feelings and he wants to tap that again but she's hesitant. What could be holding her back?" Mira narrows her eyes and gazes at the women around the table.

"Oh! Maybe she had his child and never told him. I mean, if it's a one night stand they probably didn't exchange anything more than bodily fluids," Vi's sister Jazz offers.

"Yes!" Mira points her pencil at Jazz before jotting down notes.

They keep rabbiting on and I zone out as I watch the body language of the guy we're surveilling. He and his buddy are at a booth near the back, which is perfect because we needed uninterrupted access to the truck. As we speak our team will be tagging it so we can follow its route to its final destination point.

The piece in my ear makes a quick series of beeps indicating that comms are going wide.

"We've got a problem," Dex's voice says. "I got a guy still inside the truck we're meant to be tagging."

Gus curses over the line, and shooting a look to the MC shows them all tensing.

"Who the fuck is in the diner with our driver then?" Rhodie mumbles under his breath from his place in the booth.

"A second truck pulled in alongside our target a minute or so later," Savage replies.

"So a trucker friend then?" Gus asks.

Dex lets out a sigh. "Sure. Although his truck has traces of blood on the door. We hit it with heat detection, and found at least five heat signatures. Smaller than livestock, bigger than a dog."

Those of us in communication share looks with each other, the trucker fucks none the wiser.

"Place the tracker as best you can and focus on the second truck. The heat signatures sound child-sized and the presence of blood makes that truck our priority as we don't know where it's heading," Gus barks down the line.

"Got it," Dex replies. "Tav gave me an extra tracker, we'll place it on the new target and shadow him."

Nat and Ana burst into laughter over something Jazz has said, pulling my attention away from the shitshow and to the women at the table. Namely the one sitting next to me. Vi looks up at me with her chocolate brown eyes, she has lighter flecks that run through them and I love how they glow when she gets fired up.

"What's wrong?"

I shake my head. She doesn't need to know shit. "Nothing. Just a work thing."

She narrows her eyes at me, her delicate hand lands on my thigh and I try not to tense. I don't want her to know how much my body likes her touch. Her hand travels up my thigh, then back down, settling at the top of my knee. Then squeezes. Hard.

"What the fuck are you doing?" I growl in her direction, ignoring the stares of the Davies sisters, Nat, Ana and Mira around the table.

"I can read you like a book, dickhead," she hisses under her breath. "There's something wrong. Tell me or else I'll keep squeezing until you can't feel your leg."

"Yeah, look, I don't mean to butt in, but you should really listen to her, Jules," Jazz says, staring me down.

"You should. She did that to Moss once and it was so bad he couldn't compete in the state long distance champs because he had nerve damage," Lily adds.

Mira stares wide-eyed at Vi before her eyes glaze over and she starts to scribble in her notepad again.

"Our mission has taken a turn," I say through clenched teeth.

Vi looks at Juno, who is dozing off in her little chair, then at her siblings and the Ol Ladies. "Hey, I gotta get Juno home for her nap. Do you ladies want to continue this at Jules' place?"

Violet smirks at me and I nod once, fucking ecstatic that she's leaving this shitshow before it fully starts. The MC women pack up their things, saying they'll pick up some wine before heading to mine and are out the door before I can let out a full breath. The Davies sisters are slower due to bags of Juno's crap, but still, they're going to be getting out of here. Thank fuck. Flicking my eyes around the full diner, they land on Tank who gives me a nod, probably thanking me for getting his Ol Lady out of here too.

One of the truckers stands, claps the other on the back and moves to leave the diner. Knowing Vi is going to be heading home with Juno has me feeling a shit ton better about the situation. I wait until he passes me, then I too stand, ready to tail him to whichever vehicle is his. I'm hoping it's the one we've now set sights on. This guy is scrawny and going to be a fuck load easier to throw him into a trunk as a present for Dayz.

I lean in to Vi, "Thank you," I whisper into her ear, ignoring the shiver that goes through her.

I ignore how much my body wants her. How much I want to sit my ass back down and bask in the glow that she emits, even if part of her glow is rage at my shitty move last night. Making my way to the door, I lift my chin to Rhodie, knowing he and the MC will know when to make moves.

I walk to the back lot, trailing behind the greasy trucker, far enough that he hasn't clocked me yet. Or Flack and Dex in the shadows.

"Eyes on, this is our guy," I say in a low voice. Whoops come over my comms, almost deafening me.

"I'm going in," Dayz's voice calls out, my brother's curses filling the empty air she left behind.

I quicken my steps, eager to get to this guy before Dayz. If she gets her hands on him we're gonna end up with a mess on our hands. My fingers work the lid off of the canister in my pocket, allowing my fingers to grip the nasal spray by the handle. I stop abruptly as he stops to piss about with his boot, before straightening and then banging the sides of his truck, chuckling to himself. Asshole.

I let out a shrill whistle, startling him enough to have him spin in my direction. By the time I stop moving we are toe to toe with each other.

"Who the fuck-"

My hand shoots up, shoving the spray canister into his nostril, depressing the trigger and filling his nasal cavity with Midazolam. The medication my sister uses to sedate her unwilling victims.

"Night night, asshole," Dayz's voice coos from behind me as he hits the ground.

Violet

I watch as Jules follows one of the crusty truckers out the door, then gather my 100 bags quickly, anxious to get Juno home now that I know that his operation has gone sideways. Lifting

Juno's carrier and slipping the handle into the crook of my arm, I'm assaulted by a hideous scent coming from her tiny *las pompis*.

"Jesus hell! Is that coming from her?" Jazz asks, pulling the collar of her shirt up over her nose.

"Hey! You work with kids all day, don't tell me they don't have accidents!" I snark.

"Yeah, but they eat people food. This kid eats formula and smells like that? Imagine when she eats food!"

I stare down at the angelic frowny face with the ass of Satan and have to admit, she has a point. "OK, let me get her changed and then we can go. But we gotta hustle."

"You take the diaper bag and we'll get your stuff packed up," Lil offers, starting to load up.

"Be back soon," I say over my shoulder as I hot foot it to the bathrooms, looking for the one with the picture of a woman and a baby.

I move to lock the door and realize that the lock is broken. Shrugging, I get Juno on the changing table and start unbuttoning her snaps.

"-Yeah, there's a ginger kid in here. Double check that we need a ginger and I'll get him-" a gruff voice says outside the door.

I frown and start to clean Juno up as quickly as I can.

"-yeah, thought so. He's a little older, maybe 9?"

There's only one ginger in here that's around that age and it's Rodney.

"-yeah man. Got it." There's some rustling outside the door. "Hey kid, wanna see something cool?"

"No." That's Rodney's voice. He was sitting at the second to last booth before the hallway and the bathrooms.

"Nah, it's super cool. You play video games?" The male voice says, less gruff than when he was on the phone.

"Yeah. What kind of games you got?" Rodney's heavy footsteps make their way closer to where Juno and I are and I make sure Juno is clean and changed, then I place her in her seat, strapping her in. I move her off the table onto the floor for her safety while I deal with the guy in the hallway. Rodney may be a little terrorist, but he doesn't need some perv messing with him.

I fling the door open, "Rodney, do you know this man?" I ask him, not taking my eyes of the tall, thin trucker type. How many truck drivers does this diner have? Sheesh.

"Pirate! What are you doing here?" Rodney asks, a grin on his face.

"Rodney, answer me. Do. You. Know. This. Man?"

"Aw come on lady, just mind your own business and take that fat ass of yours back to the table."

"I'll do that as soon as you mind your own business and take your skinny ass back to your table," I counter.

He ignores me, instead turning back to Rodney. "How old are you, kid?"

I place my body between him and Rodney, "He's none-of-your-fucking-business-years-old."

"You're a mouthy bitch. I was planning on letting you walk. Not anymore." Quick as a flash he grabs Rodney's chubby hand and yanks him from behind me. He pulls a gun out of god knows where, holding it to Rodney's messy, red hair. "You're going to do exactly what I say, when I say it. Now move your fat ass toward the back doors. Make a sound, and Fanta pants gets it."

"I ain't got nothing in my pants you asshole!" Rodney huffs indignantly and I really want to laugh but I can't.

We shuffle out the door, Rodney pressed up against me, smelling slightly of playdoh and wet coins. As much as he gets on my nerves, I can't let him be taken. I stumble forward as the guy with the gun shoves me, making me walk faster, dragging Rodney with me as this guy talks to someone on his phone.

I need to use the fact that he's slightly distracted to get Rodney out of here. "Psst, Rodney," I whisper in a low voice. His freckled face turns to mine before he grins and then flips the bird. "I need your help. I left my baby in the bathroom at the diner. I need you to run and get help. Ok?"

His eyes narrow at me, until they're little slits with a hint of blue peeking out. "What will I get if I do that?"

"Not kidnapped?" I offer. I stumble on a rock and manage to catch myself, only to have trucker guy poke me in the back with his gun. "Fine. I'll buy you a hot glue gun." I hiss at him under my breath.

"Not a cheap one, Pirate. A good one. Cordless."

"Fine!" I agree. "Run now, Rodney!" I whisper frantically.

A part of me thinks he won't do it. He'll just follow along in his smart ass little world. But the ginger surprises me. He dodges the gun guy and takes off as fast as his short legs can take him, only turning to flip the bird at the dickhead.

"You shoot that and everyone will come running," I yell, trying to keep the attention on me. I know as soon as Rodney alerts someone there will be hell to pay. The Tombs and DRMC will be all over his ass. Although glancing around there isn't much of a sign of any one.

"Whatever bitch. I got you now. I'm sure with the right cocktail you can birth the ginger I need." He fiddles with something on the back of his truck before rolling the door open.

I'm struck with the smell of old rotting fruit mixed with sweat and something else, something metallic.

"If you want to live, you'll get your fat ass in there right now." He presses the muzzle of the gun into my hair, hard enough to make me whimper.

I spin around, ignoring the gun at my temple, pressing my face closer to his. "You will fucking regret this. Mark my words. When you least expect it I will come for you. *Eres hombre muerto*," I say through my clenched teeth.

He laughs in my face, then hits me with the butt of the gun, stunning me enough to make me stumble, but that just spurs me on. "Get in the fucking truck NOW!"

I glare at him, memorizing his face, his features, everything about him. I meant what I said. He's a dead man. Climbing into the back of the truck I try to hold in my nausea at the smell in here. I'm not sure what the hell this guy was carting, but it absolutely reeks. The roller door slams down, effectively cutting out most of the light. It's deathly quiet until I hear a whimper.

"Hello?" I call out, hoping like hell adrenaline isn't making my mind play tricks on me.

"Are you a mommy?" a little voice asks. My eyes are adjusting slowly, but not quick enough to find the source of the question.

"I'm a nanny. Are you here all alone, sweetheart? What's your name? Are you OK?" My heart starts beating out of my chest and I bombard the inside of this manky truck with questions.

There's some sniffling and then a sob breaks through the darkness. "I want my mommy!" a voice, different from the last cries.

Looking around, I can vaguely make out a huddle of shadows, in the far corner. The sudden rumbling of the truck and movement makes it hard for me to walk so I drop to my knees and shuffle my way to where I think there may be someone.

"Are, are you OK? What's your name sweetheart?" My voice sounds panicked to my own ears but I push that aside and try to breathe, remaining calm for whoever is sharing this hellhole with me.

"I'm Maddy. There's five of us here," another voice, this one sounding older says, before gently reassuring the others.

I swallow down the bile, trying to keep my head. "How old are you and your friends, Maddy?"

"I'm ten. Bella is seven, Stevie is five, and the two little ones I don't know their names but they're small."

"It's going to be OK. I'll look after you," I say.

I sit against the wall next to them and they all huddle around me. If Jules and the MC don't tear that man limb from limb, then I will.

Chapter 13

Jules

"Fuck! It's animals," Rhodie curses, kicking the back tire of the truck that Rider drove to the clubhouse.

"What the fuck?" Tav snarls, pulling his bulk into the back of the truck to see for himself.

Marx stands, feet apart, arms crossed over his broad chest, seething. He's been in a mood since he and Lovely arrived back at the clubhouse. Lovely on the other hand seems her usual self, which is great because it means we won't have to kick Marx's ass. Lovely is, well, lovely. She's a gentle soul and if Marx had hurt her or even so much as growled at her there would be all hell to pay. Instead, he's brought his foul mood to the back of a truck that was a fucking waste of time. Although something feels off. Why the fuck would he be carting near dead animals in a large truck? Glancing at my sister I can see she has come to the same conclusion. Her eyes are narrowed and she's squishing her lip between her thumb and forefinger, staring into space.

Shaking her body she looks around at our brothers, and

the DRMC brothers that are here. "Rev Room time. I need answers."

She turns on her heel and starts walking toward the back shed. Well, it's a little more than a shed, what with its metal hospital table, autoclave for her tools, floor drain and high tech sound system. I follow Tank and Judge into the space, no one having asked Judge what happened today. He's usually fucking steady, so it must have been fucked up to cause him to lose his cool.

"OK my little friend, you got some 'splainin to do!" Chewy singsongs, walking right up to her victim and mussing up his hair. "Baby? I think I need my samba beats."

Rhodie drops a kiss on her lips and fucks about with his phone. He taps the screen and the quick, upbeat drums and peppy melody flow through the room, the LED's pulsing in time with the music. Groans sound out from behind me, the brothers more often than not hating Dayz's music choice. Normally her pulling this shit doesn't bother me, but today? Fuck today it reminds me of Vi's plump ass and thick thighs gyrating to the beat.

"I need you to tell me what you're doing transporting near dead animals. And no bullshitting, because my man will know." Dayz waves toward Rhodie, arms crossed, scowling and looking like an all round mean fucker.

The trucker leans back and tries to headbutt my sister, but she's faster. She dodges to the side then sprays something in his eye. He freezes in place and then starts to scream, his eyes squeezed shut. White froth oozes out from under one of his eyelids and he squirms in his seat. Dayz watches him for a moment, leaning against her ol man, waiting for the yelling to subside.

"Take your time, buddy. I got all day. Unfortunately you probably need medical attention, so if I were you I'd spill so I can get you the help you probably need," my sister says in her caring voice. Which sends a shiver down my spine because she only uses it when doing horrific things to bad people.

"Fuck, shit, OK. I got paid double to follow Maurice."

"The guy you were sitting with at the diner?" Rhodie asks.

"Yeah, him," the trucker whimpers.

"Who paid you?" Marx growls, causing the guy to jump.

"It's all done through Snapchat. Jobs come up, I apply, they Venmo the money and I Uber to the pickup point. The truck is ready and waiting to go, along with the appropriate customs papers and I drive. That's all I know!"

Dayz rummages in the guy's pockets, ignoring Rhodie growling behind her. "Ha!" she yells, victorious, holding the dude's phone high in the air.

Ringing sounds out, giving Dayz a fright and she fumbles the phone before looking at the screen. "Crap. It's not his phone."

"Babe?" Gus's voice says, "What? No, Jules is here with me. And she's not home?"

Who's not home? Marx's phone goes off and he walks to the corner, jabbing at his screen before he turns to look at me. "When was the last time you saw Vi?"

My brows pull low. "At the diner? Why?"

"Chewy, put him on ice. Everyone else? Common room. Now."

Dayz pops a hood over the guy's head, patting him lightly as the rest of us file out of the Rev Room and make our way into the common room. I call Vi, but it keeps ringing out and I can feel my blood pressure begin to rise. I make my way to the bar as soon as I make it inside, spreading my hands on the cool, dark wood bar top. I take a breath and let it work through me. I'm in control of my body, not the other way around. Feeling calmer I figure that Vi is probably just busy. I mean, Juno probably had a blow out. That kid's ass is pretty dangerous.

"Where is my *niña*? I don't care if you're built like a *Quinametzin* with a taste for chalupas, you will tell me where my baby is!" Spinning around I'm met with the sight of 4'10 Flora Davies poking Marx in the chest.

Moss's gaze lands on me and he storms over, finger at the ready, looking to poke me. Must run in the family.

"Don't. Fucking. Think. About. It," I growl.

The doors burst open and Pops, Mama Debs, Ana, Mira and Nat rush through the door. "Are they here?"

The energy in the room is bordering on frantic and I can't fucking think. Flora is yelling at Marx, her husband trying his best to calm her down. Jazz and Lily have tear streaked cheeks. Moss is ready to tear my fucking head off and the women are frantic. My hands shake when I realize that I haven't laid eyes on Vi or Juno.

"Where's Violet?" My voice sounds like I'm in a tunnel, hollow.

"That's what we're asking you, asshole!" Moss barks, shoving me, "The girls said she went to change Juno and she never came back. So where the fuck is she?"

The whole room quiets and my head spins. I close my eyes. I'm in charge of my body. I am in charge of my body. I let out a breath, before shooting a look at Jazz and Lil. "Are both Vi and Juno missing?"

Lil nods and I let out a breath, thanking fuck they're together. I tap my phone screen, bringing up my tracker. The carrier is showing as here, at the DRMC, but that can't be right.

"Tracker says the baby carrier is here, but that can't be right."

"Oh, we packed her bags into our car. She took Juno's carseat and diaper bag with her," Jazz sniffles, leaning into her father.

Nodding I check the location for the diaper bag and car seat. I frown at the coordinates. "It says she's at the diner."

"No, she can't be. We looked everywhere. We waited an hour and she never came back. That's not like her," Jazz argues.

"It's not. I know my *mija*, and she wouldn't just disappear," Flora says, voice full of conviction.

"Not unless there was a good fucking reason," Moss says quietly.

"You sure that's where she is, Jules?" Marx, ever the voice of reason, calls out.

"That's where the trackers are."

"Good. Let's roll out."

Violet

I curse that I like my curvy, lazyish body and don't have one of those fitness watches. If I did I'd have a way for Dayz or Wire or Remy or damn near anyone to track me. I've seen it on the news, some woman who was tracked thanks to her watch. But not me. I'm in the back of a moving vehicle with no watch, no cell phone. Nothing other than a group of scared little kids.

I have my arm wrapped around Maddy's shoulders, and the two little ones, who I managed to find out are called Max and

Jett, are curled up in my lap. I don't even mind the smell anymore. It may have turned my stomach earlier, but now I seem to have become accustomed to it. I've been humming under my breath, and cooing soothing words at the kids. If I'm crapping my pants about the situation, these kids must be downright terrified. So far I have found out that they all have parents, and they come from all over. I'm not sure where this truck came from, but I do know there's a port nearby. How the hell they came through there with no one noticing is beyond me. And where the hell they had even been before coming through there is another mystery. All of these kids are from the States so why they were there is one of many things playing on my mind.

"Maddy, where were you before you were taken? I know your family are from Kansas, but is that where you were taken from?" I ask, quietly, so as not to wake the boys in my lap.

"No," she whispers back, "I was on holiday with my family in Cabo."

My brows pinch, "How did they get you, sweetheart?"

In the dim light I can see her lip tremble. "We were at the kids' holiday program."

My frown deepens. "We?"

She nods. "Me, Max and Jett. I think they might be brothers."

I pull my arm tighter around her as I try to piece things together. If they took Maddy and the boys from a kids' holiday program at a resort, chances are they did the same to the other kids. Why take American citizens then smuggle them back to the country they came from? That doesn't make any sense. Although, is this the type of thing that usually does? I mean, they only took me because Rodney ran off.

Speaking of, I hope like hell he went and found help. My gut clenches thinking of Juno asleep in her car seat in the diner bathroom. I'm glad that she's safe and far away from here, but I still worry about her. I soothe myself with thoughts of Rodney getting help, or my sisters realizing I've been gone for too long and they'd go looking for me. The quicker someone realizes I'm gone, the quicker they'll find me.

Leaning my head back on the cool metal behind me, I try to estimate the length of time we've been driving. It doesn't feel that long, and yet it feels like a lifetime. That one gross dude mentioned using me to pop out a ginger and I shudder at the implications. I'm like every other woman in the world. I've seen enough true crime to know that shit like this doesn't usually end well. So what I need to do is pull from my hours of crime watching to come up with a plan.

So far I know there is only one driver.

"Maddy, does the truck stop often? And for how long?" I know she won't know how long between stops, but knowing that it *does* stop every now and then would be helpful.

"Um, yeah he stops sometimes. That time, when he got you, that was a long time. He sometimes stops for little bits and gives us water and snacks."

I nod, my thoughts bouncing around. OK, that's good. The fact that he gives them water and snacks means they shouldn't be too malnourished and weak. If we want to make a break for it I need them to be in some type of good health.

The rocking of the truck starts to slow and we pull sideways a little. With any luck this will be a stop and I can maybe get the kids to cause enough of a distraction to be able to get the upper hand. He's not a huge guy, and the fact that I'm pissed off, in a truck with these babies will make me a worthy opponent. Besides, I made a vow to him, and I intend to fulfill it.

The door slides up, bathing us in light so bright spots dance in front of my eyes. The little boys whimper and I pull them closer, Maddy doing the same with Bella and Stevie.

"Out. Now," he booms, gun pointed in my direction.

The kids look at me as I rise, gently placing Max and Jett on the filthy floor. I hold my hands up, trying to look small and afraid instead of murderous.

Maddy grabs onto the back of my shirt, "It'll be OK. Just do as the man says," I whisper down to her, hoping my voice is calm, so as not to scare them.

I jump down onto the ground, trucker man grabbing me roughly by the bicep as soon as I land. He holds me in front of him, gun to my head. Darting my eyes around I realize we're in some type of warehouse. It's a huge empty space with two other trucks parked nearby. There's a set of stairs and what look to be offices that have windows looking down at where we are. There's a tap with a hose connected close to where I'm standing and I try to take in as many details as I can. I can't seem to see anyone else apart from this dickhead and the kids still in the back of the truck, so I take that as a good sign.

"All of you, out. Now."

He watches with beady eyes as Bella and Stevie jump down onto the ground, Maddy passing the little boys down to them before jumping down herself. He uses his gun to line them all up before marching me in the direction of the tap.

The muzzle of his gun pokes into my temple, "Turn it on." I begrudgingly do as he says, not wanting to do anything to anger him. I need to keep my brains inside my head if I have any hope of keeping these kids alive. Water spurts out of the end of the hose. "Pick it up, and aim it at the kids. Those filthy little fuckers need to be cleaned off."

"Whose fault is that?" I say through clenched teeth.

He leans close, so close I can smell his rancid breath as he breathes into my ear. "Blame the childless rich fucks that'll pay for them."

Something powerful is rising inside me, half bile and half pure rage. I hate rich people more than I hate good looking people. Money should be used to help people, not fucking buy children to fulfill some sick need or fantasy. Kids aren't the latest accessory. They're a fucking gift.

I shake the arm in his grip, trying to get his sick breath away from me. He tugs me harder, reminding me of what I should be doing. I lean to pick up the hose and give the kids an apologetic smile.

"Sorry kids," I say gently before spraying them with the cold water. It may be spring in Texas, but this water is still cold and these kids have been in a stuffy truck for god knows how long.

I get them cleaned up as much as I can before I make out like I'm done. He still has one arm in his vice like grip, so I don't have much space to maneuver, but it's enough. I wait until Maddy wipes the water from her eyes with her hands before I spin as much as I can and shove the hose as far into his face as possible. His grip releases from my arm in shock so I wrap it around his neck, holding him closer as I force the hose as close to his nose as I can, essentially trying to waterboard him. He's sputtering and coughing, his body thrashes in my hold, trying to fight against me. His legs try to kick mine, so I wrap one of mine over his hip, pulling him in as tight as I can, my thunder thigh keeping him in place.

His movements start to slow, and his body weight feels heavy but I keep going. I told him he was a dead man and I fucking meant it. I'll protect these kids with my life and I will kill for them if I have to. He makes a weird gurgling noise and then his weight drops, almost taking me down with him. I stumble back, dropping the hose from my shaking hand and spin to check on the kids. Maddy stares at me wide-eyed, one of the boys in her arms, his face buried in her neck. Bella has the other, doing the same thing, trying to shield them from something they'll hopefully never remember.

"OK, kids, we gotta get outta here. Come with me.," I take Max out of Bella's arms and rush with him to the driver's side.

"Ah, ah. Stop right there."

I freeze in my tracks, so fucking close to freedom. There, in front of the truck is a tall, thin blonde woman, with red nails like talons. Behind her are four seriously built men, dressed all in black and holding guns trained on me. I place Max on the ground and move him behind me, trying to shield all the kids with my wide hips and ass.

"Now, I don't like when people mess with my business. And you, you little bitch," she spits, "have not only cost me a little ginger shit, but also one of my best drivers." She strides up to me on impossibly high heels and backhands me, her huge diamond ring scraping across my face.

"Please, don't hurt the kids," I plead, trying to speak to some type of maternal nature she may be hiding in her thin as hell body.

"Oh, I would never hurt them. They're my money makers. You, on the other hand, have cost me and I don't like debts. Yours will be paid on your back, breeding me fresh stock." A grotesque grin pulls across her face. She turns to her men, waving in our direction. "Take the kids to the dorm, tell Magdalene to get them cleaned up and fed."

"And the bitch, ma'am?"

She turns to eye me, taking me in from head to toe, before turning back to address the guy. "The breeding pen."

Chapter 14

Jules

I could have a heart attack at any moment, with how fast my heart is beating. I've tried breathing and clenching my toes, fists and thighs before slowly releasing, in hopes that would help and so far it's done fuck all. The ride to the diner may be short, but it's a hell of a long time knowing that Vi and Juno are missing. Gus screeches to a stop, all us Tombs including Pops piling out, while the roar of motorcycle pipes drown out any other sounds. I walk through the door, the bells jingling, not even stopping to acknowledge the teenage server wanting to seat us. I storm through the seating area, heading for the bathrooms where the trackers are going off. Bypassing the mens and womens, I slow when I get to the mothers and baby bathroom, the door slightly ajar.

"Vi?" I call quietly, so as not to startle anyone.

I push the door open gently, slowly revealing an empty room. Walking into the room I turn to see Juno's car seat and diaper bag are lying on the floor in the corner behind the door. My heart beats so hard and fast I can hear my pulse, the noise of it drowning out anything else. I take a shaky breath, then another and another, clenching and unclenching my fists. I control my body. It doesn't control me. I am in control. My legs give out and someone grabs for me as I slide down the wall behind me, landing in a heap on the floor, my legs askew, eyes burning and throat tight.

Gus and Tav are squatting in front of me but I can't understand what they're saying, it's like we're all underwater. Gus grabs at my shirt and starts unbuttoning the top few buttons and it feels like I can breathe a little easier. Still can't understand anything they're saying but I feel less like I'm choking.

Pops shoves my brothers out of the way. "Ah, shit kid, not doing well are ya?"

He stands over me and then my head jerks to the side, a warm burn spreading over my cheek, bringing everything back into focus.

"My daughter, where the fuck is my daughter?" My voice sounds breathless and strained to my ears, but I don't give a shit. I need to find my baby.

My eyes and throat burn, and I feel like my heart has been pulled from my chest. Marx steps into the bathroom, grabbing my shirt in his giant fists, pulling me to standing. I get my legs underneath me, Marx holding me until I'm steady. His resolute stare burns into mine and I'm hit in the gut by the revelation that what Dayz said is right. I need people, and yet I push them away thinking that I don't deserve this. That I'm not built for it. That I'm broken. Yet each and every one of these people - the DRMC brothers, Ol Ladies, my family, they're all like me. Not broken, just a little bent.

Marx gives me a little shake, slapping me on the shoulder

once he sees I'm steady. "We'll find her, brother."

I nod, turning to look at everyone who rode out, for me, for my daughter and for Vi. "Please, find my baby." My eyes flick to Moss Davies and his family. "And my woman."

"Bout damn time. Sheesh," Dayz says, shoving past me to walk through the doorway, headed to god knows where.

She stops abruptly, spine stiff, waving a hand at everyone clogging up the hall. "Shhhh, can you hear that?"

I strain to hear anything other than my own heartbeat. Everyone else shrugging. Dayz walks down the hall, and then back again, before heading through a door.

"Well, what the fuck are you all waiting for? Let's go," Pops says, following Dayz, me hot on his heels.

I come to a stop behind Pops. Dayz is standing in front of a wooden door, a cupboard or some shit. And that's when I hear it. A snuffling sound. It can't be, can it? Dayz holds a finger to her lips. The DRMC brothers moving silently behind me, along with the Davies. Dayz holds up three fingers, then two, yanking the door open on the last one.

"Piss off!" A tubby ginger kid hisses, curling himself tighter into a ball, angling himself further into the cupboard.

"Rodney! Is that how we speak to people?" Vi's sister Jazz steps forward, pushing her way through a wall of Tombs to stare at the kid.

"Ms. Davies! There was this bad guy and Pirate told me to run and protect the baby!" He turns his body around and there in his arms is Juno, brows pinched into a scowl and I've never seen anything more beautiful in my life.

I drop to my knees and hold my hands out to this Rodney kid.

His eyes narrow at me, "How do I know you're not some type of weirdo?"

"Rodney! This is Jules, he's Juno's dad," Jazz scolds.

Rodney takes one look at my face, then looks down at Juno, then back to me. "Yeah, that makes sense." He holds her out and I snatch her from him, wrapping her in my arms, her little face nuzzling into my neck. She lets out a sigh and relaxes into my arms.

"It's OK, Juno, Daddy's got you." I whisper in her hair, smelling faintly of her baby shampoo, Vi, and Playdoh, which I'm guessing is Rodney.

A hand lands on my shoulder, "Fucking knew you had it in you, kid. Didn't think it'd take your baby being kidnapped before you pulled your head outta your ass, but you're a stubborn bastard so I should have known." Pops gives me a grin and a nod before sliding his hands in between me and Juno. "Now give me my grandbaby." He gently tries to pry Juno away, but her little fists grab onto my shirt as she tries to burrow closer to me. "Well, shit," Pops huffs. "Looks like the feeling is mutual."

"You're a daddy's girl, huh?" I coo, holding her a little too tight, but fuck me. I'm sure today's events have taken about ten years off my life.

"I'm glad you have your *niña*, but where's mine?" Flora asks, her eyes glistening with tears as she watches me with Juno.

"I promise you, I will find her," I vow.

"And when you do, *I* want to look them in the eye." Flora answers, her tear filled eyes switching to pure unfiltered rage. Mr. Davies doesn't look any better, his expression mirroring Moss's.

"So, where's my hot glue gun?" Rodney says, standing in the middle of all the adults.

"Huh?" Gus grunts.

"Pirate said if I did what she told me to do she would give me a hot glue gun. Not a crappy one either. A cordless one. So, where is it?"

"Tell me exactly what happened and my brother Tav will take you to Hobby Lobby and get you one." Tav glares at me but I don't give a shit. I need information.

"Some dude wanted to know if I played video games, and then told me to follow him into the toilets. Pirate -"

"Why do you call her Pirate?" Dayz asks.

"Cos that's her name?" Rodney answers as if Dayz is simple.

"I'm not sure I like you," she replies, stepping back, leaning into Rhodie.

"Anyways, like I was sayin', Pirate came out and told him to piss off but then he pulled out a gun. He made us go out the back and walk to his truck and then Pirate told me to run so I did," he finishes off.

"Tav, take the kid to Hobby Lobby. Dayz, get Remy and Wire onto surveillance from two hours ago, coming and going from here. DRMC and Tombs, I need you at the clubhouse to go over this shit," Marx orders.

"I'll be fucked if you freeze me out of this. That's my sister out there." Moss stands toe to toe with Marx and I'm seeing the man in a new light. So is my sister who murmurs "interesting" under her breath.

Marx's eyes narrow, before he nods. "Fine. But you gotta know what we're going to do may not be totally above board."

"You mean like that boat that sat at the back of your property covered in flies for months? Or that explosion Mary Carpenter complained about when she was sure she saw a foot on the clubhouse roof?"

"What?! Foot? No way," Dayz says in an overly chipper voice

while aggressively staring at Moss.

"I think I'm good," he says, nodding.

"Oh, we're good too, aren't we my love? Our lips are sealed." Flora mimes zipping her lips, locking and throwing away the key.

"Fuck, fine. Everyone roll out," Marx orders then stomps toward the door.

Everyone files out, but not before clapping me on the shoulder and giving Juno's thick head of hair a rub on the way past.

"Come on, brother. Let's go find your woman," Fox says, on his way out the door.

"I cannot fucking wait until that woman finds out you claimed her," Gus chortles.

I can only hope she lets me keep my balls. I have a whole lot of making up to do.

Jules

"Tell me what you know," Marx's voice booms through the common room.

Dayz, Wire and Remy all tap away at their computers, bringing all manner of things up on the full screen so we can all follow along. Everyone is congregated in the room, my whole family, all the MC brothers and their Ol Ladies, and the Davies family, sitting in a row on the couch. Well, Vi's sisters and parents. Moss is standing with his hands on his hips between Marx and Gus.

"We went back through the footage from this morning until half an hour ago," Wire says, tapping a few things on his keyboard. "Watch the trucks."

The screen enlarges and we watch a truck come down Main Street, then pull around the back of the diner. The cameras switch to the diner lot, and Trucker No. 1, our original target, waits in his cab, talking to his passenger. Remy speeds up the footage until another truck comes into view, pulling in next to the first.

"That's the one we got out back, with the animals." Rhodie points out.

Wire nods, then the footage speeds up, showing Trucker 1 meeting up with Trucker 2, walking around the front of the diner, and entering. He speeds through around twenty minutes more footage when a third truck arrives. It tucks itself on the far side and is smaller than the other two large haulers. This one looks more like a smaller food delivery truck. I remember Dex updating us that it was there, but as no one saw anyone come or go from it and we were a little preoccupied with a change in our operation, well, it was overlooked. We watch the screen as I knock out Trucker 2, throw him in the back and then all disappear from the area.

"Now, watch," Remy says, and we sit, eyes glued to the screen.

The back door to the diner bursts open and out come Rodney and Vi, a man at their back holding a gun to them. He shoves Vi roughly, and I can see how hard he's pressing the gun to her head, her head drooping forward as she walks. He pushes them toward the back of his truck, stopping to answer a phone call. Vi shoves Rodney and the kid takes off.

"Shit, tubby little fucker is faster than I expected," Pops

remarks, getting the death stare from Jazz.

"That's one of my kids, thank you," she says, eyes narrowed.

"And he's faster than I thought," Pops replies, a shit-eating grin on his face.

I try to hide my smirk by burying my face in Juno's soft hair. I take a deep inhale, breathing in her baby scent wondering how the fuck it took me so long to realize what everybody else did. That I'm a dumbass and I love this little girl. I mean, I knew that I would kill for her. She's a defenseless baby. I'm the person charged with keeping her safe. But over the three months she's been with me, she's wormed her way into my heart and soul but I never realized it until it was close to being gone.

A soft hand lands on my forearm. Mama Debs leaning her curly head against my bicep as she's not tall enough to reach my shoulder.

"It finally clicked, huh *tama?*" she says gently, running a finger along Juno's fist, the fist still holding tight to my shirt.

"Yeah," I nod.

"I knew all along what a good papa you would be. You just needed to believe it yourself," she whispers.

"I don't think that was it. I just," I swallow. "I–"

"Are deserving of everything good in the world, Jules."

"But I'm not like the others. I'm broke–"

Mama Debs stops me with a glare. "Don't you dare say it, Jules Tombs. I know you and Chewy share similarities. Anyone can see it. But where she embraces hers as a superpower, you're terrified. Do you know why that is?" I shake my head. "It's because where Chewy struggles with empathy, you have the opposite. Why do you think you push people away? Put up your walls? Sleep with multiple women at a time?" she raises her brow at me, "It's because if you let them in, really let them in, the feelings would be too much."

I stare down at her, her dark eyes boring into mine.

"How do I fix it?"

"Can't fix something that ain't broke, *tama.*" I watch her as she shuffles off back into the kitchen, leaving me with a shit ton to think about.

"She's right, you know." Gus murmurs, leaning against the bar beside me. "When you were a kid you'd cry all the time. Over bruised fruit or having to only choose one teddy to take places, sad the others would feel left out. Elderly people in the street, worms on a dry pavement. Then one day you came home from school and just...turned it off." His hand lands on my shoulder. "Turn it back on, brother. It'll do you good. Besides, we think Dayz and her sense of justice is scary? Imagine what would happen when you actually feel things for the people we help."

My eyes narrow. "Are you trying to weaponize autism?"

He grins at me and turns back to the common room, the images still on the screen showing the back of the small truck, Vi climbing in. But it's what's behind her that sends rage pulsing through me. There, huddled in the corner, are children.

"Can you zoom in any closer?" Savage asks, the women gasping as the kids in the still become clearer.

"That son of a bitch!" Sniper rages, hands fisted.

"It's a shell game," my sister says, brows pinched before she looks around the room. "Three trucks pass through the docks at the same time. Two have live cargo, dogs, goats, whatever, the last has children."

"The FBI uses heat signatures to decide which cargo to track. Animals that size, especially when sedated are around the same size as human children. They choose the larger truck, the one most likely to be shipping something illegal, leaving the smaller, less suspicious truck to carry the cargo," Gus adds.

"Well, it worked. The FBI searched the first truck and we nabbed the second," Rhodie's gruff voice breaks through.

Dayz pinches her bottom lip before her eyes flick to Marx. "What did you and Lovely find out?"

"Not a lot. Candice Rogers is a smarmy bitch who offers childless couples the world. She runs a tight ship. Employees seem to love her, she has pictures of happy families plastered all over the walls." Marx says, running a hand down his face. "Said me and Lovely would make wonderful candidates."

"We asked how long it would take to match us with the right child, she told us that she could have the match and contract done in a week," Lovely adds.

"Fuck, a week?" Flack asks, appalled.

"She's kid farming," Dex growls.

We look around the room and the rage I was feeling is just growing. Juno whimpers and I loosen my hold. "Sorry, little miss," I whisper to her. She lets out a sigh and relaxes her body.

"She did say something a little weird," Lovely looks at Marx who looks confused at her words. "She said something like 'you know, if you were happy to wait a year, I'll have a dark haired little one on my books by then."

Recognition dawns on Marx's face. "Fuck, you're right."

Lovely nods, "I wrote it off as a weird comment, but if she's kid farming, is there a chance she could be baby farming or whatever it's called?"

"And now she has Vi!" Moss grumbles, drawing a gasp from his father and sisters and a wail from his mother who recovers quickly and starts cursing in Spanish.

Marx's whistle splits the air, silencing the room, everyone's attention on the Pres. "Jules, tell me she had a tracker?"

I shake my head, fucking kicking myself that I didn't think to tag something, anything that she may have on her.

Moss slumps, shaking his head. "I can get the station on to it, but, fuck, Sheriff Kelson only gives a damn about being seen at galas and shit. He won't place a priority on this."

"Not to mention he has a problem with Lettie," Vi's father says. We all stare at him, waiting for the story. "He waited two days to take his kid to the emergency room with a broken arm. Vi threatened to run him over the next time she saw him so he could feel the pain his kid was in."

I snort. That sounds a lot like my Vi. She's a fucking firecracker. Which makes my cock thicken, but also has my heart racing with fear. While there is no better protector for those kids in the truck than Vi, I also know she'll put herself in harm's way to protect them. It's the right thing to do, but I selfishly want her back here, at home with me and Juno.

"Who cares what this so-called Sheriff says? We have to get Vi back. Screw her having to birth babies so that bitch Candice can profit from them," Blanche growls.

She stands and starts waddling toward the door, calling for the Ol Ladies to follow her, saying they're on a hunting mission. Tav catches up quickly, takes her by the elbow and uses her momentum to steer her back to her seat.

"Settle down, babe. We'll find her," he soothes.

"And how the fuck are we going to do that? Do we have anything on the truck? The driver? Happy Value's businesses?" Moss demands.

Wire lets out a sigh. "None of the businesses were able to be raided after Agent Dansen pulled rank and opened the back of truck number 1. Happy Values lawyers came in and barred the FBI from searching."

"We have nothing on the truck, or the driver, either," Remy adds in her quiet voice, looking heartbroken.

Blanche is now crying., Mira is teary eyed. Nat and Ana look pissed and Chewy is frowning, squishing her lip.

I step forward. "We may know someone who can help."

Pops let's out a long groan behind me. "Not the Manwitch, that fucker is creepy as all get out." I stare him down. "Ugh, fine! But I'm not going anywhere near that big, creepy bastard. Nope, not doing it. Get him here to find Vi, and then tell him to piss off immediately after."

Rider gives me a funny look and I know he's going to somehow use this against Pops for the foreseeable future.

"Hey Jules, tell me more about this Manwitch?"

Chapter 15

Violet

"You fucking bitch!" The tubby guard yells, gripping the side of his neck. I can see the blood seeping through his fingers, and I spit a hunk of skin from his neck onto the ground.

I grin at him, ignoring the searing pain in the side of my face where I was punched by the thin guard when he tried to tear my clothes off. If these fuckers want to try and rape me they'll have to fight me first. I would rather die than have their hands all over me.

"You fucking wait. You won't be able to fight forever little girl. And when you can't? One of us will put a baby in you," he sneers.

Gross. Who the hell would want a kid he fathered? He shoves me onto the bed and glares before storming out the door, leaving traces of blood on the handle. I pick up the bottle of water he delivered and throw it at the door, getting little satisfaction when it explodes on impact. I refuse to drink anything the guards give me after I noticed the tamper seal was broken. They've probably spiked it. Luckily there is an adjoining bathroom so I'll just drink tap water.

I lie back on the bed, and hope like hell that someone out there is looking for me. Or at the very least that Jules has found Juno. There's no way that man wouldn't be tracking her every move. I roll to my side and curl up, my adrenaline leaching from my body, making me feel every ache and pain since this whole ordeal started. I tuck my shaking hands under my head, and take deep calming breaths.

"I am in control of my body," I whisper to myself. I've overheard Jules doing this every now and then, and I think it's working.

I mean, it seems to work for him, so why wouldn't it work for me? My heart rate settles as I focus on Jules. He can be a pain in the ass and impossible and yet, I can't stop thinking about him. Even when he makes me mad enough to spit there's still something about him, deep down that I'm drawn to. That makes me want to wrap him up in my arms and tell him it'll all be alright. I snort, thinking about him like that. A big, strapping man with a "dont fuck with me face" that somehow, if you look really closely, gives off lost little boy vibes.

He also gives off filthy sex vibes and I feel my heart begin to speed up again, but for an entirely different reason. If he could just stop being so guarded, I think we could perhaps be a good match for each other. Instead he gives me the best night of sex I've ever had then freaks out and watches me walk out.

Shaking those thoughts off I look around the room for the thousandth time. There has to be something I can use as a weapon, or some way out of here. Something that can improve my chances of leaving this hell hole un–pregnant.

My eyes snap toward the door as I hear the lock disengage.

I stand at the foot of the bed, feet planted, ready for round number three. I've injured two guards so far, may as well make it a hat trick. Also, I need to remember to thank Jazz and Lil for forcing me to take self defense classes with them. So far it's come in handy.

"Follow me," the gruff guard barks. He's new. Probably because the other two are licking their wounds somewhere.

"No,." I answer him plainly.

He makes a growling sound in the back of his throat so I echo him. I maintain eye contact the whole time. His eyes narrow and he stomps forward, gripping me around the bicep. I think about going boneless and dropping to the ground, but I also kinda wanna see where this is leading to. I want to know more about the inside of this building and see if I can find any weaknesses.

"I said, follow me," he grits through clenched teeth, so I cooperate. Slightly. I may be dragging my feet, but I'm moving.

We head down a long hall, doors lining both sides, the only clue to the occupants the whiteboard's hanging on the doors with their attributes scribbled on them.

Short, blonde, blue eyed. 18

Tall, black. 23

Average height, brunette, brown eyes. 27

There are at least a dozen of them and I start to feel a little nauseous. This isn't some hick setup, this is an actual real fucking deal. We reach a large hall, dining tables and chairs set up and along one wall a serving hatch. There are women here, some of them pregnant, some not. All look well looked after and yet there's a stench of fear and shame to them. It's stifling, making my heart both beat out of my chest and clench in pain.

"It's dinner time. You better fucking eat or else we'll administer a feeding tube." He shoves me into the room and I stumble, falling knees first on the grey linoleum floor.

"Are you Ok?" a small voice asks, holding a hand out to help me up.

I wave her away, not wanting to put any extra weight on her as she has a large, round belly to take care of.

"Thank you, but I'm fine." I smile at her, and she gives me a small one in return. She's young, like maybe early twenties, and she's a pretty thing, if not looking a little too thin for her condition.

"You don't look that fine. Your face is all messed up," her blue eyes show concern.

"Oh this? This is nothing. You should see the other guy," I grin. I probably still have chubby guard in my teeth but I dont give a shit.

"I'm Phoebe."

"Violet.

"Well, seeing as you're here you may as well eat. We get fed three times a day, more if you're pregnant." She walks toward the serving hatch, so I trail behind her, smiling and trying to look friendly to those who are giving me curious looks. "You don't have to worry about them poisoning you or anything. It hurts their bottom line if our babies aren't healthy," I can hear the sneer in her voice and I feel a little better knowing that this woman may seem like she's beaten down, but she still has some fight in her.

"Well, if you say it's safe," I shrug and follow her in the line. "I was too afraid to eat or drink what they brought to my room."

"You're smart," a tall, redhead says from behind me. "I did and I woke up bleeding." I stare at her distended belly before meeting her eyes.

"I'm so sorry. But they will pay. I'll make fucking sure of it." She gives me a sympathetic smile, like I'm some delusional woman. I mean, I could very well be, but if I'm going down, I'm bringing this whole place down with me. I take my tray of surprisingly good looking food and follow the two women to a table. Sitting down at the head.

"So, tell me everything."

Jules

"He's here isn't he? I can feel it in my waters. My balls are crawling their way into my belly just knowing that fucker is here," Pops grumbles, earning weird looks from everyone around the clubhouse.

Pops has been bitching nonstop since it was agreed to call in Dima, or the "Manwitch" as Pops calls him.

"Look, we've been listening to you whine for close to two hours now, but what exactly is your problem with this guy?" Flack asks, looking at me and my brothers because he'll get a straight answer out of us.

Gus lets out a sigh. "There's nothing wrong with the guy. Other than he has visions, I guess you could call them."

Brows raise around the common room. "There's no such thing as 'vision'. He just has great pattern recognition," Dayz scoffs, snuggling with Rhodie and Chomper. "When will the Landrys be here?"

I roll my eyes. My sister wasn't on the job where we met Dima. The Landrys introduced us and they'll be travelling with him to vouch for his character. It's bad enough we have the whole Davies family here, the last thing any of us want is to be bringing in another new person. Marx has been generous enough as it is, but at the end of the day this place is an MC full of families.

"They're here," Wire calls, eyes glued to his screen.

"Tell TumTum to let them through," Marx rumbles.

TumTum may be a patched member, but turns out he likes gate duty. Moments later the doors open and in walk the Landrys, beelining for their sister, and then mine. Dima follows them in with TumTum bringing up the rear.

"Dima," Gus says, shaking his hand. He turns to Marx, "Marx, this is Dima, Dima, the Pres of Devil's Rose MC, Marx."

Marx sizes him up for a moment, clearly impressed with his size. The Russian is tall, very close to Marx's 6'4. He's not quite as broad, having more of a swimmers build. Dima nods in acknowledgement and looks around the room. His eyes zero in on Juno, still in my arms, hours after finding her. The only time she's let me put her down is when I needed to change her. Otherwise she's clinging to me with her chubby little fists.

"We are looking for her mother, no?" Dima asks, his shock of blonde hair falling into his eyes as his head tilts, looking at Juno.

"Fuck no, I don't know where her mother is, and I don't care," I growl at him.

He frowns for a moment, his eyes flutter before he locks onto mine. "Not the mother who gave her life. The mother who loves her." He looks around the room, before gesturing in the Davies direction, "Their *sem'ya*, family."

The mother who loves her. Violet. I swallow the lump in my throat and nod. "Um, yeah, Violet."

"I fucking told you!" Pops hisses at Rider who looks impressed so far.

Actually, looking around the common room everyone looks either impressed, or suspicious.

Dima walks toward Flora, stopping in front of the couch, his shiny black shoes just touching the base. He lowers to kneeling and takes Flora's hand. Moss shuffles closer to his mother, hand hovering over his service weapon.

"Your mother is safe with me,." Dima murmurs. "She has a strong connection to your sister, it will help me with her location."

"See?" Pops whispers. "He's like a creepy fucking dog. Actually, no, dogs are better. I'd be less creeped out if he sniffed Vi's clothes and turned bloodhound." Savage stares at him before rolling his lips between his teeth.

The Ol Ladies are all staring and Mira is taking notes. She's even moved closer to the action. Everyone looks intrigued other than Dayz, who seems to be in an intense conversation with Dom Landry, probably about their gators.

"Roman incoming," Wire calls, his eyes glued to his laptop. He remotely opens the gate as TumTum is at the bar watching the Russian kneeling at Flora's feet.

"I have her location." He stands to his full height, before stiffening.

"*Brat?*"

He turns slowly, looking toward the door. Sasha rushes forward, stopping when they come toe to toe. My eyes widen slightly when I realize why Dima always seemed somewhat familiar. Same hair, bone structure and build.

"You'd think his vision would have told him his brother was on his way, huh?" Pops whispers, loudly, to anyone within hearing distance.

Dima swallows. "I'm here to help find a missing woman."

A smile grows on Sasha's face. "You got your vision back, little brother?"

Dima's demeanor relaxes, before he nods at Sasha. "*Da*, just took a while."

Sasha clasps his brother by the back of his neck, pulling him in close enough to rest his forehead on Dima's.

"Marx," Roman nods at him. "It would seem that yet again we cross paths."

"And what brings you here?" Marx replies in a bored tone, not giving away how alert his eyes are, watching the scene happening between the two brothers.

"Strangely, not Dima's presence. I have the name of the contact Candice Rogers was using. He was driving one of the three trucks that came through the port." He turns to look at his husband. "Finding Sasha's brother after all this time is a welcome surprise."

"You're the *pakhan*. How do you not know where your people are?" Dayz asks, her brows pinched.

"Because I am not bratva anymore," Dima answers.

"He's more, shall we say, bratva adjacent," Roman says, waving his hand in the air.

Marx crosses his arms over his chest. "And what the fuck does that mean?"

"The bratva has always been good to me and my brother," Dima interrupts, his eyes darting to Sasha. "However, my gift cannot be used for ill. That I learnt the hard way," he says, shedding no fucking light on anything.

"Well, that's all and good but where the hell is Vi?" I growl. I can only be polite and patient for so long.

He stares at me for a moment, "You will need help," he looks around the room, his eyes assessing before nodding. "Everyone here will have a role to play. There is more at stake than Violet."

"What do you mean?" Dayz asks, handing Chomper over to Rhodie.

Dima closes his eyes, his lips moving slightly. "There are twelve women, at least nine are heavily pregnant. There are children in a neighboring building." He looks around the room again. "Everyone will be needed."

"Well, you all heard the man," Pops says, clapping his hands. "Thank you, Dima. You can go now." He stands and tries to shoo the Russian away, Dima smirking at his efforts.

"Sorry, Pops. I need to be here. It's my calling."

Pops whispers, "Creepy motherfucker" under his breath but sits his ass back down. Marx turns to open his mouth but I'm scared and worried and impatient as fuck so I beat him to it.

"So, what's the plan?

Chapter 16

Violet

I don't want to be ungrateful or whiney, but what the hell is taking everyone so long to find me? I mean, I know I'm not a Tombs or MC, but come on! Moss is a damn police officer and still I'm stuck in this place. I let out a sigh and try to concentrate on what the women around me are saying. It's not much. Although this one girl, Holly, at least she tries to keep morale boosted. She's 18 years old and talking to her I've managed to pick up that she's had a rough life so far. A runaway, she was picked up on the streets by a woman who wanted to "help" her. Instead, she brought her here and she's now onto her third pregnancy. I can't imagine being raped until I'm pregnant and then having to hand my baby over so they can be sold to some rich douche. Listening to her story makes my blood boil but it's not like I can fly off the handle and go on a rampage in her name. Not when it seems like she herself hasn't even grasped the situation. I guess to a kid who survived on the streets a place like this, with a warm bed and catered meals is a great deal better than where she came from.

Holly rubs her belly and tries to engage some of the women in a puzzle in the "recreational" area, but no one is wanting to join her. The women are too preoccupied with their own thoughts to do much more than sit here and stare blankly at each other.

I side eye the guard closest to us as he moves in our direction. There are four of them in the room, so one in each corner, all staring, and then periodically tilting their heads and talking into their walkie talkie things. I have no idea what they could possibly be reporting on, given that all anyone has done was line up, eat, and then sit at the tables, having minimal conversation. And that's me being nice because I managed to find myself at the most outgoing table. Jeez.

"You need to come with me." The guard barks down at me.

"I don't respond to people barking at me."

"You're going to get your fat ass up, and come with me," he says through clenched teeth.

I slowly turn my head to the side, then tilt upwards so I can look him dead in the eye. "I. Don't. Respond. To. People. Barking. At. Me."

He grabs me roughly by the arm, pulling me to standing. I'm standing toe to toe with the man and he sneers down at me, his eyes focussing on my boobs. He sucks his teeth, choosing not to say anything else, other than to tell the other women not to expect to see me for a day or two. I glare up at him but don't say another word. I need to save my venom for later.

He half marches, half drags me out into the hall, heading toward my room. We get to the door and I expect him to shove me through it, however he doesn't, He walks on further, stopping at a completely different door. He unlocks it with some key card type setup and shoves me through the door, stepping over me and crushing my fingers with his boot when I lose my balance and hit the ground. I grit my teeth, not giving the bastard the satisfaction of hearing me scream. Between their less than gentle treatment and the "discipline" they've been handing out, I feel like one big bruise. My face aches and I'm sure my cheek is swollen as my left eye feels a little squinty. It's tender to the touch so it wouldn't surprise me if it's bruised as well.

I brace myself and push up to sitting, glancing around the room. There's a bed, because of course there fucking is, but it also looks like one whole wall is a window. Standing, I get a better look. It's looking into another room, this one also has a bed, and Maddy, the little girl from the truck is sitting on it, looking clean and fed, but still fucking terrified. I rush to knock on the glass with my good hand, trying to get her attention to tell her I'm here, and I'll find a way to help her.

Laughter sounds out from behind me and then a hard body is pressed up against mine, forcing me into the glass. "The only way you can help her is by doing what you're told."

"Get. Off. Me." I growl, my teeth gritted.

He presses further into me, a hard cock pressing into my ass and I can feel the bile rising. Flattening my hands on the window I use all my strength to push off, shoving him off me. I spin to give him a piece of my mind when my head snaps back, ricocheting between his fist and the glass behind me. Stars burst across my vision and I feel my legs buckle, my body sliding until I'm on my knees in front of him.

"Good girl," he leers, moving to his belt buckle.

I try to shake off the dizziness, "If you put that thing anywhere near me I'll bite it off." My voice sounds weak to my ears, but I don't care. As long as I can speak I will continue to do so.

"Oh really?" He grips my hair in his fist, yanking upwards until I have no choice but to follow, getting shakily to my feet. He presses my cheek into the window, the cool glass feeling like heaven on my bruised and battered face. "What would you do to save that poor, innocent little girl your fate, hmmm?"

My gaze drifts to the side. From my periphery I can see that fat guard I bit sitting on the bed next to Maddy, his doughy hand on her thigh.

"No," I whisper, desperately trying to claw my way out of his grip. "No! Let her go! She's just a kid!"

His breath is hot on my ear, "That kid has started her period. That means that her little girl body is ready to fuck," he says with force, "and have babies. If you don't want to do it, then she will have to take your place."

Tears pool in my eyes and not from fear, but from pure, unadulterated rage. Fat Guard looks toward the window, probably at the fucker behind me, and smirks, before gripping the back of Maddy's head and smashing his lips to hers. She beats his chest with her fists but that does nothing to deter him. There is only one person who can help her, and that is me.

I breathe in deeply, I am in charge of my body. Clearing my mind I think back to self defense and what to do when an attacker is behind you. I maneuver myself a little, moving to stand directly in front of him. Due to our height difference I know that I'm about nose/mouth height, so I tilt my head forward and with all the strength I can muster I snap it back, hitting him square in the face with the back of my skull.

He lets out a yell and stumbles back, giving me enough time to spin around and kick him directly in the balls. He hits the ground and I whale on him, punching his face with my good hand over and over. When he falls back I keep going until he stops moving. I stand over him admiring my handiwork before I look through the window, seeing Fat Guard gripping Maddy's thigh, and tears falling down her plump, freckled cheeks.

I rush out of the door, not caring who is in the hall, on a mission to find the room I need to be in. Stopping at the door directly next to the room I was in I don't even bother trying the handle knowing the guard used a key card to enter. Instead, I rear back, aim for directly next to the handle and I kick. Hard. The door makes a terrible noise and I see a little bit of give, so I try once more, this time even harder, the door flying open and bouncing off the wall behind it.

I don't say a word, instead I launch myself toward Fat Guard, his surprise at my entrance momentarily leaving him open. I do everything within my power to get him off Maddy. I punch him, whaling on his face with my fists, when that doesn't affect him as much as I would like I use my feet and my teeth, using anything and everything at my disposal.

There's noise coming from behind me but I don't care. I don't stop, I can't stop. I have to get him off Maddy, I have to help Maddy, keep her safe.

"Violet!" Maddy screams and I turn to find her tossed over some guy's shoulder. She's kicking and screaming and there's a roaring sound. A painful sound as if it's being ripped from the very soul of the person. It's not until I'm restrained that I realize the noise is coming from me.

The air leaves my lungs as a boot kicks me in the stomach, then a fist follows, hitting the already bruised flesh of my face.

"I'll kill you," I gasp out. "I'll kill you all, *dios de muerte* motherfuckers!"

Then everything goes black.

Jules

"And you're sure this is the place?" Tav asks, for the hundredth time.

"*Da.*"

"OK, just checking." Tav rolls his shoulders, the leather seat of the SUV creaking with the movement. "Chewy, you guys in yet?"

There's dead air on our comms and we all know to just wait my sister out. If she's busy working on something she'll talk when she's damn well ready.

"We're in. Images being sent to your phones along with building schematics."

I pull up the live feed from the Computas and watch as the camera flicks to a new angle and shot every 15 seconds, giving us a real time idea of what's happening where.

"Plan still stands. Easiest and safest way in is through the front door," Wire's voice says over comms.

"Sniper, I want you, Dex, Savage, Tank and Judge breaching the back entrance at the same time the Tombs, Fox, Nitro, Rider, and myself breach front. Dima, Moss, Rhodie, Flack and Landrys will breach the building holding the kids," Marx orders.

"Yes Pres," voices reply, including mine. Shit, maybe Tav had the right idea prospecting. I would, but I hate being told what to do.

"His path isn't yours," Dima murmurs beside me before opening his car door, and slipping out into the darkness.

"You know, maybe Pops has a point," Tav says, watching as the Manwitch stops in the beams of our headlights, meeting up with Rhodie and the others.

Backing out of the clearing I head slightly further down the road, flicking off our lights and going dark. We slowly crawl through the outskirts of the building compound, pulling up in a blind spot Wire found. We exit, weapons already strapped to us. A rustling sound has me reaching for my weapon, only stopping when I recognise the scent of Rider's gum.

"On edge there, brother?" he says in a low voice, grinning.

"You would be too if your woman was in there," I answer, eyes on the front door, itching to breach.

"Like that huh? Does she know that?"

"No, she fucking doesn't!" Moss growls over the comms.

"Well, she is. I'm claiming her. Or whatever the fuck the MC says."

Congratulations sound out over comms and now I've got to get my woman back. Then find some way to convince her to forgive me for my shitty behavior. I need her on side before she finds out that I've claimed her. Fuck. Maybe I shouldn't have given Tav so much shit when he claimed Blanche without her knowledge.

"Don't worry, brother. It'll work out. Look at me and Blanche." Tav slaps my shoulder, almost a little too hard. Dick.

"Breach in t minus 45 seconds," Marx says, circling his finger in the air, then pointing to the door.

We follow in close formation, Marx at the head, the MC brothers flanking him. My brothers and I have our own formation, from years of operations together, so we assume our formation and pull in tight behind the MC. We hold, my eyes on Marx's fingers as he counts down the last 5 seconds.

There's a flash of light from the stun grenade Marx tossed into the building lobby, effectively taking out the four guards on this floor.

"Fan out. Find that hall Wire has been watching," Marx barks, striding over to the nearest guard and cold clocking him with the butt of his gun before moving to the next.

"Hallway is second floor. Elevators are all on Level 1, waiting for you to board," Remy calls over the comms. It's actually fucking nice hearing a sweet voice for a change.

I don't wait for anyone else, I run to the nearest elevator, mashing the button to get the doors open. Vi is somewhere on the next floor up, and I will find her. Stepping into the car I turn, catching sight of the DRMC men zip tying the unconscious fuckers.

"Ready for this brother?" Gus asks, standing shoulder to shoulder with me.

I give him a chin lift, no words needed. The elevator doors begin to close, narrowing my view of Fox and Nitro, before disappearing completely. There's a thirty second wait and then elevator jolts, the doors dinging and opening to reveal some fucker with a child tossed over his shoulder. She's screaming Vi's name at the top of her lungs and fighting with all she has.

A growl erupts from my chest, the fucker spins, eyes locking onto mine. He pulls a gun, keeping it trained on me as he slides the girl from his shoulder. He moves her until she's standing in front of him, his hand tight around her throat. She's shaking like a leaf even when he calmly tilts his head and speaks into the comms clipped to his shoulder. He grins at me, his hand moving to aim the gun at the girl.

"I wouldn't do that if I were you," I tut at him.

"Yeah? Why's that?"

"First off, it's currently three against one," I tell him, in a bored tone.

His brows pinch as he thinks through my words. "What do you mean by 'currently'?"

I'm not one for smiling, but right here right now? My lips pull up, the grin getting wider and wider until I'm beaming at this motherfucker.

"What the fuck are you smiling at?" he yells, "Tell me!" He points the gun at the girl in his arms, the one that is turning an alarming shade of red and gasping, clawing at his hand. He presses the muzzle into her dark hair, hard, hard enough to make her moan around the lack of oxygen she's currently getting. "If you don't tell me I'll blow her brains out!"

"How about I tell you?" Rider whispers in his ear, gun to his head. "Please let the little girl go and I'll let you live."

The guard or whatever the fuck he is releases his hold on the girl's throat and she starts to crumple to the floor. I lurch forward, catching her in my arms before she hits the ground. I hook her legs over my forearm, her back leaning on my shoulder and I cradle her, letting her get in gulps of air before asking about Vi.

I'm not usually good at shit like this, letting Gus and Tav take the lead, but this little girl, she was fighting tooth and nail to get back to Vi. If Vi means that much to her then the feeling is probably mutual. Anyone that is Vi's is now mine.

I clear my throat and try to soften my voice like Gus does when he handles the children and women we sometimes have in our care. "It's OK sweetheart. We're here to help." Her whole body relaxes as she lets out a sob and lets the fear and adrenaline drain from her body.

"Please, you have to help Vi, she was trying to save me!" She starts clawing at me, trying to get out of my arms at the same time she's trying to burrow deeper, the thought of Vi sending her into a panic.

"Alright, shhhh. It's okay honey." Tav kneels down beside us on the floor. He has all those fucking kids, so he's definitely going to be better at this than me. "Take a deep breath, that's a good girl," he croons. "Can you tell us what happened?" There's some banging coming from down the hall and the girl jumps.

"Hey, sweetheart, look at me," I say, my gaze boring into her dark brown eyes, puffy from crying. "That noise is our friends, they're going to help everyone here, get them back to their families."

She nods up at me, before taking a deep breath, her gaze flicking between me and my brothers. Rider gives me a chin lift as he walks past, the guard that had been choking the little girl thrown over his shoulder.

"I'll keep him on ice for ya."

I grin knowing that Dayz won't be the only one who gets to play tonight.

The little girl takes a deep breath, then lets it out slowly. "There was a man, he put me in a room and said if I did everything they said I would get to see Vi. She tried to save us but she was taken and brought here." Her lip wobbles, but she clenches her fists and looks up at me. "Anyway they took me to a room and the guard man said I was pretty and then he put his hand on my knee and I was really scared. He grabbed me and started kissing me and I fought back because those were bad touches and I didn't want them. He was gross and I tried to get him off but he was too big." She's breathing erratically and I do the only thing I can think to do. I start to rock her, the way I do with Juno when she won't settle. "I was really scared and fighting and then the door slammed open and then

Vi was there and she's hitting and biting the man and got him off me and then some other men came in and hit her and then that other guy took me away. Then I saw you." She looks up at me and then bursts into tears again, her wail making my heart clench.

"We know where the others are being kept?" Gus asks Marx who has just stomped into the hall.

"This section is clear. We are yet to breach the eastern sector. Wanna join?"

"Fuck yes I wanna join!" I look to my brother and Tav knows what I'm asking without saying the words.

Wordlessly we transfer the brave girl in my arms to my brother, who coos nonsense to her, settling her a little as he carries her to the elevator and waiting safety.

"Which way?"

Rhodie

"She is not here," Dima the Manwitch says, looking confused.

"What the fuck? You said Violet would be here!" I growl, throwing yet another unconscious guard in the back of Chewy's van. I had to promise all sorts of sexual favors to borrow it, but shit, there's nothing I wouldn't do for or to that woman.

"No, not Violet. She is here, along with some others who have families waiting for them."

Dima looks at my handiwork as I hog tie the guard, making sure that when he wakes up he doesn't get any bright ideas.

"Then who the fuck are you talking about?" The guy talks in riddles and I dont know if its because his English is crap, or if it's as Pops says and he's just a creepy fucker.

"Your daughter. I had a vision that she was here but she must have been moved on."

I whirl around, staring at him in disbelief. "What the hell did you just say? I don't have a kid!"

What the actual fuck? Please, please don't tell me I've done a Jules.

"You don't have one yet. But you will." His eyes go cloudy for a moment, scaring the shit out of me. Dude looks like he has cataracts for a split second before they clear. "She is waiting for your old woman to find her."

"Ol lady," I correct him, my voice weak.

"Yes, that's what I said." His head snaps to the side, staring up at the building we've just left., watching. "Violet has been found."

He climbs into the back of the van, moving things around, stacking up Chewy's equipment neatly.

"What the fuck are you doing?"

"We need more room for prisoner transport. It's going to get messy and I believe the clubhouse is the best place for it."

Chapter 17

Jules

I follow Marx down the hall to what he called the "eastern sector". I wanted to be in the lead, but Marx pointed out that his rank and training is superior to mine so to shut up and get in behind.

"Fucking sons of bitches," Nitro murmurs, stopping and pointing to the sign on the door.

Black, 5'9, brown eyes, 21

"They've labelled the fucking doors like they do at the animal shelter," Fox says in disgust.

He reaches for the door handle but Marx stops him. "Not yet. We don't know what we're releasing them into." He looks around before settling his gaze on our group. "Notice the guards?"

"Lack thereof you mean. It's fucking weird," Gus says under his breath.

"Seen it before," Marx grunts, "Either they've given up their stations -"

"Or?" Gus asks.

"Or they're all in the same place."

"Fuck," my brother curses under his breath.

"Exactly. Lets find those fucks, then once they're neutralized we help the women."

We nod in reply and start moving forward again. I try to ignore the signs on the door, but fuck, there's at least a dozen of them all stating the stats of the women held prisoner behind them. I walk by a door on my left and I freeze.

Brown hair, brown eyes, 5'3, 27

That's her. It has to be fucking her. My eyes flick to the touch pad at the side of the door, the light flashing green. Dumbasses. Gripping the handle I turn it, pushing in as silently as I can. I get my first look at the room and fury pulses through me like I've never felt before. Because, there, on the bed, her face bruised, battered and swollen is Violet. Two guards have her feet, another two are holding her arms down, her shirt has been cut down the middle. Thankfully the lace of her bra is still intact, her breasts covered. What it doesn't cover is the bite mark on her left breast, one that I know for a fucking fact wasn't there last night when she left. A guttural roar leaves my body as I lunge forward, ready to fight with everything I have to protect Vi.

Grabbing the guy closest to me, the one who had Vi's jeans down to her knees, I yank his head back by his hair enough to smash his nose with the butt of the gun in my hand. He splutters as his own filthy blood runs into the back of his throat before throwing him to the ground kicking him for good measure. Moving onto the next son of a bitch I sidekick him directly in the gut, enough to have him fold in half, fist height, perfect height to pistol whip, cutting open his cheek in the process. I ignore the shouts from the other men in the room, knowing my brothers, both biological and MC have my back and will take care of the rest of these fuckers in the room.

I continue to growl and bash this one guy in the face, ignoring his hands clawing at mine until a firm hand grips the back of my neck.

"That's enough, brother. You don't want to kill him here," Gus says in a low, calm voice. "Go take care of your woman, I got this."

I nod at my brother frantically, too keyed up to do anything in a calm manner just yet. Stalking to Vi who's still lying on the bed, her bra covered breasts exposed, I drop to my knees, my breath coming in pants. I shuck off my tactical jacket, grip my tshirt behind my neck and pull it off in one movement, leaving me in my thin kevlar undershirt. Gently I lift Vi, my brave woman, leaning her against my chest as I find the head hole of my shirt and try to pull it over her head without hurting her battered face. She lets out a whimper and I rock her slightly, shushing her as I try to get her arms in the arm holes.

"Jules?" Vi's hoarse voice whispers as she turns her head into my chest.

"I'm here, Firecracker, I'm here."

Her dark head tilts back and she cracks her left open, this one slightly less swollen than the right.

"Took you long enough." Her busted lip curves up before it wobbles and she bursts into tears.

I wrap her in my arms and hold her, hoping the pressure will make her feel safe, secure. It works on Dayz so I'm hoping to employ the same reasoning. The sounds of flesh hitting flesh plays in the background, at one point Fox laughs, joined by Nitro. Before long Rider is back, bringing with him Flack, Savage, Dex and Rhodie who have all the kids secured and handled by Moss and the FBI.

"Load 'em up boys, we'll take this lot with us. I think Jules may have plans for them," Marx says, giving me a chin lift when I nod. "We'll take care of getting these doors open for the women held here."

"Moss has emergency services on standby for them. Dansen is outside along with half the bureau." Rhodie informs him as he tosses one of the guys I beat over his shoulder.

"Any word on Candice Rogers?"

"In the wind along with three of her staff. Don't worry brother, Chewy is on it," Rhodie says on his way past, with Flack, Dex and Rider with their cargo in tow.

Vi has started to settle in my arms, her sobs slowing, even if her breathing is still a little dysregulated. All of a sudden she sits bolt upright, fighting to get out of my arms.

"Maddy! I have to get Maddy!" She starts scrambling up off the bed, her movements awkward and pained.

She turns too quickly and her breath catches as she falls to her knees, a whimper escaping her lips, her hand pressed to her rib cage. My fists clench and my hearing warps, sounding like the inside of a seashell - crashing and swirling as my anger rises to the surface. My fists clench and I want to find whoever did this and make them hurt until they're begging at Vi's feet for forgiveness, but I can't. Vi needs me. I take a deep breath, I am in control of my body. I am in control of my body. My fists unclench and I reach for Vi, cupping her face gently in my blood-stained hands.

"Maddy is safe. We got her out of here, along with the other kids. She told us where to find you." I whisper gently, my forehead pressed to hers.

"She's so brave," my Firecracker murmurs, ignoring how

her bravery saved Maddy in return.

"So are you. What do you say we get outta here?"

She nods, her movements moving our heads as we're still pressed together. "Can you walk?"

"I wouldn't say no to being carried by a big, strong man," she replies cheekily. "Even if that big strong man is an asshole sometimes."

I huff out a breath, "Yeah, but I'm yours." She stares at me with her one good eye, and I'm fucking scared to look deeper, in case she doesn't want an asshole like me. I mean who would? I'm rude and my communication sucks. Fuck, I only started feeling shit after my kid was stolen and my nanny kidnapped. I have no business -

"And Juno's."

"Huh?"

"You. You're mine and Juno's," she says, a little shyly.

I swallow, "Yeah, and Juno's. Let's get you home, she'll be waiting."

Vi nods and I lift her gently from the ground, cradling her in my arms. She rests her head against my chest and it feels like this is where she was always meant to be.

Now all I gotta do is try to convince her to stay.

Violet

He found me. He found me and he said he was mine. I have no idea what the hell happened over the last however many hours it's been, or even if the declarations are a good thing for us given what's transpired in the past 24-ish hours, but at this point I don't care. A man I like, even more than like, came for me. As did all the men he has at his back.

He walks down the hall, cradling me in his arms and I'm sure he's taking gentle steps so as not to jolt me and my bruised body too much. This alone is enough to make a woman fall, but I know with someone like Jules, it'll be one step forward and maybe two steps back, even if he does seem more emotional and in touch with himself than I've ever seen him before.

Nitro opens a door ahead of us and Phoebe, the pregnant woman from the dining room, peeks around it. Her eyes widen when she sees me in Jules' arms.

"Violet! Oh my god, are you OK?" She looks at Jules. "Is she going to be OK?"

"She'll be fine now that we've got her. You all will be," Jules answers gruffly.

I bury my face in his chest, trying not to giggle. It seems like he's still the rough, abrupt Jules to anyone else by me and Juno.

"Come with us, ma'am. We've got emergency services waiting outside," Nitro says, gently taking Phoebe by the arm and guiding her down the hall to the elevators.

Fox has Holly who looks like this is all a new adventure for her. The rest of the freed women are huddling together in a pack, not wanting to get too close to the men and I get it. If I'd been held against my will and raped I'd never want to see a penis owner again in my life, let alone trust one.

We make our way downstairs and I marvel at how strong Jules really is. I'm not a small girl, more plump than I'd like but holy crap, this man has not faltered once in his care of me, not even having to do that thing where he gives me a little hoist up to have me in a better position. He scooped me up and that's where I stayed. Until I hit the ground floor and see the kids from the truck surrounded by people dressed in suits, looking bewildered.

"Put me down, Jules."

"Not on your fucking life," he grits out.

"You need to put me down. I have to go settle the kids, and I don't want them thinking I'm hurt really bad."

He tilts his face down, staring at me like I've lost my ever loving mind. "You *are* hurt really bad. Fuck Vi, I don't even know if there's a part of you that isn't bruised."

I pat his chest gently, "It's not as bad as it looks. Trust me, I'm a nurse, remember?"

A snort sounds out behind us, along with a muttered "Good luck with that, brother," as Nitro slaps his hand on Jules' back, passing by us with some of the women following.

"Look, just put me down for now, and you can boss me around later. Deal?" I would wink, and try to look cute, but even I know I'd be pushing it.

He lets out a long sigh, then gently places me on my feet, his large hands on my hips, bracing me until I'm steady. I turn to look at him, placing my hand on his cheek, trying not to wince when I get a good look at my torn up knuckles.

"Thank you, Jules. Give me ten minutes, OK?"

"Ten minutes, then you're getting seen by Switch." He raises his thick, dark brow and I nod, knowing full well that if I didn't he'd wait the ten minutes and drag me away anyway.

I make my way through the suits, police and MC brothers milling about until I make it to the small group of children I recognise.

"Violet!" Maddy yells, throwing off the silver emergency

blanket the kids all seem to be wrapped in. "Are you OK? I tried to help, but I couldn't, I'm so sorry!" She starts sobbing and I pull her into my arms.

Bella, Stevie and the two little boys all run toward me, wrapping their little arms around anywhere on my body they can touch. My ribs are still a little tender, nothing broken, probably just bruised, but I ignore the pain of them when Maddy wraps her arms around my waist, holding tight.

I lean back as far as I'm comfortable with, and cup her face, "You did good, Maddy, so good. You were so brave." I look at the children around me, and make sure I rub my hands through all of their hair, getting their attention, so they can see the sincerity in my face, "You *all* were so brave and did so well. I'm proud of you for sticking together and looking out for each other." I hug them to me.

I can feel the adrenaline leaching out of me, and I know it won't be long before I crash.

"Come on kids. Let's help Vi to the ambulance where Dr. Hansen can look after her," Moss says, looking down at me with tears in his eyes.

I lean my head toward him, managing to rest it on the side of his arm without squishing Max and Jett.

"You did good, Pirate," he blinks the tears out of his eyes, giving me a thin lipped grin.

"Damn Rodney," I huff out gently, not wanting to hurt anything.

"Yeah, he managed to get Tav to take him to Hobby Lobby for the hot glue gun you promised him. Came out with enough shit to fill a craft room," Moss barks out a laugh and I grip my side as I join him, not heartily, but enough to get my giggles out. "Come on, Lettie. Let's get you cleaned up."

I follow my big brother, kids in tow to where Switch and Jules are waiting for me at the open back of an ambulance.

"Damn girl, hate to see what the other guy looks like," Switch booms, shaking his head.

He puts his hand out to gently guide me into the back of the ambulance, chuckling when Jules shoves him out of the way and wraps his arm around my back, making sure I don't jiggle myself as I sit where Switch indicated. He then stands beside me, the heat of his body seeping into my side, holding my hand as Switch gently works on the left side of my body where I took the most amount of hits. The kids all huddle together, on a spare stretcher, watching me intently. Knowing their little eyes are on me I try not to flinch too much when Switch presses on my nose, checking for breaks and what not. Rolling my lips between my teeth, I bite down a little when he feels around my tender eye and cheekbone.

"So, nothing looks broken, just hella bruised." He places an icepack on the left side of my face and before I can raise my hand to hold it for him, Jules' arm comes around me, his hand gently holding it in place.

"He needs to deal with your hands, babe." he murmurs in my ear, sending a thrill through me. Which is fucking ridiculous when you think what I've gone through today. Later on my vagina and I will be having a talk about appropriate times and places.

Switch gently takes my left hand, cleaning it and wrapping it in soft gauze before gently placing it in my lap and moving on to my right side.

"Shit girl, this hand is mangled," he shakes his head and goes about his business, giving Jules a dirty look when he refuses to move out of his way so he can continue his checks.

I'm starting to slump, and whatever brave face I was putting on for the kids is starting to slip. I'm exhausted and all I want is to crawl into bed and fall into a deep sleep for the next 24 to 48 hours.

"Come on, let's get you to the clubhouse. We're all staying there tonight, I have some...stuff I have to take care of, and Juno is there with Mama Debs. And your mom."

My brows raise at Jules' comment. "Mom? My mom? Flora Davies is at the clubhouse?"

Jules smiles wide. "She practically kicked the door in, looking for you."

I drop my head and lean it on Jules' hard stomach, my shoulders shaking with my repressed laughter. "Of course she did."

"You're free to go. But take it easy. I'll give you something for the pain and I'll be in to check on you in the morning. I'm fairly certain you have a mild concussion so you need to take it easy."

"I'll check on her in the night," Jules says seriously, before scooping me up in his arms.

"Wait! The kids!" I look to the stretcher where they were all sitting and see that Moss has them, loading them into a vehicle. "Where are they taking them?"

"All the kids have families that are desperate to see them. The FBI and the Landry brothers will be travelling with them to the field office to meet them."

My brows pull in slightly. "Who are the Landry brothers?"

Jules looks down at me for a moment. "What do you know about Blanche and Lovely?"

"That they escaped a cult their father and uncles ran."

He nods once. "Blanche and Lovely's brothers have taken

it over, they run a safe haven for mainly women and children who have escaped shitty lives. They also have a network of people, kinda like an underground railroad that helps move people to safety. The kids will be safe with them."

I let out a relieved breath, feeling exhaustion take over me now that I know everyone is safe. "Take me to Juno, Jules."

Chapter 18

Jules

"And where do you think you're going?"

I look down to find Flora Davies staring up at me, her foot tapping impatiently.

"To see my sister," I hedge.

"Good. Take me with you."

"Ummmm," I shoot a glare at Moss who is smirking behind his tiny mother. His sisters are with the rest of the Ol Ladies, keeping an eye on Violet for me.

"You promised me that I'd be able to look those men in the eye," she says, her eyes narrowed. "Take. Me. There. Now." She punctuates each word with a poke to my chest.

"Flora, I'm not sure it's a good idea." I say, holding my hands up to try and placate her.

"I think it's a wonderful idea. Lets go," she nods decisively, looping her arm through mine, tugging me toward the door.

I look to Moss or even Steven Davies for help and they both shake their heads sadly. "Good luck with that, Jules," Moss says, waving at me.

"Davies! You don't want your mother in there," I hiss, on my way past him.

"In all honesty Jules, you probably want her in there less than I do."

What the fuck does that mean? She tugs me through the kitchen, then stands outside the door, waiting for me to give her directions. I let out a sigh, drop my head and then lead the way down the path to the door of the Rev Room.

"Flora –"

"I'm sure. Now open the door." Her dark eyes glint up at me and I shrug, opening the door and holding it for her.

All chatter inside the Rev Room ceases as soon as Flora walks in. Marx looks like he's going to have a heart attack until Moss steps in. "It's fine, Johnny. She just wants to look at the men who had the audacity to take her daughter, then I'll take her home."

Marx eyes Moss, then Flora and gives a curt nod. I'm sure he's still pissed though. Two people who don't look pissed are Pops and Chewy, who take Flora on a quick tour of the room, and even let her choose the soundtrack for this evening. The sounds of early 2000s Pink ring out in the Rev Room, the LEDs lighting up to the beat.

"Right, which one of you *culero* took my daughter, hmm?" Flora plants her feet, hands on hips as she stares down at the four men that Dayz has secured to metal chairs. Usually the Rev Room is used for single occupants, however tonight it looks like it's going to be a party.

All the men stare at Flora. Well, three of them do. The one I attacked first with the butt of my gun turns his head in her direction, his nose crooked and his eyes swollen shut. Flora moves closer to the men, leaning down to stare them in the eye one by one. The MC brothers watch on with interest. Shit, even Roman who has made it for the interrogation, watches the scene with curiosity.

Flora comes to a stop, intensely staring at one particular guard. He was one of the guards holding Vi's hands down. Instead of cowering under Flora's glare, he stares her down, smirking up at her. Quick as a flash Flora brings down her hand onto the guy's thigh and he starts to scream, writhing in pain.

"Mom! Fuck!" Moss yells, lunging for Flora as she pulls a goddamn knife out of the guard's leg, then spits in his face.

She yells obscenities in Spanish as Moss carries her toward the door, the rant only broken up by her laughter at the guard pissing himself and whimpering in pain.

"Don't worry Mrs. Davies! We'll take good care of him!" Dayz calls cheerily after her before turning to me. "Wanna split 'em? Two each?"

I run my gaze over the four men in front of me, then look at my sister with a grin. "What have you got planned?"

Groans sound out behind us from the MC brothers. My own brothers are leaning against the wall, big smiles on their faces. So far all anyone has seen is what my sister can do. Usually I leave her to it, but in some instances, with especially dangerous people, I like to help. It's a great stress reliever. Sue me.

I follow Dayz to her cupboard, Rhodie moving to take Chomper from her so she has her hands free for whatever she is going to pull out. Pops sidles up as well to offer his two cents worth.

"So, I recently got this little beauty made up," my sister says, holding up a pear shaped contraption with a handle and some type of twist mechanism.

"What in the fuck is that and please tell me you're not going to put it inside someone," Rider whines, running a hand down his face.

Dayz stares at the contraption in awe for a moment, before beaming at Rider. "It's the Pear of Anguish and yes, it's going inside someone. I'm just not too sure which end," she frowns at it, then at the first guy, he's still blinded by his swollen eyelids so he has no clue what's happening. "I guess I could use it in both ends really. Ass first, then mouth," she shrugs, then hands it to Pops who moves to place it gently on the stainless steel tool table. He whistles along to Pink's "Funhouse", then claps and dance shuffles his way back to the cupboard.

"Well, kid, what are ya after? Chemicals? Inserts? Ropes and knives?" He cocks a brow at me, waiting for me to make my choice.

I eye up the offerings, before turning to Rhodie's wall of devices. My eyes land on some knuckle dusters, and I think that's how I want to start my evening. Switch gave me a run down of all of Vi's injuries, so I want to replicate that before I get onto anything more...permanent.

Raising my brows in question at my sister's Ol Man, Rhodie lifts his chin in reply and I remove the knuckle dusters from their designated spot on the wall. Be rude of me to not ask before using another man's tools. Pops rolls his eyes and mutters "boring" under his breath. Dayz nods her head and they both turn back to their cupboard, heads bent together in serious conversation.

I stop at the man nearest me. I know that Dayz and I had agreed on two each, but I don't think she'd mind if I rough them up a little first. This guy, Baldy, has a black eye and his nose is looking a little crooked thanks to one of my brothers' handiwork. And yes, I did mean MC as well as biological. The MC had my back when I needed it, and I'll have theirs. That seems like brotherly shit if you ask me.

Baldy smirks up at me when I come to a stop in front of him. I grin back at him, the knuckle dusters fitting snugly on my hand, and I throw a right hook, hitting him exactly where I wanted - his left cheek. I move on to the next injury Vi's body had. A split lip which I deliver with precision. Vi's right cheek had marks where I'm guessing she was backhanded, so I do the same, dragging the dusters over his cheek, splitting it with little effort. His ribs are next, as a well-earned punch has his breath whooshing out of him as he starts to pant due to the pain.

The swelling and bruises are starting to come up on his pale skin, and yet he still doesn't look as bad as my Firecracker. I continue to work him over, hit for hit, kick for kick until he's battered and bruised and looking a lot less smug than he was.

"Ah, brother, are you going to ask him anything?" Tav asks, sounding a little nervous.

"That's Dayz's job," I reply, over my shoulder. "So, who's next?"

Violet

I wake with a start as Juno's cry sounds out. Shit, did I fall asleep on the job? I move to sit up and then fall back, pain shooting through my head and ribs for a split second. The pain is what brings it all back - the truck, the kids, those fucking guards, all of it. I lay back with a tiny groan, taking shallow breaths until I'm in a more comfortable position.

"Shhh, it's OK Vi. We got you," a gentle voice coos, and my eyes, well, eye, flies open.

I'm met with the stares of my sisters, almost all the Ol Ladies and one big, blonde guy. Mama Debs has Juno in her arms and they're all staring at me.

"Um, what are you all looking at?" I mumble, my face quite tender.

"At your face, holy shit Lettie you look TERRIBLE," Jazz exclaims, not even quietly either. Loudly so that it reverberates through my head a little.

"Thanks, next time I get kidnapped I'll try not to stop any punches with my face." I roll my eyes at her.

Jazz bursts into tears, sending Lily down the crying hole, then Blanche.

"It's the hormones so you better not give me any shit!" she threatens, trying her hardest to suck up her tears. She even has her hands on her hips as she stomps around the room, blinking double time.

"You do look pretty shitty," Nat agrees. "Is there anything we can help you with? Switch left your next lot of pain meds so you can take those now, but they will knock you out a little."

I nod, feeling tightness in my shoulders along with other aches and pains. "I'd like a shower. I feel filthy at the moment."

"Good idea, do you need help?" Lil asks, sniffing a little.

I look at her like she's lost her mind. "Lil, I love you, but there's no way you're getting up close and personal with my jiggly bits."

I move myself to sitting up in bed, feeling weirded out a little. "Ah, don't mean to be rude, but why are you all here?"

Mama Debs bounces Juno in her arms, settling her back to

sleep, "Jules had business to take care of and didn't want you alone,"

"Yeah! He went all alpha on us and told us that we all had to be here to support you and under no circumstances were we to leave you alone. It was actually kinda romantic. He had 'burn the world down' vibes going on," Mira adds excitedly.

"Yeah he actually did!" Jazz agrees, "Like that man was on a mission! Rounded us all up, barking instructions and all that."

"Ugh, I hate when he barks at me," I mumble.

"He does it from a place of care," Lovely says, resting her hand on my leg. "But I could see how it would be annoying," she smiles.

"That's because you have your very own bossy alpha barking instructions," Ana cackles.

Lovely gives her an odd look, "No, I have a very bossy MC Pres who thinks I'm a damsel in distress all the time. He has no idea what I survived to get to this point," she says quietly.

"Yes, but we do," Nat says, pulling her into her side.

"Boys are dumb," Blanche says, flopping down onto the bed. "Tav is convinced we're having a boy because he has spent years wearing loose fitting boxer shorts."

I frown. Well I think I do, it's hard to tell what my face is doing at the moment, but I'm sure my expression mirrors the other women.

"What? How?"

"Some men think that by keeping their testicles unrestricted, that the sperm are stronger, healthier, and more manly." The big, blonde tall drink of water says in an accented voice.

"Who are you?" I breathe out, then clear my throat because since Josh dumped me I've turned into a hussy.

"Oh, this is Sasha, he's Roman's husband and one of my best

friends," Ana says cheerily. "And his brother found you."

"He's a man witch," Mira whispers.

I stare at her and try to wrap my head around all the craziness that's happening. Then decide that I'd rather hide in the shower and get clean. I'll worry about everything else later. I slowly move the blankets off my legs, and swivel my body, being careful not to move too fast. Jazz jumps up to help pull me to standing, and now that I am I feel a little better about life.

"Here, take these," Lil shoves my overnight bag into my hands and confuses me. "Jules made us go home and pack you some clothes. I packed you a soft sports bra and your fave stretchy pants."

"Oh, good call on the stretchy clothes," Remy says, holding her hand up for a high five.

I pull my sister in for a gentle hug, "Thank you," I whisper, blinking the tears away.

"Hey! Don't leave me out!" Jazz muscles her way into the hug, and the next thing I know I'm being embraced on all sides by the women and the giant man who is married to some guy named Roman and has a warlock for a brother.

After a long, long hug they let me shuffle my way into the bathroom, Remy having already started the water for me so it'll be nice and warm by the time I get in. I discard my dirty clothes in the empty hamper and move to stand under the water, letting it beat down on my sore body, washing away all the grossness of the day. Or yesterday. I have no idea what time it is, or even what day. I pick up the generic body wash that's sitting on the shower stall shelf and lather it in my hands. There's no way I'm using the body puff knowing that this is an MC. Who knows who else has rubbed that on their body. I work on cleaning everywhere I can reach, getting rid of the grime and the ickiness I feel. I also take stock of my injuries and bruises. I'm actually impressed at how I'm looking so far. Don't get me wrong, I took a hell of a beating, but apart from some bruised ribs, and my tender face, of which icing and painkillers have numbed a lot of it, I'm not looking too bad. Put it this way, I look better than some of the women who would come into the ER while I worked there.

I continue cataloguing wounds. Some bruises on my wrists from being yanked around, some on my legs from kicking at people. Hot water hits my tense shoulder muscles and I relax into the water, checking to see if there are other bruises anywhere. Looking down at my chest I freeze. What the fuck? Rubbing soap suds and sluicing water out of my way to get a better look I stare at my bare breast.

Teeth marks. Fucking teeth marks! I know for a fact that Jules never bit me when we were together, so some other motherfucker out there bit me. I check between my legs and feel nothing, letting out a sigh of relief knowing that they didn't get that far, but still. Some fucker bit my tit and I'm going to find him. I twist the shower taps off harder than I should do then wrap myself in a towel, drying myself as carefully and quickly as I possibly can. I yank on my clothes and my care for my aches and pains goes out the window. I need answers and I need them now. I burst through the door into the bedroom, making everyone in the room jump.

"Where is Jules?" I seethe.

"Ummm, he's working on something right now," Lovely says, her eyes darting to Nat who is staring at me with narrowed eyes.

"I don't care. Where is he? Better yet, where is Marx? I have a motherfucking bite mark on my boob and I *know* that they have the people that did this. Where are they?"

The women all share a look, Mama Debs gives me a nod then leaves the room. "Violet," Remy starts but I hold my hand up, stopping her from trying to placate me."

"No, she has every right to know where they are," Nat says, Blanche nodding.

The Ol Ladies and one Ol Man have a full conversation with their eyes as my sisters stand by my side, holding my shaking hands.

"I'll take you to them, but your sisters have to stay. It's for the safety of the club," Nat says, looking toward Jazz and Lil.

"Stay here, yeah?" I squeeze their hands gently, then drop them. Jazz opens her mouth to say something, but I stop her. "No, Nat's right. They put their lives on the line for me, the least I can do is respect their rules."

My sisters nod. "I guess we should go check on mom and dad then," Jazz murmurs, giving me a kiss on my check.

"I saw your mom not long ago, she's doing just fine," Blanche grins.

"OK, show me the way ladies."

Chapter 19

Jules

This fucker's eyeball is taking a little longer than I expected to come out. I mean usually those things pop right out, but either this guy has the strongest ocular muscles known to man, or I didn't break his orbital bone enough when I punched him with the knuckle dusters. Doesn't matter, one way or another he's losing an eye.

I drop the bloodied dessert spoon on the tray Pops placed on the table for dirty tools, and pick up a scalpel. One of the prisoners starts to sob so I give him a quick slash along his cheek to shut him up. I have serious shit to do. I lean over my victim, grinning into his good eye, as I grip the left side of his face, holding him still as I slowly let the scalpel descend into the corner of his eye socket. The door is thrown open, bouncing off the wall, stopping me from going any further.

Turning to look over my shoulder I see Vi, my woman, my Firecracker, standing in the doorway, looking like a fucking Valkyrie. Her gaze travels the room, taking in the men, and woman, all in various stages of relaxation, leaning against walls or on the couch. Her gaze comes to a stop on me, my hand poised, blood covering the front of my shirt and my hands. She surveys the situation, her eyes glancing over the four men lined up, tied to metal chairs, positioned over the grate in the floor. All have severe facial injuries and one is on the verge of losing an eye.

I brace myself. Now is the moment that she realizes that I am exactly what people think I am. Cold. Unfeeling. An asshole. Instead she steps closer, one step, then another, until she's standing in front of the men, hands on hips, exactly like her mother did an hour ago.

"Which one of you filthy assholes bit my boob?" she seethes, her balled fists shaking with fury.

"Oh oh! Pick me! I can answer that!" Dayz waves her hand in the air and comes rushing around to stand between Vi and me. "Jules told me about the bite so I took photos of it while you were asleep. Then Pops made dental impressions of these guys' mouths. The winner isssssss-" Dayz points to all the men in a Meeny Miny Moe fashion before stopping at the guy still sobbing even after I gave him a warning. "This crybaby!"

Pops' leans between two of the prisoners, the crier to his left, my guy to his right. He holds up the dental impression he made. "Hello," he says, using the plaster teeth as a puppet.

Vi stares at him before slowly turning to look at my sister. "You took photos of my boob while I was asleep?" She looks both confused and fucking livid.

"Yup. You're welcome." Dayz says before flouncing off to continue lubing up her Pear of Despair or whatever the hell she called it.

Vi turns her stunned face toward me, and I wait for her to lose it. In fact, I'm sure everyone in this room is waiting for the same thing. Roman has even moved closer to the action, so to speak. She's quiet for a long time, a very long time. The only sound in the room is the snivelling of the men tied to chairs and the squelchy sound of lube being applied. Vi stares at me, for so long in such silence that I start to worry that the one woman I can actually picture myself with is going to find me fucking repulsive. Nerves swirl in my stomach and I feel nauseous at the thought that I could be losing the one person who makes me want to be a better man. A man who shares who he is. A man that can love one single woman with his whole being.

"There's probably a shard of orbital bone holding his eye in place," she says in a hoarse voice.

What the fuck? I open my mouth to say something, anything, but nothing comes out.

"You're trying to remove his eye, right?" I nod, still stunned at the situation. She steps closer, looking down at the guy about to become a Cyclops. "The orbital bone is smashed in. Chances are there's a shard keeping the eyeball in place. Here."

She moves slightly, placing her small, soft hands over my hand holding his head, and the side of his face. She presses outward, as if stretching his face, tugging the broken bones away from the eye socket. With a little grunt that makes my cock thicken, she lets go, stepping back out of my space, making me feel cold and empty.

"Try now."

I eye her suspiciously, not wanting to do anything that will make her look at me in a different light. I hesitate, unsure what to do next. Looking up I catch my sister's steady stare. She gives me a small smile and a little nod. She wants me to test Vi. A soft hand lands on my cheek, and I lean closer, soaking up the contact in case this is the last time Vi touches me.

"I won't think any differently of you if you do this. But I may think differently of you if you don't."

"What?" I grunt out, because clearly I've gone back to being mute Jules.

"I've always known that you," she stares at me for a moment, before looking around, "all of you, do bad things for the greater good. I'm not an idiot. And neither is my brother."

"Whoops, my bad," Dayz says under her breath.

Vi turns back to look me in the eye, her thumb running across my stubble. "Tonight you saved those kids, those women and me. These men don't deserve to live. They kidnap and rape and do evil shit. You can not only stop it, but you can make them suffer."

I swallow, my throat thick. I know now what Dayz feels for Rhodie. What Tav feels for Blanche. They've found people who have seen their darkness and instead of being disgusted they embrace it, they embrace what we are and what we do. My gaze shifts around the room, the looks on the men's faces are that of acceptance for Vi. Fucking beautiful, brave, easy to irritate Vi.

She takes my hand, and guides it where it needs to be. The orbital bone now no longer impedes my access to the side of the eyeball, allowing me to pop it out, leaving it to hang down the face of the guard who has done unspeakable things to people. His screams rend the air and are the perfect soundtrack as I cup Vi's face, lean in and gently press my lips to hers. I hold right there, breathing her in, her scent, her taste, her feel until there's nothing left of this world but her and I.

She deepens the kiss slightly, her tongue tasting mine in a lazy duel, sipping from each other until we have to come up for air.

"Well done, brother. Now, can we please get on with the fucking interrogation?" Marx grumbles.

"In just a minute, please, Mr President," Vi says, holding up a finger. "Chewy, what do you have that'll leave a nasty bite mark on someone?"

Dayz grins wide, moving to lift Chomper out of his stroller. "This do?"

Violet

I hesitate for a moment. Am I really going to do this? Use an alligator to maim a man? Looking down at my chest my anger rises again. Yes, yes I fucking am going to do that. And I'm going to do worse. Now that I'm back to my senses and not kiss drunk on Jules' lips, which by the way are fucking heavenly, and I will be revisiting that as well as trying to figure out whether me entering something with him is a trauma response or not, I reach my hands out for Chewy's baby.

"Be a good boy and do what the nice lady tells you," Chewy says, cooing at the gator dressed in a freaking argyle vest.

My hands run over his scaly body, marvelling at the texture of him, his belly soft on my thumbs as I grip him by the underarms, as you would a toddler. He's surprisingly a lot heavier than I expected. He's a small gator, with funny feet that make it hard for him to walk, and a pronounced underbite, but I've been warned a few times that he does like to chew on things so he'll be perfect for what I have in mind.

"Jules, can you please strip the biter of his shirt?"

"Sure thing Firecracker." He presses a gentle kiss to my temple, then using the scalpel in his hand slices down the middle of the guy's shirt, not even worried when he slices too deep, causing his chest to bleed.

Chomper must smell the metallic tang because he starts to gnash his teeth, large head swaying this way and that, trying to pick up the scent. I gently place Chomper on the biters lap, the man struggling this way and that, trying to buck the little gator off, however Chomper holds fast. Besides, there's not enough time to dislodge him before Chomper lunges forward and snaps at the guard's chest, latching on in the perfect spot, right where my bite mark is. Excitement rushes through me and I grin, catching the Jules' eye, who smirks back. Chewy looks excited as well, cooing words of encouragement to her baby.

Jules sidles up next to me, his large, rough hand wrapping around my smaller one. "We can get out of here if you like? You've had a huge day, let me take care of you." He gazes down at me and for the first time I can see there are no walls up. No road blocks, no hiding his feelings, he's open and it's breathtaking.

I look toward Chomper and the men lined up, then back at Jules who is gazing down at me like I'm his whole world. Me. Violet Elena Ximena Davies. The woman that pushes his buttons to get a rise out of him. The woman that sometimes refuses to do as he asks. The woman that has been ignoring the feelings he stirs up. He squeezes my hand and I decide I need to speak my truth.

"Can we stay? I want to help."

"And how are you going to help, exactly?" Nat's Ol Man

Savage gruffly asks.

I turn to face the MC, hands on hips because for some reason that's where they like to rest when I'm being challenged. "I'm a nurse. Between me and Dr. Han- I mean, Switch, we can keep these guys alive for as long as we want."

The MC brothers stare at me, then turn to Switch. "How come you've never offered that?" one of them whines. I think it's Rider.

"Because I figured there was no point, Chewy was going to get rid of 'em anyways," he shrugs.

"Yeah but we could have had more fun with them!" Rider argues. "I'm on Vi's side." he says, turning to Marx.

Marx gives me a chin lift and I clap my hands, then turn, beaming up at Jules.

"Let's get this party started then," he says with a grin. I find I quite like putting that smile on his face.

* * *

"OK, maybe I was wrong, maybe I prefer Switch not keeping these guys alive," Rider says from his corner where he's standing, his face turned to the side not watching, but not not watching either.

"You said you wanted this," I remind him, as I push a little adrenaline into this guy's veins. I'm not too sure which guard this is given that his face is so battered, but it doesn't really matter. Also, I have no idea how or why Chewy has adrenaline, but whatever. I'm a nanny now, I have no professional laws to uphold.

"I said I wanted them to be around longer so we could have fun with them! Not watch their gaping assholes get even more gapey!"

I glance down at the man Chewy has tied to a table, and yes, his asshole is a little gape-y.

I shrug at Rider, "Sorry, not sorry."

And I'm not. These men tortured and tormented women and children for some bitch out there making money hand over fist. They have to pay. All of them. I'm on hand for this and I'll be on hand again as soon as we get this Candice Rogers woman. No way am I missing that little party.

There's a gross wet sound followed by a muffled screech and I turn just in time to see the body fluid covered metal pear enter Gapey's mouth. I wince a little, then flick the blood pressure cuff to "on" and check his vitals. I keep an eye on them as Chewy cranks the pear open wide, while Rhodie interrogates the poor bastards left to watch what will happen to them next. Well, not the one whose eyes are swollen shut but the other two. Although the biter doesn't look like he has much left in him after Chomper went to town. Looking at all four men I realize that none of them are looking all that great and this could well be over soon.

The monitor starts to frantically beep, sounding like a 90's rave, so I turn to Chewy with my brows raised.

"Let him go, we got enough outta him," she waves dismissively.

"I think we got enough out of all of them." Marx says, "Wrap this up Chewy, it's late."

Chewy gives him a salute then goes back to her cupboard, looking for what, I don't know. A warm hand runs over my shoulders, giving one a little squeeze, drawing a moan out of me as the tight muscles relax a little.

"You've had a massive fucking day, Firecracker, lets get you to bed," Jules says quietly in my ear.

Now that these guards have paid the ultimate price, my adrenaline and anger have ebbed away, leaving me exhausted. How Jules knows this, I have no idea, but for once I'm going to listen to him without a fight.

"OK, Jules, take me to bed."

Chapter 20

Jules

Taking Vi by the hand I lead her out of the Rev Room. I'd love to have her in my arms again, but after months of getting to know her I know she won't want to look weak in front of everyone. It seems crazy that a few months ago I was living my best life working and fucking to my heart's content, and now, now I'm living a better life. One I didn't realize I loved until it was almost ripped away from me yesterday.

We get to the room I use whenever I'm in the clubhouse and I lead Vi in. Shutting the door quietly behind us I turn her toward me, then run my hands up under her oversized shirt, careful of her bumps and bruises.

"Jules–"

"Shhh, let me take care of you." I whisper, stopping any protest with a soft kiss to her lips.

She raises her arms as best she can with her sore ribs, and I work her shirt over her head, throwing it into the corner hamper to be burned. Who knows what she has on it after helping Dayz? I drop to my knees and gently tug on the stretchy waistband of her joggers, willfully ignoring the outline of her pussy behind her pink cotton panties. Her thighs touch and I can't wait to have them pressing against my face sometime in the future. If she lets me, of course. I was an utter asshole, freaking out about what I was feeling for her, but no more. If it takes me weeks, months, fuck, even years to win her over, I'll do it.

I toss her pants and panties into the corner, followed by her socks. I've never been a foot guy, but looking down at her cute blue tipped little toes I lean forward and press a light kiss to the top of each foot before pressing my forehead to her knee, gripping the back of her calves in my hands.

"Vi, fuck, I'm sorry for how I treated you. I, shit, I don't know. I freaked out. I –"

"Jules?" I look up at her, her gaze shining down at me, her hands threading through my hair. "I don't exactly know what's going on with us so why don't we put a hold on it, get cleaned up and sleep on it?"

My heart sinks and my head hangs. I fucked it up. I fucked it up so fucking badly. Pity party, table for one.

A soft snort sounds out, my head tipping back to look up at Vi's smirk, "I'm not saying I don't like what you were saying. I'm saying that in the past two days I've been dumped, been fucked to within an inch of my life by my boss, and been kidnapped."

"It's been a lot."

"It's been a fucking lot."

I rub her calves then move to stand, so close that her bare breasts now rub the top of my abs. Saying nothing I remove my clothes, toss them into the pile, then taking Vi by the hand

I lead her into the shower. I know she was freshly showered when she burst into the Rev Room, but I have a feeling she showered herself, not wanting anyone to help her. She may have let her mom, but little Flora was busy stabbing bad guys. I let out a snort and Vi gingerly turns her head to look at me.

"What's so funny?"

"Did you know your mom came into the Rev Room and stabbed a guy in the leg?"

"She what!?" Vi screeches, staring at me in horror before her face morphs and she wraps her arms around herself, holding on tight as she laughs, the sound a fucking symphony. "Actually, I can believe that. Lemme guess. Dad waited outside and Moss had to pull her away?"

I grin down at her and she rolls her eyes, turning back to face the spray, letting it wash out the blood and lube and whatever other body fluid she came into contact with.

"I don't have a problem with it, you know?" she says quietly.

"With what?"

"With who you are." She turns her head to the side, speaking to me over her shoulder but not looking me in the eye, and I appreciate that at this moment. "I know you're not comfortable with yourself a lot of the time. I pretty much guessed that you like to push stuff down, but you seem different now."

I fist my hand, and clear my throat, "Yeah, almost losing you and Juno was a huge wake up call. Turns out pushing shit down can only last so long before it comes out in a fucking deluge."

"Well, I liked the old Jules, even if he acted like a bossy dick sometimes. But this Jules, this Jules is someone I can see spending more time with, maybe watching movies with," she raises her dark eyes up to mine, a small smile playing on her lips.

"Maybe dance with?" I hedge.

"Maybe," she shrugs, and I can see by the rise in her cheeks that she's smiling.

"Does that mean my bad behavior is forgiven?"

"Hell no! You're definitely going to pay for ruining my afterglow by freaking out. I will require dates. Both with you and Juno, and alone. Oh, and you'll volunteer to be a life model for my sister's class. On three occasions."

I turn off the water, leaning out to grab a fluffy towel, moving to wrap it around Vi, tugging the ends in, leaving her beautiful, but damn battered face exposed. "Deal."

She beams, her good eye almost closing, and where I would feel rage at this, I feel gratitude that I'm getting a second chance. I press a kiss to her forehead, then her temple, then her lips, and then, because we're alone, I scoop her up and move her to the bedroom, gently placing her down, her dark hair splayed over the pillow.

I pull on some boxer shorts, knowing that I need to keep my cock under control. She'll hurt even more in the morning, and I'm not going to do anything to make her even vaguely uncomfortable, so the dick, he's going away, locked up tight behind fabric. I settle into the bed, pull the covers over both of us and maneuver myself until I'm pressed as close as I can get to my Firecracker without hurting her.

"Jules?"

"Yeah?"

"Thank you for coming to get me. I always knew you would."

"Anytime and everytime, Vi."

Violet

I roll over and wince a little, yesterday's memories rushing back.

"Ugggghhhhhh," not caring how loud or long it is.

"Bit stiff there Firecracker?" Jules asks, standing in the doorway with Juno on his hip, her little dark head topped with a ginormous bow.

I widen my eyes, glad that ice, ibuprofen and arnica have done their job. I can open both eyes now, so both are staring at Juno, a bow sitting on a jaunty angle on her head, and her trademark frown.

"What the hell is on her head?"

"Cove and Jovie bought Rosie and Juno one each so they can all match."

I stare at it a little longer, "It is kinda cute. In a slightly scary way."

"It keeps tickling my nose and I keep sneezing on her,"

As if on cue Juno moves her head, the bow brushing Jules' nose. He lets out a terrifyingly loud Dad sneeze, causing Juno to burst out into giggles.

"That's the only upside. Juno thinks it's funny," he says as he jiggles her in the air over his head. She laughs again and he makes his way to the bed, softly sitting down, so as not to jar my sore body too much. "Morning, babe," he leans forward, giving me a sweet kiss on my lips.

"Babe, huh? So, ah, we're really doing this and it's not just a trauma response to what happened yesterday?" I look at him with a belly full of butterflies.

I mean, this man, this super hot, stupidly gorgeous man

wants to be with me. Me. It's freaking nuts.

Jules leans back and lets out a sigh, looking at Juno for a moment, who beams up at him. He turns his dark gaze back to me, clearing his throat. "I'm going to say something that might scare you. I hope you take what I say as something I have thought deeply about, and it's not just because we fucked or because I thought I had lost you. OK?"

I eye him, not having any clue where he's going with this. "Ooookay," I agree.

"I've never felt anything like this for anyone outside of my family. The feeling is... big. So big that when I was with you, *really* with you, I felt like I was drowning. I pushed the big feeling down and pushed you away because I'm a dumbass." He inhales deeply then in one breath blurts, "Iloveyou."

His large palm gently covers my mouth before I can reply. "Don't say anything yet. I didn't tell you that to force you into saying it back, I just wanted you to know that's how I feel." He frowns.

I sit there, wide eyed staring at him, and I'm certain the kidnapping has broken him. Well, maybe not broken *him*, more like broke down his walls.

"I want you to join mine and Juno's family. But I don't want you to say it if you don't feel the same. I'll understand if you don't." He slowly removes his hand from my mouth and I shimmy to sit myself up. Important discussions like this have to be done with both parties sitting up, at least.

"Jules, we may not have seen eye to eye to begin with, but over the past few months I've gotten to know you. The real you. The version that you hid from everyone else. I knew you had it in you to feel deeply and intensely, but I never thought I would ever get to see it."

He stares at me and when I open my mouth to say the words, the words I've been feeling underneath all the emotions he brings out in me, he covers my mouth again.

"Don't say it. I don't want to hear it until you know. Completely."

I frown at him and he laughs, jiggling Juno who copies her daddy and laughs too.

"Fine. But mark my words, it's coming," I threaten.

He leans forward, giving me a quick peck before Juno can get her hands into my hair. "I'll give you a week and then we'll both be coming." He winks as he leans back and my panties combust with a heat so intense I'm sure it's probably singed my pubic hair clean off.

"Mamama."

Jules and I freeze and stare at one another.

"Mamamamama," Juno continues to babble.

"Did she just?" I ask, shocked and delighted and on the verge of bursting into tears.

"Fuck! I think she did!" Jules says, holding his daughter up, staring at her like she's Einstein.

Her chubby legs kick as she squeals, "Dada."

"What the fuck!" Jules yelps, holding Juno up even higher, staring at her in wonder.

"Dada," Juno's cute little voice rings out loud and clear.

"That's right, I'm your Dada," Jules voice is thick with emotion, tears in his eyes as he looks at me.

Leaning forward I rest my head on his shoulder, gripping Juno's hand as she babbles "Mama" and "Dada" and my heart is full. Who knew that when my mother fired me I'd fall in love with a little girl, lose a boyfriend but gain a good man who loves me. The only thing marring that experience would be being kidnapped with a truck load of kids.

"Hey, what happened with the info Chewy found out last night? I ask, wanting to make sure that nasty bitch Candice Rogers is going down.

Jules swings his legs up onto the bed, maneuvering himself so he's leaning against the headboard, the left side of his body pressed against mine. He places Juno between his legs and she lays there, kicking and blowing raspberries at her feet. I lift his left arm, slipping my head under so I can lean against his hard pec.

"The kids spent the night in the ER for observation, and their parents were found and contacted. The Landry's contacts are working alongside the FBI in getting the women back home." He swallows, then continues, "Dayz found out that Candice is just a small link in the chain. In the state of Texas she's a huge trafficker, but she's part of a larger group of scumbags."

"So we didn't shut down anything?" I slump, taking one of Juno's feet in my hands, leaning forward to blow a raspberry on her foot, leaving her giggling and squirmy.

"Yes and no. Happy Values is finished. The employees are being questioned by the FBI and they have APB's out for Candice, as well as alerts at all the airports."

"I guess that's good then," I say, the disappointment surprising me. It seems after a night in the Rev Room that I've gotten a taste for making people pay for their crimes. Candice is on my shit list and I want her taken care of.

"The guy yanking the chain is who we're going to focus on looking for in the immediate future. We don't want any nasty surprises if we bring Candice in."

"Fair enough. But you better let me know when you and the team have her. I have things I want to say to her."

Jules side eyes me as if he knows that I'm talking shit. My stomach rumbles causing Juno to make a weird growling noise in reply.

"Looks like it's time to feed my girls," Jules says, his lips lifting at the corners, "Come on little Miss Grumpy Face,"

I stay sitting in bed, watching that hot hunk of man move to stand, baby in his arms.

"I was talking to you, Firecracker," he winks. I flip him the bird and gingerly get out of bed, stretching this way and that to loosen things up.

"Get dressed, babe and I'll go get your breakfast set up." He drops a kiss to the top of my head and leaves the room, his resting bitch face back in place with Juno frowning at me over his shoulder, but still giving me a wave on the way out.

I chuckle to myself as I move to find some clean clothes, taking them into the bathroom to freshen up. Looking in the mirror I gasp so hard I choke on my own saliva, coughing like I'm dying and moaning with every cough as it jars my ribs.

"Oh my god you look terrible!" Jazz gasps, falling backwards onto the bed.

"Ignore her, you look beautiful as ever, just a little bruised," Lil says because she's the not evil sister.

"*Mija*! My baby!" my mom wails, coming at me with outstretched hands, moving to cup my face but Dad beats her to it, pulling me into his warm arms.

"Thanks Dad." I snuggle into him, ignoring Mom slapping Dad's arms to get him to move.

Dad lets out a sigh and releases me where I'm roughly scooped into my mother's arms, her strong hand forcing my head down to rest on her boob.

"My girl, my beautiful baby girl." She holds me at arm's

length, getting a good look at me before grinning, "I stabbed the man that took you!"

"I heard, Mom. You were very badass,"

"That's right. I'm thinking of getting a motorcycle. Maybe DRMC will let me join!" She bustles off out the door, all our eyes following her.

Dad lets out a long suffering sigh, before following in Mom's wake.

"Soooooo," Jazz says, waggling her brows at me as I pull on my soft pants.

"So, what?"

"So, we heard what Jules said to you. That man loooooves you! Are you going to move in with him and make more cute babies?" Lil asks, lying on her stomach on the bed, her chin propped up on her hands.

"Maybe. But, like, isn't it too fast? I had a completely different boyfriend two days ago! Then me and Jules slept together and he got all weird about it. He's my boss! And sometimes he's stubborn and it pisses me off. And then last night he took care of me and actually talked about his feelings and said sweet things and I don't know! He can be such an asshole and then such a sweetheart. Ugh." I throw my hands up and then regret the movement.

Jazz eyes me. "You do know there's a very fine line between love and hate, right? Let me ask you this: Even though Jules can be a rude dick, in the times he wasn't like that, did you have fun?"

I think back to the dinners we shared or the lunches where Juno and I would visit Jules in his office. "Yeah, I did have fun. He's thoughtful and comfortable to be around and we had good conversations." I shrug.

"OK, and when you were taken, who did you have faith in to find you?"

"Jules." Without a doubt.

"And when you think of him what do you feel?" Lil asks softly.

I think about how I feel when he walks into a room. When he laughs at my jokes or frowns at my teasing or does that little smile thing when our eyes meet. "I feel everything," I whisper.

"There it is then," Jazz says with a decisive nod.

"Nothing is too fast, Lettie. Mom and Dad only knew each other for two weeks before they got married and I've never seen two people more in love," Lil says. "Apart from the couples here at the MC."

"They're sickeningly in love," Jazz says.

"We heard that!" Blanche's voice booms down the hall.

"She's pregnant, between the three of us, we can take her," I say loudly enough so she can hear me.

"Bring it on!" she yells back.

"You sure about joining the Tombs family?" Jazz asks, peering down the hall.

"Second to our family, I couldn't think of a better family to be a part of."

Chapter 21

Jules

I place a few toys on Juno's high chair in the MC kitchen while I plate up pancakes for Vi. I even get creative and add strawberries in the shape of a heart. Feeling eyes on me I look up to see Fox, Nitro and Flack staring at me in shock.

"What?" I growl, my "fuck off" face in full force.

"Nothing, just wondering what the fuck happened to you?" Nitro asks, as if I've had a lobotomy or some shit.

"Nothing happened," I frown, adding in a stink eye for good measure.

"Dude, we only knew you as the surly asshole who can fuck two or three girls in one night. Now you're making love hearts on pancakes." Fox says. Flack leans against the door jamb, nodding his head.

I look down at what I'm doing, then my heart does somer- saults when Juno's little voice calls out "Dada" getting my attention. I shake her fat little hand, smiling at her before glaring at the men giving me shit.

"That boys, is a man in love," Pops says, coming out of the

pantry with Mama Debs. I shiver, knowing full well that me and Juno have been the only people in the kitchen for the last twenty minutes. "A man can be out there, sowing his wild oats with any woman, or man he pleases. But when he finds that one that makes him want to give up all that willing pussy and ass? Well, he grabs onto it with both hands and never lets go. Proud of you son." He slaps me on the shoulder as he moves past me.

He stops in front of Fox and Nitro, staring up at both of them, "Mark my words boys, one day a woman is going to walk into your lives and be willing to love the both of you numbnuts. When that day happens, those orgies of yours," Pops makes a whistling noise, drawing his finger across his throat, "Doneski."

Fox and Nitro snort, watching Pops leave the room, "Happy for you brother," Fox says, slapping me on the shoulder, much like Pops did, then rubbing Juno's head on the way past. Nitro nods in agreement and follows after him, giving Juno a rub as well, but clearly she has had enough because she shakes her head at him and then scowls when he chuckles at her.

"I agree with them Jules, you're lucky. You found a good woman to not only love you, but your daughter, too. Make as many heart pancakes as you need to keep her," Flack says before giving me a chin lift.

I have no idea why people think bikers are badasses, it seems they're always up in each other's business, handing out advice, gossiping and supporting their brothers. I'm fucking glad my sister broke into this place all those months ago.

Hearing the women's voices in the common room I scoop up Juno, nuzzling into her soft, chubby neck, letting her grip my face in her sticky hand as she squeals. I do this a couple more times before settling her on my hip, and grabbing up Vi's breakfast. Entering the common room my eyes search for her, landing on her bruised face tipped back laughing at something Cove is saying.

I beeline for her, staring down at Ana until she moves from the seat she's sitting in, to the next one over.

"You're a caveman."

"And you're my favorite sister-in-law,"

"I heard that!" Blanche growls, Tav covering her ears too late.

I smirk at her until she rolls her eyes. Placing Vi's food down in front of her I press a kiss to her temple and breathe in her citrusy scent.

"Right, we're heading out," Vic Landry announces, gaining everyone's attention. They spent all last night getting the kids to their various contacts for transport back to their families before crashing at the clubhouse last night.

We all line up to shake hands and slap each other on the back. Dima stands off to the side, giving his brother and Roman a polite head nod before they leave the room.

"Who is that man?" Vi whispers when I return to my seat. "I've met Blanche's brothers and the bratva guys, but not that guy."

"That's Dima, Sasha's brother. He's the one who helped us find you."

"The Man Witch?" Vi's eyes widen and she pushes away from the table, gingerly walking as quickly as she can across the common room, coming to a stop in front of the Russian.

Dima dips his head and they have a conversation before Vi reaches around his waist and gives him a gentle squeeze. Dima's lips turn up, and I realize this is the first time in the encounters I've had with him where he looks lighter. Huh. Finding missing people probably weighs a lot on a man.

Vi makes her way back to me and Juno, gently sitting her luscious ass down and taking a bite of her food. "Thank you for my breakfast, honey," Vi says, my heart skipping a beat at the endearment.

"Anytime and everytime," I whisper back.

She beams up at me, and then it morphs into a smirk. "Remember what you promised me?" I give her a puzzled look, "You agreed to pose three times for Jazz's class?"

"Oh yeah, Elio is in that class," I reply.

"Yes! He is. Well, Jazz said she'll need you next Wednesday at around 10am."

"Done. I mean, what's the worst that could happen?"

Violet

I check myself once more in the mirror admiring how good the midnight blue lingerie looks on my golden skin. I check the time once more, fluff my hair out and perch on the end of Jules's bed, waiting for his return. Mama Debs and Pops have offered to have Juno for the night, my bruises have faded to a yellow that's not really so noticeable anymore, and my ribs are feeling ready for all sorts of sexy athletics. All I need now is my man. The man who has been showing me all the layers that he had kept locked down for all those years. I have a feeling a lot of the way he was is due to not knowing how to handle his emotions. Add in losing his parents and I'm guessing the depth of feeling probably scared the shit outta him, so instead of working through them, he pushed them down. It seems that thinking he lost Juno and me broke the wall that was holding all that back and now he regularly has moments where he feels everything. Anger, fear, sadness, happiness. That's my favorite one, seeing Jules smiling and content.

The door opens and closes and I wait for him to make his way into the bedroom. Instead of the sound of his heavy footsteps, I'm met with moans. What the hell? I quickly wrap myself in the short silky robe that matches my lingerie and race into the lounge. I come to an abrupt stop when I see Jules sprawled on the couch, his legs at impossible angles.

"What the hell happened?" I shriek, concerned for his health.

His eyes raise to look me in the face, a deep frown marring his good looks, "Your damn sister happened! And that little shit Rodney." He takes a deep breath before giving me a pitiful look, "You know that I don't wax my brows, right?"

My brows pinch in confusion. "Um, yeah? I guess. Why?"

"Because Rodney called me a 'metrosexual' and teased me about waxing my brows and then it escalated and now the kids think I get waxed. Everywhere."

I roll my lips between my teeth, and try not to laugh. I should have warned him those kids were feral.

"And then a really cute little girl asked why my shirt was a weird color in the armpits and then Jazz explained about sweat patches and how it's a part of life and then the little girl started sobbing hysterically because she didn't want 'crying pits'. She lost it even more when Rodney told her that because she had German ancestry that she'd grow hairy underarms and not be allowed to shave them."

I snort and Jules gives me a death stare. One that would scare any other woman, but not me. I know that deep down Jules is more afraid of me than I am of him.

"Um, so, why all the moaning?" I ask him. I'm curious to know the answer now that my blood pressure has lowered.

He lets out a long, sad, sigh. "My body is all locked up after holding a pose for almost an hour. I thought I'd just have to stand there! Instead that rat bastard Rodney suggested I pose like that Gollum guy, so Jazz piled some crap up to look like a rock and I had to squat on that with my arms spread out in front of me and resting on my fingertips." He looks at me with eyes full of sorrow before they narrow and then look me up and down. "Babe, what are you wearing?" he looks around the room, "and where is Juno?"

My fingers play with the silky belt, loosening it just enough that he gets an eyeful of the way this balconette bra is framing my ample breasts. "Well," I answer him, "Juno is with Mama Debs and Pops for the night and, do you mean this old thing?"

I let the fabric slide down off my arms, letting it pool at my feet, and Jules sits bolt upright before groaning and falling back onto the couch.

Letting out a sigh I walk up to him, hands on hips. "Well, it looks like I'm in charge," I shrug.

Jules grins up at me, his large, rough hands running up the backs of my thighs, gently squeezing my ass cheeks, then running them back down again. He repeats this motion twice more, however with each time his fingers get closer and closer to brushing my core.

"I want you up here, Firecracker, I need to taste your cream," his voice is thick with lust and who am I to question the man?

I place my right foot on the couch beside him, then move to stand, placing my left foot on his other side, my pussy in line with his mouth. He leans his head back, his hands on my ass bringing me closer to him until I'm straddling his face. He runs his nose up and down my slit before sucking me through the wet fabric of my lingerie.

"Fuck you taste so good, baby."

He hooks a thick finger through the side of my panties, tugging the gusset to the side, allowing his mouth full access to my dripping core. He sucks gently at my lips, nibbling at them while a thick finger rubs my empty hole. My hands grip his hair, holding him in place as he slurps at me, the sounds of him devouring me and me moaning for more create a chorus of pleasure.

I whine when his finger leaves me wanting as his hands disappear, only to feel a tug before my underwear is in tatters.

"Hey!" I yelp, staring down into his heavy lidded eyes.

"I'll buy you more," he says before thrusting two fingers all the way inside me and latching his mouth to my clit.

My lingerie troubles cease to exist as Jules brings me closer and closer to the edge. The hand holding my ass, pressing me closer to his mouth moves to spread my lips wide, allowing deeper access to my clit, batting it with his tongue. This coupled with his fingers hooking and hitting the perfect spot has stars bursting behind my eyes, my legs shaking and my core gushing. My breath is coming in pants and I'm screaming to high heaven but I don't care.

Jules

Vi's body twitches as her hands rest on my shoulders, keeping her semi upright over me. It's a fucking hot sight, my woman's legs shaking and the wet spot on my trousers from her orgasm, but I want more, I need more, even if my body is broken right now. I take my hands off her gorgeous fucking body, dropping them to my button and fly, undoing both, tugging them down under my ass so I can free my aching cock.

I run my hand over the crown of my cock, using my precum as lube, jacking myself as I gaze at Vi's beautiful pussy.

"You're in charge, baby. Come ride my cock."

She smiles gently at me through blissed out eyes, but she complies, squatting over me as I line my cock up with his home. Vi informed me that she's on birth control and that she trusts me, but I still got myself tested and showed her my clear paperwork. Whether she trusts me or not, it's up to me to protect her.

She lowers her body down, wrapping my cock in her soft, wet core and I let out a long, low groan as she sighs in bliss. She moves back and forth a little, grinding on me before lifting up, hovering, hovering until I get impatient, and then she drops down, engulfing me. She does this a few more times, teasing me, to the point where she smirks at me until I slap her ass, trying to get her to stop taunting me. Instead of going faster, she stands, my desperate cock slapping against my stomach. She turns her back to me, smirking over her shoulder as she grips my base, lining me up and then sitting down, slowly, so damn fucking slowly.

She tests out the position before riding me in earnest, her

thick ass jiggling with the movement. It's the best fucking sight I've ever seen, and I grip her ass cheeks, spreading them slightly to find that this, this right here is an even better sight. Her pussy lips are spread wide around my cock, and everytime she pulls up, I can see her pussy gripping me, her cream coating my throbbing length and I know I'm not going to last.

Moving my hands to her glorious breasts I grip them, more than a handful in my large hands. Pulling her back until she's resting against my chest I hold her to me and thrust up into her from below. Vi turns her head and I drop my mouth to hers, tongues tangling, nibbling, duelling until my Firecracker rips her lips from mine, moaning deeply as I hit the right spot inside of her. Knowing that I need her to come, and soon, I release her tits, grip her under the knees and pull them to her chest, spreading her wide as I drop lower on the couch. With my feet planted I can thrust harder and deeper, the sounds of our lovemaking loud and frantic.

"Touch your pussy baby, make yourself come," I growl into her ear.

She does what I demand, one hand going to pinch her hard nipple, the other moving to her mouth, where she sucks her fingers and then trails them down to her gaping pussy. I watch as her fingers make contact with her clit and she tips her head back, letting it rest on my shoulder. Her movements feel jerky, and I can feel her pussy start to tighten. Gripping her legs harder, and wider I power into her, once, twice, three times before she screams my name and her pussy milks the come directly from my balls, pulling a long groan from me.

I wrap my arms around my Firecracker, holding her to me, my cock still nestled deep inside her. Our breaths start to calm but I still don't want to let go. Not yet. Nuzzling into her neck

I use my nose to move some tendrils of hair out of my way so I can drop a kiss to the part where her shoulder meets her neck.

"I never thought I'd find my person, but Juno found me, and you found us. I love you Vi," I whisper in her ear, meaning every single fucking word.

"You found me. In more ways than one. I love you, Jules."

My heart skips a beat everytime she says those words. Over the past week I'd stopped her on three occasions, wanting her to be really sure of her feelings. When she yelled and threw Juno's teething ring at me for being a stubborn asshole, I had to let her speak her truth, and it gets me every time. I angle her head toward me and we kiss, pouring our feelings into our movements. My cock softens and slips out of her, our combined juices dripping onto my leg.

"Ew. Come on, let's get cleaned up then order pizza. I need sustenance before I can fuck you again," Vi says, with a wink before sashaying her gorgeous ass toward the hall. Looking over her shoulder she gives me a look. "Are you coming?"

"Baby, I would love nothing more, but thanks to Rodney, I can't feel my legs."

Epilogue

Jules

"So why are we here?" I grumble. It was meant to be date night but Vi postponed because she needs to be at the clubhouse.

"Because I have stuff to do with the ladies," she says.

"What kind of stuff?"

"Oh, the Girl Gang has been tasked with a couple of projects so, you know, we want to have a meeting about it."

I nod and lean into the car to unlatch Juno. Blanche and Lovely's new community center opened two months ago and the goal is to help women, and some men get back on their feet. Whether they've escaped religious cults or abusive relationships or even been medically discharged from the military, it's a place for people to rebuild their lives. The women have made contacts with people in Rose Grove willing to help with training or jobs. Vi's sisters Jazz and Lil have been helping with literacy, while Flora has two jobs open for anyone wanting to learn floristry. The community center is more important than me taking Vi to the movies, so I get it.

"Come on little Miss Grumpy Pants," I coo to Juno, who still hasn't outgrown frowning all the time. Vi says she's perfect the way she is, and I agree. Besides, she saves all her smiles for her mommy and daddy so what do I care if she stink eyes everyone else?

"Yo, has anyone seen Chewy?" Rhodie's voice booms out in the common room as we open the door to walk in.

"She mentioned something about having an errand to run," Ana says, rocking Chomper in his stroller.

"What kind of errand? Did she say where she was going?" Rhodie's voice rises and I know that something is wrong.

Vi reads me so well that she holds her hands out for Juno so I can get a read on my sister. We transfer Juno, who places her head on Vi's shoulder and snuggles in. I use my thumbs on both hands to tap on my phone screen, bringing up our tracking software.

"Why the fuck is she headed toward Roxburgh?" I ask, confused at my sister's movements?

"What the fuck?!" Rhodie explodes, "She never said any-thing! Her phone is off and her go bag is gone! Pops!" he yells, looking around the room wildly.

"Keep your hair on kid, shit. What's your problem?" Pops growls.

"Fuck, you're here. I figured it was some bullshit idea you came up with," Rhodie says.

"Gee, thanks asshole," Pops rolls his eyes.

My sister has disappeared, her go bag is gone and her phone is off. "She's hunting." I raise my eyes, catching Tav's gaze first, then Gus's. Both nod, knowing full well that's what she's doing.

"Yesssss," Vi says under her breath, a little fist pump action going on. "What?" she asks, wide eyed.

"Tell me where she is, I need to get to her, what if she needs help?"

"I saw Moss leave with her," Lil says, looking confused over what's happening.

"What the actual fuck!?" Rhodie explodes.

Before he can demand that someone call Moss, Jazz holds up her hand. "His phone is off, too."

Marx stands in the doorway, hands on hips, watching the whole scene go down. He turns to look at me, "How long did you let her hunt before you stepped in?"

"She knows to check in after 6 hours. Then 12, 18, and 24. If we hadn't heard from her we'd go in," Tav answers.

"Well, let's let her hunt," Marx says, nodding.

"But–"

"No buts, brother. Your woman is dangerous, fearless and a fucking genius. She knows how to do this. You need to trust her," Marx says, staring his younger brother in the eye.

Rhodie's body deflates slightly. "She doesn't need to hunt anymore because she has me to do it for her."

"We love when our big, strong men do things for us, but sometimes we like to do it for ourselves." Ana says. "Chewy is more than capable of doing this, Rhodie. Trust her. Besides, if she's left you here, it's for a reason."

He nods, but looks heartbroken nonetheless, leaving down the hall, his shoulders tight.

Gus steps up to my side, Tav beside him. "She hasn't done this in a long time,"

I nod in agreement. Since she's been with Rhodie she's been a lot more settled.

"Something either spooked her, or pissed her off," Tav says, eyeing his very pregnant wife.

"Whatever it is, it's going to need the Rev Room," Gus sighs.

"I'll get it ready." I move to press kisses on the cheeks of the two loves of my life and make my way outside.

I have work to do.

Tuesday

Chewy

My senses are being raped by florals, the smell giving me a headache as I sit in this shitty, hard chair. Why do fancy people have such uncomfortable furniture? Jules used to have uncomfortable furniture too, but now he has Violet and Juno to love so he had to get comfortable stuff. Stuff for families to sit on, closely, maybe even hugging or letting their legs touch or something.

I'll add that to my list of things I need. I have a comfy couch, it's very soft, but it's light colored and that's not family friendly. I type "dark colored soft couch" in my notes app and then turn my phone off.

"Need anything?" Moss's voice calls over the comms we're using.

"Yes. I'll need some coffee grounds to sniff once I get out of here."

"Ooookay," Moss mumbles and I smile to myself.

After rescuing Vi I've seen the sergeant in a different light. Hence why I've brought him with me instead of Rhodie. Rhodie will be all Hulk smashy and I need subtlety. Well, someone more subtle than Rhodie. And probably me.

I tilt my head when I hear the jingling of keys and I know it's almost showtime. The door opens and a spicy scent cuts through the sickly florals and now all the scents are mingling and making my throat feel thick. I close my eyes and take two breaths, in and out, through my mouth, to refocus.

The light flicks on and I open my eyes to stare at the person I've been hunting for two months now.

"Hello, Candice. I hear you have my Ol Man's daughter."

What the heck did she say?

Kotiro – Girl
Tama – Boy
Mija – My daughter, sweetheart
Mi amado hijo – beloved son
Eres hombre muerto – You're a dead man
Quinametzin – Refers to a race of giant men

Thank you for reading

Thank you so much for choosing to spend a little time with the characters I made up. What a wild ride!

If you want to know more about me or what I'm reading you can find me all over the place –

Follow me at my author page on Facebook

Friend me on Facebook

Join my group Cleo Browne's Babes

Follow me on Instagram

Keep your eyes peeled for upcoming books in the Devil's Rose MC Series, The Tombs Security Series, and a new series, because I can't just write two concurrently, The Davies Family Series – Small Town Romance set in Rose Grove. There may even be cameos from some of your fave characters.

Cleo Browne books

Rhodie - Devil's Rose MC Book One

August - A Tombs Security + Devil's Rose MC Crossover

Wire - Devil's Rose MC Book Two

Tav Devil's Rose MC Book Three
DRMC - Devil's Rose Merry Christmas

Tank - Devil's Rose MC Book Four

Jules - A Tombs Security + Devil's Rose MC Crossover

Tuesday - DRMC Novella
In progress

About the Author

Cleo Browne is the pen name of a neurospicy geeky girl from Aotearoa New Zealand. As a child, she realized very early on that she wasn't a people person, so she would spend all her time reading and writing her own stories. These stories usually ended with the line "and then they died". As an adult, she has gotten slightly more people-y (not much) and better at not killing all her characters off when she writes.

Cleo loves to write about women who don't need a man to do their dirty work and the hot alpha men who turn to mush when they watch their women handling business.

When she's not writing romance novels about strong, curvy women and the men who adore them, she hangs out at home with her hubby, her boys, and her ancient greyhound who likes to creepily watch her write

Acknowledgements

First off, I'd like to thank all the wonderful readers who took a chance on a kooky little autistic woman and read my first offering, Rhodie. Without you all reading it and loving it, this book would never have happened. I would have just faded away into obscurity, never to be seen or heard from again. So, thank you. I appreciate you all.

Second, I'd like to thank my book besties who all have a hand in helping me get these stories to you guys, the readers. Thanks to Shaye Torrel for the Book Bitch meet ups, Courtney Clarke Michaels for the speed talk meet ups, Gabi Brocklesby for the proof reading because holy crap, without you these books would be a hard read, Sally Howells for the AMAZING alpha advice and chapter breakdowns, and last but not least Gretchen Calder for helping keep me somewhat organised on social media. Thank you all from the bottom of my weird little heart.

Thanks to my partner PN. Without his constant words of encouragement, "I really didn't think MC books were a thing," I would never have finished this book. Thanks also go to my boys. Ronnie, for being completely disinterested, and Louis for your two hour long phone calls that would eat into my writing time. Love you guys.